Corker's Freedom

Corker's Freedom

John Berger

VERSO

London • New York

First published 1964
This edition published by Verso 2010
© John Berger 2010
All rights reserved

1 3 5 7 9 10 8 6 4 2

Verso
UK: 6 Meard Street, London W1F 0EG
US: 20 Jay Street, Suite 1010, Brooklyn, NY 11201
www.versobooks.com

Verso is the imprint of New Left Books

ISBN-13: 978-1-84467-641-5

British Library Cataloguing in Publication Data
A catalogue record for this book is available from the British Library

Typeset in Garamond by Hewer Text UK Ltd, Edinburgh
Printed in Sweden by ScandBook AB

For Anant and His Mornings and Paul Lawton at Christmas

Contents

Part One

Corker's of Clapham

(William Tracey Corker, bachelor, aged 63, has this morning, April 4th, 1960, walked out on Irene, his invalid sister, in whose house he has lived for the last twelve years. He has no intention of returning. Alec Gooch, Mr Corker's junior and only clerk, will be 18 in two months' time. Last night he went to bed with a girl for the first time in his life. The girl, with whom he is in love, works in a florist's shop and is called Jackie.)

Although Alec is six feet tall, when he sits at his table the window on the wall above him is so high that it seems almost like a skylight. Alec has two jobs to do simultaneously. The first he does in order to be paid, to satisfy his employer and in the hope of gaining good references which will enable him to get a better job. The second he does for his own satisfaction. The first job involves cleaning out the office, opening the post, filing, typing, addressing envelopes, cutting out adverts. The second job is secret. To do it properly he must observe everything that happens in the office (whilst still carrying out the duties of the first job) and having observed it, name it. A great deal of what happens is repetitive in the same way as a simple game played many times becomes repetitive. The repetitions do not have to be separately named. So long as they comply with the rules of current practice they can be subsumed under *Office Day*. But Alec must still check that they do so comply, and having checked, tick them in his mind as a schoolmaster ticks a correct answer. Accordingly he is constantly ticking the responses of his

I

employer, phrases used over the telephone, clients' questions, the vocabulary of letters, ways of answering, calculations concerning money. The ticking affords him a kind of satisfaction: the satisfaction of seeing a plan working according to plan. Several times each day, however, something new happens, something for which he can find no precedent. He then has to decide whether the new event can or cannot be accommodated by *Office Day*. He has to ask himself whether, if it occurred often, it would threaten the basic principles of current practice or whether it is merely the result of an insignificant chance contingency. If he considers that it probably can be accommodated, he marks it *Funny*, and then waits to compare it with similar events which nevertheless do comply with the rules. If he thinks it unlikely that it can ever be accommodated he marks it *Unknown*, and then gives it an abbreviated descriptive name such as *Unknown: Younger Woman Taking Mickey Out of Whole Business*. The descriptive name is necessary, for it may be that finally this event will be seen to belong to a third category of events. These occur seldom during office hours but when they do they are of considerable importance. They are events which quite clearly and immediately have no connexion whatsoever with *Office Day* and for which the rules of current practice are utterly irrelevant. If Alec's employer fell down dead it would constitute such an event. Less dramatically, if a client started crying or if he saw up a girl's skirt that she was wearing no pants, both these events would belong to the third category. Events in this category, for which there is no set of comprehensive rules and which exist independently, have to be named for what they are. Thus: Dead-Never-To-Talk-To-Again: Crying-Too-Much-To-Stop or, Hair-Where-Want-Is. Outside the office events in the third category can occasionally come so fast and furiously that they overwhelm. But inside the office, where Alec spends more waking hours than in any other single place, there is always enough time for him to think and to arrange his mind methodically. Often before now he has tried in the calm of the office routine to take an event in the third category and construct a system, a set of rules, a practice around it. If he succeeded in achieving this he would be in a position to challenge *Office Day*. He would like to challenge it, for the challenge would be a vindication of his own experience, it would allow him to feel a closer connexion between daily life and his being alive. It is really *Corker's Office Day* and is as it is because Corker is exempt, in Alec's opinion, from the experience of any event in the third category. Everything that interests Corker has already been written into *Office Day*. It is part of *Office Day* for Corker to ask Alec to go and change his books at the Public Library: books on gipsies and the lives of great men. Often he has four or five out at a time. It is part of *Office Day* for Corker to tell Alec about his trips abroad, to Finland and Greece and Italy. When Corker gives a lecture at the church hall about one of these trips, and Alec goes to listen, this is also a kind of extension of *Office Day*, like working late. If they have lunch together in the kitchen and Corker talks about Pelmanism and asks Alec about his family, this is also part of *Office Day*. Even when Corker goes to the doctor about his headaches or a pain in his foot, it is part of *Office Day*. *Office Day*, as Alec sees it, is Corker's life. Alec has never succeeded in challenging *Office Day*, for he has never been able to see enough sustained promise in any event in the open third category to justify an extensive enough system being built round it. *Office Day*, despite its remoteness, still promises a good deal: knowledge, status, security. This morning he is trying, with higher hopes of success than ever before, a new system based on a new event: *Having Jackie*. He is bent over his desk. A leather jacket hangs over the back of his chair. He is entering post in the Post Book. Each envelope is slit open with a silver-bladed letter-opener which belonged to his employer's father. Then name of letter writer and place of origin is entered in Post Book with full particulars of enclosures, if any, and in a separate money-adding column, if cash. There are six more letters to enter, all twenty-three having been slit open. Vaguely towards the bottom of his stomach and precisely in his penis he is conscious of a sensation. The sensation almost amounts to a pain. It is the sensation one has when a wound or a scar is healing and one presses on it to remind oneself of the pain that has gone and to rejoice in the fact that it is mending. For the hundredth time since he woke, Alec checks that this near-pain is indeed the greatest reassurance he has ever known. And having checked it, he ticks it as belonging to *Having Jackie* with a sweet golden tick. Mr Corker, plump in a grey tweed suit, holds the telephone to his ear. Whilst listening to the voice, female, at the other end, he turns the revolving chair in which he sits with cushion placed specially at the back where he has been known to feel a draught and takes from a shelf of large books one which is marked Domestic Staff Male. Mr Corker is in fact searching for a Married Couple, the Wife of whom will be employed as a Cook General and the Husband as Chauffeur and Gardener, both of them living in the Lodge rent free, with the Midday Meal Found and a joint wage of £12 a week. He is searching in Domestic Staff Male because, the times changing, the number of married couples prepared to enter Domestic Service together does not justify them having a book exclusively of their own. His clean forefinger runs down a list of names, occasionally slowing down and almost stopping at one and then, like a dog whose curiosity is sometimes satisfied by a single sniff taken in passing, albeit slowly, hurries on to the opposite page. There Mr and Mrs Box are found. Mr Corker remembers them specially, although it is five weeks since Mrs Box registered for them both, on account of their name. By the side of the name is an index number and it is for this that he is searching, since his memory, being good but not phenomenal, is unable to retain CA/9342/60 in the same manner as it has retained the piquant and also short BOX. The voice, female, at other end, becomes silent. Mr Corker is as deft with phrases as he is with his books. He now makes two selections simultaneously. He swings round in the swivel chair to the shelf on the other side of him, that is to say his right, and without a second's hesitation chooses from the twenty books assembled there that one in which he will find CA/9342/60 and thereby more information about the Boxes, at exactly the same moment as he says to the voice, female, at the other end: We would not, Madam, dream of sending you anyone in whom we did not have *reason* to have confidence. Reason to have confidence, ticked, belonging to *Office Day.* Alec duly blots his entering of the eighteenth letter, an inquiry from a firm of tent manufacturers in Mitcham, and leans back to stroke the sleeve of the leather jacket hanging on the back of his chair. He does this to verify that the evidence of his senses is reliable. He can feel the leather sleeve: what he feels is true. He can trust his body and so, triumphant, he ticks his whole body with a great thrusting tick as belonging to *Having Jackie.* The exact ages and the anticipated wages of Mr and Mrs Box are verified by reference to the book that was unerringly selected. He is 57 and his wife, somewhat unusually, is 61. They are asking £14 a week. At this point Mr Corker draws upon experience accumulated over a period of seventeen years in this identical office – he assumes without hesitation that the difference of £2 is negotiable. The Boxes will be persuaded to accept less in view of the fact that the Lodge has a garden wherein Mr Box can grow his own vegetables or in view of some equivalent as yet unmentioned attraction which in such cases can always be discovered, whilst the voice, female, at other end, will be persuaded without great difficulty to offer a trifle more considering especially the shortage of Married Couples today. He proceeds to read out the history of the Boxes; they are genuinely a country couple and they remained in their last happy place of employment for twelve years until their respected and now much mourned employer passed away. Whilst talking, he takes a light-green coloured card from the top of a pile of light-green coloured cards. These are the Interview Cards printed according to Mr Corker's own design and now requiring that only the details of place and time be filled in upon them. Alec has entered the twenty-third letter and it remains for him to add up the postal orders, stamps and legal tender which have accompanied them. Having ascertained that £3 14s. 3d. is indeed correct, he opens a small black money box with a red line round the edge of the lid. The key for this box is always returned to the right-hand drawer of his desk. Into the box he deposits 2s. 3d. worth of unused stamps received as enclosures. He remembers her navel. The degree of his pleasure which he cannot speak about makes him grunt in his throat like an infant. No single word has meant more than this grunt which comes from the time before he could talk. Mr Corker confirms the details of the meeting which through his agency will take place in two days' time. His voice falls into the Winding-Up Phrase and he touches the bridge of his tortoiseshell spectacles with his right thumb: There is one thing which we do like to ask, Madam, if you should decide to take the people we are sending you into your employment will you please inform us immediately. Way of Saying Good-Bye ticked under *Office Day*. Domestic Staff Male is returned to its shelf and Employers Domestic is taken out so that it may be recorded that the Boxes will be sent in two days' time to the owner, female, of the voice. The third book, the source of information about all those seeking work who have been indexed under the prefix CA, is handed over to the boy so that he may type the address of the Boxes, set out therein, on to the envelope in which will be sent the light-green Interview Card.

Mr Corker straightens the blotter on his desk and turns round to speak to Alec. The office is small. There is not more than a yard between them. On the whole Alec enjoys Corker. He is his employer, but he often talks unexpectedly and treats Alec like a friend. Alec doubts whether Corker has many friends. Mr Corker's mouth hangs open in a smile. What would you say if I told you I was coming to live on the premises? Alec instantaneously marks the question as a difficulty belonging to *Having Jackie*. He had left her house before it was really light, so that the neighbours shouldn't see, when the sky was the colour of her tummy, and walking he had decided that after this once they could no longer wait for her mother and father to visit her uncle again, and that since he always had a set of keys to the office they would come here at week-ends and make love on the settee in the Reception-Room. As he made this plan he had formulated a new rule: *Having Jackie* means taking New Chances. Here? he says, unable to keep the disappointment out of his voice. We have the floor upstairs too, says Mr Corker.

I know, but I cannot think, that I need Alec's approval. Yet this approval must be given without his fully realizing what he is being asked to approve of. If he knew everything the whole basis of my present authority over him would be undermined. There are times when, for a fraction of a second, I am tempted to be honest and to throw away all disguise. It happens when my heart, that is to say the physical organ itself, feels swollen and heavy in my chest. The relief of being recognized would be sweet indeed. But afterwards, as soon as it became clear that there was no further disguise to throw off, I would be reduced to shame and this shame would be so comprehensive that I would have to pretend to be dead in the hope that Alec or whoever it was who had recognized me would abandon me to fetch an undertaker. Then between the moment of his going and the undertaker's arrival I would be up on my feet and away to live again as I am now, in my old disguise. What I need now, however, is less than recognition; I simply need practice in treating what I have done this morning as normal. During the walk to the station I behaved as I do every morning. My regular travelling companions talked to me in the same way. But the more they addressed me as 'Old Corky', the more indistinguishable this morning became from any other morning, the more startling and large and far-reaching became the thing I was hiding. The secrecy makes me feel more and more abnormal. As soon as a thing can be spoken of, it acquires alternative names and becomes a matter of opinion. Only secrets seem absolute. All this I know but cannot think.

You're kidding! says Alec. No, says Mr Corker, I'm serious, do I look like a man who is joking? I never know with you, says Alec, you've had me before now. You'd better show the next client in, says Mr Corker. As Alec gets up from his chair to open the door with the frosted glass window at eye level, he formulates, regretting the hundred week-ends when he could have brought her here, another rule: Before *Having Jackie* you wasted your time. He opens the door and is about to shout Next Please when he notices that the new client is pretty. Will you come this way, please, he says.

Since she receives special treatment wherever she goes and has done for the last three years, the girl, who is small and whose beehive hair is the colour of Pacific sand, accepts it now as her destiny and the starting point of her mounting dreams in which she will finally give herself and the inlaid filigreed golden gift of her youth in marriage to the boss whose letters at first she will take down, perched tinily on the edge of his office chair, Italian shoes pointing, just as she perches now on the edge of the chair facing the elderly man whom she counts as a boss even if he clearly belongs to the humblest category, in her newly acquired prize-winning shorthand. Mr Corker, the boss of the humblest category, makes inquiries. This is her first time of coming. Whilst still under the fountain of her little answers and smiles he takes down the current volume of Office Staff Female. It is in this volume that she will always be able to be found directly, with her number. He explains to her the nature of the under-standing necessary. We give you a number, Miss Marlow. He picks up the pen, carefully chosen for the sake of the leather pad a little above the nib to prevent the blue-black ink staining his fingers, writes the number on a buff-coloured card, printed according to his own design, and holds it out to her who takes it in her magenta-gloved hand, looks at it for a moment with her head inclined to one side as though she has expectations of the number itself smiling back at her and then pops it into her white handbag with the golden clasp. And we do ask you,

Miss Marlow, to quote this number to us whenever you write to us or phone us or get in touch with us in any way at any time. If we know your number it is very much easier for us. Alec notices that beneath her powder she has two spots on her chin. Then he finds it odd to think that all girls perform in the same way as Jackie. Mr Corker is writing in the book devoted to all those with the index numbers of which the prefix is ST. She was christened Brenda and the ceremony was performed eighteen years ago. She claims three 'O' levels. Her speeds are 60 and 100. At Boothby's Secretarial and Commercial College she won a Presentation Prize. And what Miss Marlow is a Presentation Prize given for? For general availability, she says. Availability? asks Mr Corker. Alec sniffs out a little laugh. I said ability, says Miss Marlow eyeing Alec. She has been employed for six months by Dodds, Coal Merchants. She wishes to find a post which is more intrinsically interesting and which will offer Brighter Prospects. Mr Corker inquires, if he may, how much Dodds are paying her. Eight pounds, she answers perkily and in such a manner as to make one imagine that she is quoting the price of a coat she has bought rather than the money she earns by her work. He asks her whether she would be prepared in a better situation offering Brighter Prospects to commence with less. Speaking confidently from memory and without a glance at a book, he informs her of a job at £7 10*s*. with a firm of Estate Agents. The facts come so easily to him because the estate agent is an acquaintance who travels with him on the same train every morning and Mr Corker would dearly like to oblige, to fix him up, as the estate agent himself would term it. Twisting her body from above her precisely small waist through forty-five degrees so that her breasts instead of pointing at Alec now point straight at Mr Corker, she says: Why should I?

I know but cannot remember that when I was in my teens I was like this child. Not like her in manners or ideas or mischief. But like her in my awareness of my own novelty.

Mr Corker challenges her to guess how much he was earning when he was her age. She lowers her eyes, finding the question meaningless and the idea of him ever being her age totally unacceptable. I don't know I'm sure. He states the number of shillings, surrounded by a sarcastic smile. Both stare at the desk which divides them. It costs her the same amount to have her hair done each week and she reckons it money well spent. He takes up a book and begins to read out descriptions of possibly suitable vacancies. His spectacles have bifocal lenses and this causes him when reading to hold the book close in to his body, resting it, practically speaking, on his stomach. He reads quickly but not so quickly that her imagination cannot keep up with him. Alec recognizes Current Practice: whenever in *Office Day* women demand more money, Corker becomes irritated. Alec winks at the girl in order to show her that he has, in all respects, a more sophisticated attitude towards women than his employer. Typist. City shipping office. School leaver considered. She answers the wink by staring into space. Two weeks' holiday with pay. Minimum speed 50. £400. Oh dear, she says, how much is that? Mr Corker converts by reflex. Just under £8 a week. She remembers the City because at school they were all taken over St Paul's and Pat played the giddy goat in the Whispering Gallery. She remembers it as an unfriendly and bleak place. And in a shipping office the number of ships' officers to be encountered must in reality, whatever the term may suggest to the silly, be small. Shorthand typist (female). X-ray Dept. of Croydon General Hospital. Salary £430. She could never, she had previously decided, stand the training necessary to become a nurse, but as a typist she would still be working with doctors and with surgeons who work so hard at the operating-tables that they themselves die young, their colleagues helpless at their bedsides. She will lessen the burden they suffer by the calm and neatness with which she will take down and type their letters so that eventually, having thought of her as a mere machine for so long, he will suddenly behold her in amazement and see how young and slim – Manufacturers of Tyres, Rubber Footwear and Resilient Webbing. Two shorthand typists. First-class conditions of service. Girls 16–19. Salary £380. No Saturdays. On Saturdays, she is sure, he will take her out and considering that they manufacture tyres it is not unlikely that he will be interested in cars and so own a fast open one which will allow her to show him her hair streaming in the wind (she read only the other day that backcombing is bad for the hair) and which at the same time will not allow him the advantages of a saloon when, having pulled up by a five-bar gate and taken his cap off, he wishes with the darkness descending so softly to go too far. Shorthand typist. Fancy Goods Manufacturers, Streatham. Luncheon Vouchers. 9–5. £450. She says to herself that the boss who offers to pay the most probably has the most. Who will I be working for there? The tense of the question, a sign not unnoticed by Mr Corker, suggests that she has already made up her child's impressionable mind. She has decided, and she imagines her eyes like two butterflies, settled in beautiful symmetry upon the vase of her neck and face. Mr Soloveichik. Mr Corker pronounces the outlandish name with calculated blandness. Alec recognizes that it is calculated, just like the speed and impersonality with which Corker read the details, to take the girl down a peg or two. Who? exclaims the girl. Mr Soloveichik. This time it is said to diminish further, to make exceeding small. The girl concludes that the owner of the name must be a foreigner and this transforms the scene of her future office. It acquires candlelight and an unusual smell. Mr Corker's malice passes unnoticed, for a new hope has been born, a new Brenda crusade to convert the infidels has begun. It is not only that she has the possibility of attracting his attention, leading him on, and then with the promise of her priceless gift making him so docilely captive that she can even take him home to Melrose Avenue, it is also that the nature of her priceless gift, as she and she only has deduced from examining the secret splendour of it, is strange and delicate in a foreign way and altogether created for the different, wild but really gentle gentleman from a distant country, not for any of the ordinary local young men whom the other girls so predictably and self-importantly invite back to Sunday tea. What country does he come from? she asks. He is British now, says Mr Corker. How old is he? The question slips out helpless.

I am without one now. And this is true even if the one under whose auspices I have lived for so long was a denial of what woman is, and even if she was no more – and indeed far less – than what by the accident of our birth, or my father's intermittent passion, she was: a sister. Even at my age a man without a woman is marked. He is the subject of comment. (This I am even capable of thinking.) But he is also in his own eyes and in the eyes of all others, *questionable*. Nobody can quite estimate what he means and nobody can quite estimate his value. He excites the curiosity of women. This curiosity, as we call it in order to give it a household name, is not impartial. Women gossip, but their gossiping merely disposes of the useless information they have gained. The information which is useful to them they use in quite a different way. Women want to take as many men down with them as they can, like sinking ships lost with all hands. Down with them to the sharp joys of their bed. Down with them to childbirth. Down with them to keeping a home. Down with them to making cups of tea and waiting for nothing. Down with them to rock bottom. Down with them never to voyage again for ever. The centrifugal pull of the female – it could be simple enough as it is with animals, it could simply be what I feel in my member as it grows large. I could be like a bull. But here the curiosity, the information gained, the cunning of woman complicates the scheme of things. They play on our weaknesses and bind us with habit and promise and pity and age and dependence. The old are the same as the young, for no woman ever loses her skill in discovering the information which, properly acted upon, can make him think she serves him whilst in fact she holds him. I know now how wise my father was when he said: Never give your name to a prostitute. And I know too: Never give your youth to your mother: and never give your middle age to your sister. But I do not think this.

I am not in the habit, says Mr Corker, of discussing employers' ages with employees. She quickly asks another question in order to bury the last. What do they make? Fancy goods, says Mr Corker. But what sort of fancy goods? All sorts. He begins to tap his fingers on the arm of his chair. All sorts of fancy goods! She self-consciously repeats the phrase like the refrain of a song. Then there is silence. It lasts no more than ten seconds. It is, however, a silence born out of helplessness. The girl believes that the man is too old to be charmed. So far as she is concerned he is like a machine which she does not understand and which has gone wrong and now needs mending; all she can do is to wait for a young man. Mr Corker stares. She instinctively turns towards Alec for help. The gesture does not escape Alec. He has noticed her breasts which are a nice size, and the zip fastener of her oatmeal skirt which is not zipped to the very top, and her plump small toes which are not quite covered by her shoe. He has also felt her presence through Corker's mounting irritation. She is part of *Having Jackie*: not a part he has touched, not a part of him or Jackie, but a part of the world made as it is with all the sweet surprise of it not being otherwise. The only help that Alec could give her is another wink. Instantly he decides not to. More important than her being a girl is the disadvantage of her not being Jackie. What is more, she will never give her own *Having Jackie* to anyone. She may have nice breasts and tootsies and perform like Jackie. But she will never let anyone have her Jackie, or even touch her Jackie properly, because she thinks she's too good, so bloody good that if you wink at her you have to say thank you. As Alec gauges all the disadvantages of her not being Jackie and all that she must put her boys through, he begins to feel grateful for Corker's irritation. Together, he concludes, they have a good solid male attitude towards feminine frivolity. And so he pretends not to notice her glance. She turns her shoulders and her vase with the butterfly eyes upon it back to the older man. She knows that she won't be able to pronounce Dr Soloveichik out loud. So she is forced to say: I'd like to go and see the Fancy Goods job. None of the others? Mr Corker demands. And the hospital one. Asked when she can go for an interview, she replies Wednesday Afternoon in a husky but inviting voice, a voice that she has no intention whatsoever of employing on this particular occasion in this mean little office where there are no gentlemen, but which has become her unthinking way of saying Wednesday Afternoon because having to work at Dodds late on Monday evenings she has been given Wednesday as a half-day and Wednesday Afternoon has thus become the only weekday time which is hers to dispense with dusky promise to those whose longing to see her again is worthy of sweet encouragement. Mr Corker dials the number of Croydon General Hospital and makes an appointment for Miss Marlow. Likewise he telephones Mr Soloveichik. The latter has an insistent broken voice. I do not take a damn, he says, for U levels or any other levels. Can she do the work? Quick with no mistakes too. Can she do the work? That is all I ask. I want good work and I pay good money. You should know that. As he listens to the voice at the other end of the line Mr Corker stares at what he is dispatching. Although she cannot distinguish what Mr Soloveichik is saying, such open staring forces the girl to take out her mirror and study her mouth. Alec considers another rule. The girl with the toffee voice earns half as much again as Jackie on her feet all day at the florist's and Jackie was trained in Flower Arrangement. Until today he has never considered Jackie's work important. Her work was simply what kept her occupied during *Office Day*. The new rule states that Jackie is worth more than she gets. Mr Corker glowers at the girl's newly made cyclamen lips. Mr Soloveichik can't see you on Wednesday, can you go at five this afternoon? The girl nods.

She'll come today, says Mr Corker and puts the receiver down. Two light-green Interview Cards are brusquely taken from the top of the pile of light-green Interview Cards. The addresses are filled in as also the exact time. We ask you, Miss Marlow, if you are in any way prevented from keeping these appointments to inform us and the employers concerned before the time of the appointments which we have now arranged. We emphasize this because as you will we are sure appreciate nobody has time to waste. Mr Corker shuts the book on her name and number and strokes the back of it which is deep red and has leather corners. He repeats his last sentence. Nobody has time to waste Miss Marlow and the business world is a very busy one. She gets up. On her feet she is only 5 ft. 4 in. She looks through her eyeslits from the post where there is only room for one and which she will defend to the death. She says Thank You to the older man and patently ignores Alec. She holds the light-green Interview Cards in her magenta-gloved hand. She turns to begin the Walk to the Door, Through the Waiting-Room to Mr Soloveichik. She can walk herself in any way she chooses for she can sidle left and she can sidle right. Alec watches her bottom and rules again: only the girl you love with is loving. I think we'll see Miss Marlow again, says Mr Corker, quite a little bit, wasn't she? Not for me thank you very much, says Alec. But tell me, asks Mr Corker, turning round in his swing chair so as to face Alec, does anyone really like hair like that, I mean it looks like feathers or something? It can look quite good, says Alec authoritatively. But it's so unnatural, says Mr Corker, it doesn't look like hair, a woman's crowning glory they used to call it but all done up like that it looks like – it looks like what I said, a feather duster, and I'm sure it can't be good for the hair. It's a fashion; says Alec. It was very different when I was brought up, says Mr Corker. Alec ticks this sentence under *Office Day: Chatting*. We were very sheltered, I suppose, continues Mr Corker, I mean my sister I don't suppose she went to a hairdresser's until she was twenty, we used to have a retired lady hairdresser to come and cut our hair at home, upstairs in the Nursery, all of us one after the other. And do you know something else? In Switzerland they still have lady hairdressers for *men*. They think nothing of going into a barber's and having a young woman do their hair. Mr Corker laughs at the idea.

> I have known for a long time but have never thought it, that I like people to touch me, so long as their touch is gentle. I particularly like women to touch me. Peace can be the result of a very small sensation. I have often been made peaceful at the barber's. He has been rubbing my scalp and the pleasure of the sensation has travelled down my spine and then gathered my whole body to itself. To be compact, to be contained, to be suspended in a world without edges, to be swung between two trees and the blue sky to come down to my face, to be transported, to be central again, to know no differences, to be the opposite to being put on one side – such is the nature of our bodies and the logic of our growth that all this can be felt as the consequence of having one's neck gently stroked, of having one small desire respectably and quietly and regularly met.

They probably do it better, says Alec. No, says Mr Corker, the best hairdressers are men, just like the best cooks. You've only got to look at the names up in the West End – René, Claude, Marcel. All men's names they are. If they put their mind to a thing, men are always better than women. Do you think so? says Alec, in my opinion there are some things women are better at. Such as? says Corker. Well, says Alec, such as arranging flowers or making dresses or some kinds of singing. Mr Corker looks hard at Alec and announces in a loud voice: You know I meant what I said about coming to live here. In his normal voice, he then adds: The time has come, the Walrus said. But you live in the real country, says Alec, we were out Banstead way biking last Saturday and we passed your road. I just don't get it. Mr Corker takes off his glasses to polish them and says: The country's not everything, not by a long chalk. You know the word civilization, well that word comes from the Latin *civis* which means city. Will you live, says Alec, all by yourself? No, I shall get a housekeeper, says Mr Corker. Then, patting Alec on the shoulder, he continues: We'll make it very nice here, really very nice.

She could be one of Alec's mother's friends. She has chestnut hair swept up at the back and a stretched face, but she is younger than his mother. Thanks dear, she says to Alec as he shows her to the chair. She looks at the gentleman across the table and doubts whether he can be much use to her. But she crosses her legs with her dark nylons on and makes herself comfy in the chair. Then she glances down at the gas fire which is going to feel too hot. The gas fire whistles lightly. By the side of the fire is a bowl of water with a lot of dust in it. Well Mrs—and what can we do for you? asks Mr Corker. Alec looks at her hand to check that she has a wedding ring. Mr Corker is always teaching Alec that in this business you need to be as observant as a detective. I was just passing, begins the woman. Have you ever been to us before? interrupts Mr Corker. No I never have, no, I was just passing. You haven't told us your name – it's Mrs—? McBryde, she says. Mr Corker leans right back in his chair, places his hands on its arms and opens as always: And how, Mrs McBryde, can we help you? I was just passing and so I said to myself why not and so I thought I'd come up just in case. She smiles at him and undoes the top button of her coat. The skin of her neck is very fair and she has full round breasts. You never know, she says.

I know that a desire has grown within me which I cannot recognize, but which is part of my plan. It is to go down with a stupid woman.

Mrs McBryde could you please tell us what you want? says Mr Corker, articulating each word as though speaking to an idiot. A job, she says. As? shouts Mr Corker. Oh, she says, a housekeeper.

I'm a housekeeper. I see, says Mr Corker. Alec glances at his employer in the hope of seeing him react. His expression betrays nothing, but Alec is certain that inside the head with the grey hair, held so stiffly, the same question has occurred as occurred to him: Will this one do? I see, repeats Mr Corker. Mrs McBryde moves her chair nearer to the desk and to the right. The fire's scorching my legs, she says. Alec glances at them again and considers them not bad. Do you have a job for a housekeeper? asks Mrs McBryde, a little surprised by the gentleman only saying I see. Mrs McBryde, says Mr Corker, if you would like us to put your name on our books, we'll do our very best for you. May as well, she says, since we're here. Mr Corker types on a buff-coloured card. Do you spell your name with an Mc or Mac? he inquires. My husband says it should always be without the A, says Mrs McBryde, he knows his own mind about everything, Bob does. Alec observes Mr Corker taking up his conversational pose, chin in hand. He has often explained the technique to Alec: You must draw them out, get their confidence — they tell you more themselves than all the references in the world, but it's an art getting people to talk, don't you know, an art. Does he come from Scotland, your husband? he asks. No, funny thing, he was born in Cairo. Is that so? And was it in Egypt you met him, Mrs McBryde? She is gradually coming to an opinion about the old fool across the desk who runs the place. She doesn't much like the way he talks, like a patronizing old lady. She doesn't much like his nose which is huge. She is not at all sure she would trust him. But what she does like is the way he looks tired: he looks tired like a person, like a man, and not like an old pudding. I don't think I'll tell you where I met him, she says, it might shock you, but I'll tell you one thing, it wasn't Egypt. Egypt is one of the countries I plan to go to one of these days, says Mr Corker. Bob says wild horses wouldn't get him back there, says Mrs McBryde. I would like to see the Sphinx, says Mr Corker, the Sphinx of Egypt with a lion's body, if I'm not mistaken, and a woman's head. Always smiling the Sphinx is, I expect your husband told you all about it. Do you like animals then? asks Mrs McBryde. I wouldn't really call the Sphinx an animal, says Mr Corker, it's a mixture, it's a mystery – the riddle of the Sphinx that nobody knows the answer to, an enigma as they say. But do you like animals? repeats Mrs McBryde. In their proper place, says Mr Corker. I know somebody who wants to get rid of the dearest little Persian, says Mrs McBryde, and you could do with a cat, in a place like this. I wouldn't mention it normally like, because if there's one thing that makes me wild it's cruelty to animals – one hand is playing with the button of her blouse – but I'll say this for you, you look as if you'd be kind to things smaller than yourself. Mr Corker shakes his head. I'm afraid I can't take on a cat at the moment, he says. It'll get rid of all the mice for you, she says. She sniffs the air as though she can smell mice. Perhaps later, says Mr Corker. Now, Mrs McBryde, could you tell me how old you are? You put down what you think she says, I can't lose that way, can I? Mr Corker smiles as he types. Can you tell us why you left your last place of employment? I was there three years, she says, but Bob kept on at me so that I had to stop in the end, there was simply no way round it. Mr McBryde doesn't like you working? suggests Mr Corker. O yes he does, she says, it keeps me out of mischief he says and perhaps he's not so wrong at that either. But the last job then, persists Mr Corker, what was the matter there? It was the walk back at night, it was right across the Common you see, and Bob got all het up about it, though I must say I never gave it a thought – half these rapes if you ask me aren't rapes at all, it's just that the women want to get their own back afterwards. You can't be too careful, says Mr Corker, the new crime wave is a fact. They admit it. There's no respect for life or property these days. Look at that poor old lady in Brixton who was coshed the other week. You know, says Mrs McBryde, I don't think Bob would have minded if they'd coshed me. She smiles. A gap in her front teeth is quite obvious when she smiles. Funny isn't it, she continues. Are you quite sure you wouldn't like that little Persian? Mr Corker now says something which considerably surprises Alec for he has never heard him use such an expression out of the office, let alone in it. No Can Do, says Mr Corker. His tone of voice is also different. He says it archly as though it were the refrain from a slightly indecent song. No Can Do, he repeats. It's a thousand pities, says Mrs McBryde shaking her red head at Mr Corker and thinking that probably he talks like an old lady because he can't help it. Are you looking for a full-time job? he asks. All day yes, she says, but not sleeping in, I can't leave Bob, you see. I see, he says, and what hours do you have in mind? All depends, she says, who they are and where they live, if I like people I fit in with them, if I don't they find out pretty quick. And what money are you asking? he asks. Seven pounds, she says, phew it's hot in here, do you mind if I take my coat off? She takes off the black overcoat with the fur collar. Underneath she is wearing a short-sleeved green blouse, the colour of willow leaves. Her arms are plump and white except for the backs of her forearms which are freckled. Alec, who is writing out cards for the downstairs showcase, decides that she looks older with her coat off and therefore more tarted-up. She's like an aunt of his, his favourite aunt. Seven pounds with all meals found? asks Mr Corker. Oh yes, she says, you don't think I'm going to feed them and not myself, do you? Do you enjoy cooking, Mrs McBryde? This is one of Corker's favourite questions. He has explained it many times to Alec: The good worker has to *enjoy* his work. If they don't enjoy it, they're no good. Depends, answers Mrs McBryde, if it's appreciated or not. If it all goes without a thank-you, I feel like saying you can cook the next damn lot yourselves. I mean I ask you a thank-you doesn't cost anyone much does it? I once worked for a young gentleman who was really appreciative – he really noticed what I did – I enjoyed working for him, I did really. Cooking is an art, says Mr Corker. Are you particular about food then? asks Mrs McBryde. I've always said and I always will – Alec ticks this sentence before it's finished; he knows it off by heart – I can eat anything that's put in front of me – except parsnips. Parsnips! she repeats and laughs. What about turnips then? Turnips, answers Mr Corker, I have eaten with considerable pleasure. And I'll tell you something else, in Finland I ate reindeer, and it was delicious too. Ugh, says Mrs McBryde, it must have been cold. Now tell me, Mrs McBryde, says Corker, how would you cook a joint of roast beef? Don't make me laugh, she says, I'll tell you what though – I'll make you a cup of tea if you like, where's your gas ring? Mr Corker places the tips of his fingers together like a curate and smiles. Then he uses another expression which surprises Alec. Thanks dear, he says, but we haven't time.

I know without thinking it that there are women who get kinder as the day wears on.

If you want me, Mrs McBryde, to find you a post as housekeeper I must know something about your recipes. Alec considers another possibility: Why shouldn't he and Jackie have a room here as well? Roast beef, Mrs McBryde, please, says Mr Corker. You really want to know? says Mrs McBryde. Please. Well, the secret of roasts is to get your oven real hot first. And? Well, I take the griller you do the toast on and I take the thing off it – the platform thing with legs – and I pop that into the oven tin and put my meat on top because then your meat is never touching the tin so it won't stew in its own juice. If you want to get it nice and brown on the outside and keep it lovely and red in the middle you don't ever want to let it stew. She looks at Mr Corker's hands with the little bandage round the wart on the little finger of his right hand. Course you've got to have a man who can carve. And how about the Yorkshire, Mrs McBryde? You beat it up hard, she says, you must really beat it, get it real eggy, then you pop it in as high as you can. When it's risen you put it under the meat so all the juice of the meat drips down into the Yorkshire tray. Gives it a lovely meaty flavour that way. All the goodness of the meat dripping all the time on to your pudding below. She sees the feeble eyes behind the bifocal lenses of his glasses. You look as if you could do with some good meat, she says.

> I know but never remember that there is a special kind of dirt, made distinct for me by the use to which I once put it. In this particular dirt I scrabbled with my hands to hide something which I did not wish anyone else to see. I do not even know what it was. It has become so well hidden that I could never find it again myself. It is lost in the dirt. Sometimes for a fraction of a second I become frightened because I know that whatever I hid could be found and recognized by another. This woman might be prepared to look in this special kind of dirt. But I do not think this.

Mr Corker starts to consult his books. He offers Mrs McBryde a post in a large house near the Common. A businessman and his wife and two young children. They already have a nanny for the children, a gardener and a regular cleaner. They want a cook-general. I happen to know Mr Wollheim, says Mr Corker, and he's a very charming gentleman and I'm told one of the best amateur golfers in the country. What's the pay? demands Mrs McBryde. Six pounds five, says Mr Corker, but they might come up a bit. I don't like the sound of the place anyway, says Mrs McBryde. Why not just go and see, says Mr Corker coaxingly, it doesn't commit you to anything. Just go and see. What time do they want you there? asks Mrs McBryde. In time to have breakfast ready by 8.30. And then you stay till after tea. They don't expect you to stay for supper but only to prepare it. Saturdays off? she asks, not because she is in any doubt that they won't be, but because she wonders how he will put it. Mr Corker consults his book. Half-day Tuesday, he says. She can imagine Mr Wollheim and Madam his wife. Madam wears rubber gloves, always speaks softly to her when the children are present and will one day sack her and say: I've enjoyed working with you, Maggie. For Mrs McBryde her name Maggie trails out of

Madam's mouth like a dead mouse out of a cat's. That makes a long week, doesn't it? she says. I'll have to ask Bob about it. She reckons that if you're going to work in a house like that, you may as well work in a bloody factory and get twice the money. If she's working in a house, she likes to make a difference to somebody. She'll give her services but she's damned if she's going to be bought, least of all by some foreigner rotten with money. I can't see Bob agreeing, she says. That's not it at all, she argues to herself, that's not what I'm after, I'm not going to cook meals for a Nanny, life's too short for that and I'm not getting any younger, that's not what I want, I want to be able to use my brains a bit and have a bit of notice taken of me, bloody useless that type of person, I can be more than that, I can. I'm sure, says Mr Corker as persuasively as he is able, you'll find Mr and Mrs Wollheim very kind people to work for. Mr Corker suddenly looks to Mrs McBryde like a pawnbroker. She can almost see the three brass balls outside the window. If you don't mind my asking, she says, what do *you* get out of all this? He has the perpetual discontented look of a pawnbroker. We charge, he says, a Registration Fee of five shillings, that is to register you in our Books, then when and if you find a vacancy your employers pay us too. Much? she asks. Mr Corker studies her as though something about her forehead has surprised him considerably. Usually it's one week's wages, he says. Well, says she, you're not going to get very fat on that! You mightn't believe it, says Mr Corker, but we've got ten thousand clients on our books. And with his hand with the little bandaged finger he indicates the Books around him. Alec has stopped working altogether. He has never seen Corker suffer so much so gladly. In this little place, she says, ten thousand – I just don't believe it. Smiling, she looks all round, and catches Alec's eye. It seems to Alec that she shuts her own, but so quickly that he cannot be sure. And so you want five bob off me? And you'll go after the job? asks Mr Corker quickly. No, says Mrs McBryde, if you'll pardon me I won't. Then that's that, says Mr Corker standing up. Haven't you got any other jobs? she says, still in her chair. Not at the moment, Mrs McBryde, nothing at the moment, if you care to come in next week we may have something or if we hear of a vacancy which we think will suit you we will write to you, we have your address. He recites this like a priest an absolution, whilst looking over her head. She searches in her handbag and holds out two half-crowns. There's your money then, she says, I'll be back. Mr Corker, standing, takes the money and puts it straight into his pocket. He doesn't mention a receipt. Then he holds up the black coat with the fur collar and says: May I help you on with it? *Office Day* has ceased to exist. Why wasn't the client given a receipt for her Registration Fee? Why wasn't she offered another vacancy – Alec knows that there is a list of at least twenty housekeeper vacancies? Why did Corker answer questions which he would never normally allow? Why did he say No Can Do in a voice that wasn't his own? Why is he hurrying her out? Alec knows the answer which answers all these questions. There is nothing to puzzle over. But the explanation, however obvious, cannot be found in *Office Day*. Even the office itself seems different, smaller and less important. And the disused rooms above, and the Kitchen and the Reception-Room, which are at the other end of the stone landing, already seem to be inhabited: inhabited by a *we* who will make it very nice here. The *we* will also make it like a shop. Corker's desk will be the counter. And on the other side of the door at the back will be breakfast things stacked on the draining board, shirts for ironing, a kettle on the gas, a cat, a bottle of nail varnish on the window-sill, last Sunday's papers folded on top of the needlework basket, the unmistakable noise of a woman moving about. A profession, even though an unrecognized one without an impressive name, has been sacrificed. A little shop remains. Corker has changed. He has become capable of falling asleep in his armchair after lunch, of walking about in his pyjamas, of talking through the lavatory door, of reading his books in bed whilst she – another she if not this one – sips tea beside him. Corker has become the *Old Bugger*. The *Old Bugger* explains it all. Oh thanks ever so much, says Mrs McBryde and standing with her back to Mr Corker (she is shorter than him) she slips her plump white arms into the black satin-lined sleeves of her coat with the fur collar. Whilst she buttons it, Mr Corker is wedged between her and the mantelpiece on which stands the French clock under the glass dome, which belonged to his mother. When she puts her hands up to the back of her head to arrange her hair, they play in front of Mr Corker's very nose. She twists round to laugh and say to him: We're a bit cramped here, aren't we? His face remains expressionless. Only the fingers of one hand behind his back play invisible piano notes in the air. She picks up her handbag and makes for the door. He steps across and opens it for her. You've had five bob off me, she says, so mind you find me something. Something near and not too classy. She laughs again. It's a pity you don't need a housekeeper yourself, she says, just round the corner like! We'll do our best, Mrs McBryde, says Corker and eases her out into the Waiting-Room. Alec listens. Let me know if you change your mind about the Persian, he hears her say. Then her shoes clip along the stone landing and down the stone stairs. Well I wouldn't, she thinks, take his job on for all the tea in China. Mr Corker returns to the Inner Office. He has a handkerchief in his hand. During office hours he always keeps his handkerchief tucked up the sleeve of his jacket.

I know that I am not apparently lovable.

He avoids Alec's excited eyes. But Alec is too excited to notice this. Even when Mr Corker sits down without saying a word and starts moving papers about on his desk, Alec explains his behaviour to himself as the *Old Bugger*'s pretence not to be an *Old Bugger*. What did you think of her roast beef? he asks. She was a madwoman, says Mr Corker, mad. All women are mad, says Alec, wanting now to reassure Corker of their male solidarity, but they have their uses. Mr Corker turns round and stares through his glasses as though he didn't quite trust them. Don't be coarse, he says. I was only joking, says Alec. It's no joking matter, says Mr Corker, I tell you that woman was mad, we might both have had our throats cut.

In the Waiting-Room there hangs a coloured engraving which depicts a monkey dressed up in a jockey's uniform riding a horse. Underneath the picture on the mount in delicate copperplate script is written the title: Give Em All You've Got, Dobbin! In the chair directly underneath this engraving sits a man. His cap is on the seat of the chair next to him. He is wearing a wide pin-striped blue suit. It is his best and it is somewhat crumpled. He has large hands. The fingers of the right one are much stained with nicotine and seen against the light blue of his suit these stains appear to be bright orange. He is straining his neck to look out of the window. There is nothing to prevent him getting up and standing by the window or moving to the chair next to it, but having chosen which chair to sit on, he prefers, even though he is alone in the waiting-room, to stick to his choice. Outside the window it is the acres of roofs that interest him. The hundreds of chimneys serving old fireplaces with black grates and room only for three lumps of coal are like stumps of trees in a forest long since cut down. He is able to see no end to it. He is in London. Next please, says Alec in the doorway. And since there is nobody else in the room, he knows it must mean him. He follows and finds himself standing on the red and green genuine Persian rug, no matter that it is worn, in front of the desk which once belonged to the managing director of a firm of high-class cigar importers, no matter that he went bankrupt, and sees the old chappie with grey hair and a pearl tiepin, no matter that it is his only jewel, staring at him. Take a seat, my man. The man notices particularly the old chappie's large head. He has been made aware of scale ever since he arrived in London yesterday. It is the bigness or smallness of things that continually strikes him and although he is far too rational to say to himself that the old chappie has a large head because he runs a busy important office in London, the expectations that he has of the one become confused with his expectations of the other as he sits down on the chair and waits for a lead. The down-turned eyes are reading an important paper selected from a pile of others in a neat metal tray laid on the large desk. What do you want? asks Mr Corker when he has finished reading. The man puts his hand in his side pocket, takes out a piece of newspaper folded into quarter the size of a bus ticket, unfolds it, smooths it out on the desk with his orange fingers and, handing it over, says: I read this. It says you've got a driving job, I'm a driver. Mr Corker says nothing but instantly performs. The chair swings round, arm and hand raised to select and take whilst still moving the correct book, the book is opened at the right page, a cross-reference is instantly understood, the chair swings and another book is selected to be read, there is a pause whilst a finger runs down the side of a list, the finger is licked, a page is swiftly turned. For the man watching, the performance is not unlike that of a cinema organist's. One produces information about the employment situation in London, the other produces music. It is true that neither the old chappie nor his books change colour but for the watcher each book, each page suggests a hundred different possibilities and variations. In Coleford there have been two street corners to stand on since he was born. The town is like the old recruiting poster by the bus stop next to the Angel, read a hundred times and every word known. London in the books the old chappie handles with such experience is limitless. He waits for the performance to produce an answer. Flicking the two middle adjacent fingers of his left hand against one another Mr Corker eventually speaks. The job's gone. The man looks at the scrap of newspaper still on the desk in front of him. Keeping the advertisement in his pocket had not meant keeping the job. His disappointment forces him to get on to his feet. When there is no reason for being in a place it is better to get moving. On his feet he looks round the room and down on Mr Corker. He senses that London is not only the city outside the window but

27

is just as much the interior of this room. The fancy clock on the mantelpiece underneath a kind of glass cloche such as they grow early lettuce under is as much London as the crowds and the distances. Because the man has got to his feet so abruptly Mr Corker makes his face look shocked.

Not even this morning can I think that I count. But I know that I count. I know it. It is my duty to act on this assumption. I am the guardian of my own counting. Since I was a small boy I have been myself. Earlier I was also myself, but under a different sky – a sky so sweet and delicate that it soon tore: it was torn to shreds and only a few of these shreds remained to remind me of the silken sky of my infancy: they remained, these shreds, attached to certain landmarks: the bath, my mother's singing voice, a lace curtain in my bedroom, grass as high as myself. When the sky was rent the name William became me. I recognized myself in it. I lived in the name William as though it were a small house. Whenever the name was called, or even when I said it myself to refer to my own being, I went to the front door to answer. It was important to do this because the front door always remained unlocked. Anybody could place any kind of accusation or order or embargo inside my front door, in the hall, and when once it was there I had to accept it. So I was always rushing to the front door to see who the caller was and what was wanted. Often it was Liesel: Liesel who was always welcome, Liesel who was like a garden round my house, Liesel in whom I would lose myself. Sometimes I made a mistake and the William wasn't mine at all. Sometimes the caller or callers had not intended me to hear and were busy looking in through one of my windows, and I would watch them secretly spying on me. They were like a crowd gathered round an accident and, seen from the back, all faceless. Later – much later – I made a few friends of my own age. This was when I was 17 or 18. Because they were friends, I used to bring them in the back way, through the back door. But, once, two of them started laughing: You don't really live *here*, do you? they said. Or rather, that is what I knew they meant. In fact we were talking about dreams. They told their dreams and then it was my turn. I told them about a dream I had in which I saved a dog from being run over by a train. They started to laugh. And one of them, his name was Reggie and he worked in a bank, said: He's probably made it up to set a good example. And Reggie said to me: Tonight you'll dream you'll get a medal. After that I brought everyone through the front door. There are many dangers. There is the danger of housebreaking. Certain cupboards I keep locked. I only open them in the silence of the night. I do not know for certain whether I keep them locked because their contents are so valuable or because I am ashamed of their contents and would hate anyone to discover them. I do not know this. But I do know that the value or shame attached to the contents is the result of my own pleasure in them. I have kept certain things in these cupboards since I was four, kept them secret and for myself. I cannot know what is in these cupboards for I only recognize them by night, and then I recognize their familiarity rather than their identity. They are my unidentifiable toys. They are what I saved from that time, now long ago, when I first moved in and had a roof over my head instead of the silken sky. There is also the danger of fire. My house William will be ashes when I die. I shall be myself no more. The house and I must end together. But we did not begin together. I came before the house. It is uneasy for me to trace my origins back too far. It is odd for me to accept the possibility of myself as one spermatozoa in my father's testicles. The knowledge of this has made me shiver when I have seen a shooting star in the endless night. The odds against me were astonishingly high. Which is perhaps why I now know I count for so much. I treasure the improbability that made me. I have not always done so, and I have not always known what I know now.

Before I moved into my independent name, everything around me under the silken sky confirmed that I was the centre of the world and Mother the space I inhabited. (Much later she told me that God would punish me for my selfishness.) When I moved into William, I learned that my name counted, for I was continually being called upon. But my name wasn't me. It had been given me. I moved into it with all my own accessories, but I had not built it. And so I assumed that somebody had given it to me, that somebody had built my house for me. I never connected this with the straightforward ceremony of my being christened (at Christ Church, London Road, by the Rev. Jasper Chase) for I realized that my name as such might have been different – I might have been called Edgar or Roland – yet everything else would still have been the same. Indeed, later, this happened: for I ceased to be William, I became Corker or Mr Corker, and then to some I became Corky, but I still opened the same front door and I still inhabited the same person as I'd always inhabited since that time so long ago when the sky wore away. At first it seemed likely that Father had built my house for me. I never considered the mystery of how he had done so. And anyway at that time I believed that he had built nearly everything I knew. London was his to make come and go. The day was his to end when he said. I do not remember but I know that sometimes I was frightened because I feared that I was not living in the house – which was mine but which was also the house he had granted me – as he would wish. Sometimes he would come to me without my calling, he would creep up to me when I was asleep and kiss my head, and then, if I half awoke, I would pray that he had not seen what I was. It was not until my mother told me that he was wicked, a bankrupt and a drunkard and that we would not see him again, it was not until then that I knew he had nothing to do with my house. And even after that, when he died, I wondered whether he knew at the end what I was, and I hoped he did. That was the real tragedy of his death: it was now forever too late for me to tell him. But after his death, I counted even more. I became the head of the family. For a while I felt grateful to whoever it was who had arranged my being me. By now, however, I was too adult to imagine that this 'whoever-it-was' was a single person. Equally I knew it had nothing to do with God. God was a long way away when I became William. Perhaps it was not so much a question of being grateful to whoever-it-was that had supplied the house, but rather to all those who were helping to maintain it: the Prime Minister, George V our King, our Judges, my employer who assured me that I had a golden future (I was working for a firm of sock manufacturers), the writers of editorials, men who behaved like gentlemen. All these helpers were representatives of the supplier. They were there to help me to be myself and to become what I deserved to be. Others were there to prevent me: the Germans whom we were fighting, men who behaved like cads, anarchists, and (after I had become a medical orderly in France) a number of non-commissioned officers. Many opportunities slipped through my fingers. I no longer felt grateful to the representatives of the supplier – and furthermore I was no longer so certain who these representatives were – but I consoled myself by believing that if things became really bad, I could always seek out a representative somewhere and appeal to him to pass a message back: the message would have read: Things Cannot Go On Like This. William Corker Is Not Counting. That is how I lived. Life became harder and harder, but always I found consolation in the belief that whoever-it-was who had supplied me with myself would in the end see that justice was done to me. It was not until one month ago – after running my own business for years, after the Second World War, after Mother's death, after travelling to eleven different countries, after suffering Irene year in and year out – it was not until one month ago that I knew for certain that there was no supplier, that there was nobody to whom I could appeal, that whether I maintained myself or not was my concern and mine only, that the person I had inhabited since the day the silken sky was rent was mine to do what I liked with. Then I knew that I was alone. Then I knew – although I have not thought it even yet – that I counted because I was myself, the last and only possible celebration of the highly improbable event which started sixty-four years ago and is me. I matter, and now at last I know that I matter. I matter, I matter, but I do not know how to think it.

We are an Employment Agency, Mr Corker says. What is now being said, the tone of voice, is London too. If you should care to Register with us we will do our very best to help you. The *Old Bugger* playing at *Office Day*, ticks Alec. The man hesitates before putting his name down for anything. He came for the job in the newspaper. His working plan is now to look for another job in another paper. There must be a job for him in the whole of London. He glances again at the clock to remind himself how different London is from Coleford. Sit down, says Mr Corker. Within five minutes the man hands over five shillings as Registration Fee. He asks how long the five bob lasts for. Until we find you a job, says Mr Corker. The man considers that he is fortunate indeed to have come to such an office. Details are taken. Bert Immonds. Albert Immonds, Mr Corker repeats as though by avoiding the abbreviation he is bestowing an honour which is all part of the inclusive service. Laundry Van Driver. Age 32. Married. Temporary address: 12 Minsey Road, Bayswater. He is given a Receipt for Registration Fee. The *Old Bugger*, Alec decides, has always been bluffing about *Office Day* and now he is bluffing again. He is pretending that *Office Day* rules rule all. Alec now knows they don't; they don't even govern what Corker himself does in his own Inner Office. It was of course a mistake to refer to her roast beef as though it were a joke; he too should have pretended to believe in the rules. They should both pretend. The van driver folds up the Receipt like the newspaper advertisement. The telephone rings. Alec answers and says it is Miss Corker for Mr Corker. Mr Corker takes the phone and starts to smooth down the hair over his temples. I'm afraid, he says, I can't talk now. I'm in the middle of seeing a client. He adds softly: An important client. He puts the receiver down hurriedly. Now we must find a vacancy for you. What about chauffeuring – ever done any? No, replies the man. I can't say I have and I can't say I want to. Vans are my line. I like vans, you see. I couldn't take being given orders all the while from the back seat behind. You got nothing in the laundry line? The telephone rings again. Mr Corker quickly picks up the receiver himself. It is the same voice saying: I'm quite prepared to go on phoning all the morning till you have the courtesy to listen. Although the voice is shrill, Mr Corker presses the earpiece hard to his ear so that neither of the other occupants of the office shall hear the exact words being said. I suggest you send your client and your assistant into another room. Then you can listen to what I have to say in peace. Mr Corker glances at Alec and the van driver. By the expression in Corker's eyes Alec guesses that it is his sister who has rung again. Alec regrets that she is phoning. Her phoning offers the most likely explanation of the morning's events and the outcome will be dull. She and her brother have had a quarrel: he walked out and said he would not come back: he has been upset ever since: and now they will make it up and he will go back to her. *Having Jackie* will benefit. They will come here at week-ends. But Alec had hoped the *Old Bugger* would be an old bugger. From today he would like everything to be different. He is sick of all the arguments (such as he imagines Corker's sister now using) which explain why things must stay the same. He would like everything to be different and everything new to be explained by the new truth of *Having Jackie*, even Corker. The van driver asks himself whether this phone call might not be the latest news of a new batch of jobs including one for him. He has noticed the way Mr Corker always says 'we' and he believes that there may be other branches of the Agency in other parts of London. Go on, says Mr Corker wearily. I assume, enunciates the voice, that what you have done and the childish way you have done it is no more than a tantrum, a childish tantrum as I say. I couldn't believe my eyes just now when I found your childish note. You have never said anything like this before. You have never complained in any way. You never raised your voice. For every day of fifteen years I have kept house for you and I thought you liked the arrangement. It hasn't always been very easy for me. Hallo? Hallo? Are you there? Yes, says Mr Corker looking up at the ceiling, I'm listening. I've made a number of sacrifices, continues the voice mounting, but I always understood we were friends, good friends. I tried to make a home for you as you need. The earpiece held so tight to the ear is beginning to make the ear go red. The voice rises. I just can't believe it. You can't mean it because there's simply no reason for it. It's like one of those crying fits you used to have as a boy. It's a tantrum. So don't be such a silly and I'll be expecting you back for supper tonight. The presence of the other two forces Mr Corker to answer obliquely. I assure you the proposition is quite a serious one. In anticipation he presses the earpiece even tighter. How can you talk like that? Proposition indeed! Are you out of your mind or don't you realize what you're doing? It's not a proposition I tell you, William, it's a death warrant. Mr Corker returns the receiver suddenly to its rest. As he does so the screech of the high-pitched voice becomes audible. Alec becomes hopeful again. The van driver persuades himself that there must be something the matter with the telephone. Mr Corker, eyes protruding, apologizes for the interruption. Business! says the van driver to make clear that he understands the difficulties. Underneath Mr Corker's jaw a pulse is beating like a little sprat. So you drive vans you say. Ever been involved in any accidents? Not what you'd call real ones. The man laughs. The laugh is in no way the result of embarrassment. When recollecting certain scattered and surprising moments he can laugh the same way

34

even to himself. Behind the laugh is a kind of relish: relish in the way that things, solid manufactured things – roads, Commers, Bedfords – and existing natural things – fog over the Wye, grass banks – can come together and interact quite unexpectedly, can within a fraction of a second stand a situation on its head, bang around and bounce off and still you come out to tell the tale. It is a laugh about escapes. The escapes were not dramatic. A tractor came round a blind corner on the wrong side at Redbrook. An elm under snow in the Forest fell right across the road. On the hill up from Cinderford the brakes failed. The value of escapes is that they remind you how high the stakes are. After an escape you see the materials with which you work as trickier, slyer, more treacherous. But also by the token of your survival you see yourself as measuring up to anything they can produce. Staying alive increases your self-respect. The van driver's laugh is an acknowledgement of this, and of the fact that materials are as they are, tyres get worn smooth, roads get wet, often you can't see the ice till you're on it, there are some bloody fools on the road, trees don't grow with lights fitted on them, and he knows the dodges. As he laughs, he is struck by how suspicious Mr Corker's eyes look behind his spectacles. The old chappie needs reassuring. Even the little laugh was wrong. But nothing you could call serious, he says. The telephone rings. The voice in the ear is very strident. You're going to be sorry one of these days. It's not my death warrant, oh no my dear William, it's not my warrant you're signing, it's your own. You're quite incapable of living by yourself and you're far far too selfish for anyone else to look after you and put up with it for more than a week. You'll go to pieces, William. Mr Corker bares his teeth. I'm running a business, he shouts without waiting for the voice to stop. I'm running a business and I can't be constantly interrupted like this. Will you please be good enough to hang up? Will you hang up? He pauses but is not quick enough in reapplying the pressure of the earpiece to the ear. The voice saying *You are killing me, William*, is understood by all three in the room. It sounded like a voice in a distant galvanized water tank. Mr Corker puts the phone back and shakes his head. *You are killing me, William*, is still in the room. Alec remembers rows he has seen. She wrestles with him and he struggles and they fight in the absurd and horrifying manner in which a man and a woman fight, keeping their bodies far away from each other and slapping and grasping with their hands as though trying to still a slapping fish that has come between them. The van driver, well versed in matrimonial affairs and a consultant for some of the younger men at the Angel, hesitates between two conflicting theories. The unnatural truth does not occur to him. Either the voice belonged to the wife or to a piece. *You are killing me, William.* It is somewhat early in the morning for the wife to talk like that unless the wife is abnormal, abnormal with the terrible complaint of women, the complaint of complaining incessantly like a river flowing. Such women can say anything at any time; they feel it coming on them, and they start to speak. The old chappie, however, does not look like the husband of such a woman. He is too plump and convex. The husbands of such women are clenched, blasted and cracked down the middle. The van driver does not entirely discount the possibility that the wife is normal but has just discovered or heard something bad. The argument against this is that the words chosen and the tone of voice implied so little righteous indignation. Every normal wife has a rolling pin in her armoury. Despite appearances the van driver decides within a second that the voice belonged to a piece. He would not deny for one moment that he is a little surprised. The old chappie's age, his manner, his unprepossessing but mild face, the respectability of the office, all make it seem unlikely. Or all would make it seem unlikely if it were not London. But it is London. And in London even the man across the desk from him can look for and discover what he would never even begin looking for elsewhere. He can let himself out of his own front door, travel several miles in a bus, walk along streets almost indistinguishable save to the experienced from those he left an hour before, arrive at where he is unknown and cannot except with the greatest difficulty be traced, and there find the means and those willing to allow him or entice him to become somebody totally unconnected with what he is and with what he is believed to be behind his own front door. London transforms. London can affect any aspect of a man's life. If one knows where to search there is everything in London. But also – and this is the crux of one of the van driver's anxieties – in London one can come across things without looking for them, London, he fears, is full of stray chances and unlooked-for opportunities and these can erode a man. There is nothing one cannot be, nothing one cannot call oneself, nothing therefore one cannot forget in London. In London there is always somebody who knows what you want before you do. And the van driver's resistance to London is expressed in a sentence that is repeating itself far faster than words again and again in his mind: *I'm not sure now I want it.* The old chappie has found himself in a corner he never meant to be in. Did she put him in it? And who put her in her corner? And then who, who? The chimneys on the field of roofs are like the stumps of a whole forest felled. He is anxious lest when they move to London they will find themselves where they never meant to be. He is expectant because London may give them the chances they want. For himself he feels confident. His fear is around his wife. Yet it is in order not to disappoint her that he has come. Already in London he is acting despite his own wishes. Already he is going along with a plan he has not made. *I'm not sure now I want it.* For the wife London has become all that she has never had, all that she does not know. But the van driver reckons that although the fruit-bottling factory where she works pays badly, much of what she has had is worth having. He fears to disappoint her and he fears not to take a good chance for them both. But equally and also he fears that in London she may be lost. She will slip through his fingers and he will never again find her as she is now, for she will change and want different things and perhaps even then not want London any more. *I'm not sure now I want it.* But out loud and out of sympathy with the old chappie who has his own surprising difficulties of the same essence, the van driver says with some exasperation: Women! Mr Corker appears not to hear the remark.

I know I haven't the courage to face this woman. In her presence I cannot challenge her authority. Only in her absence, only in a silence she cannot violate, do my hopes turn into plans. I am not a fighter for I can never believe that the issue is more important than what I know. I need to preserve my knowledge, if knowledge it can be called, my own awareness of what is happening to me, and what is happening began sixty-three years ago and has continued ever since. This is the knowledge I have, it is the state of being alive and conscious, it is being William Corker that I know, and to be William Corker knowingly has always seemed more important to me than fighting. Irene is a fighter. What she is does not occur to her. What she says she does not realize. What she wants she does not know. She fights without thinking for what or why. I know how pointed and long her fangs are. She sits there with her sticks but her sticks are not to help her walk: they are to help her get her way in the world. Her face is white the better to accuse. Her good works are all arguments for her prosecutions. Even the name of our Mother is a tooth in her jaw. In Little Red Riding Hood she is the wolf. Yet if I see her, I kiss her and rearrange the cushions behind her back and dig the garden bed that she wants dug, for when she looks at me or speaks, she makes me feel that I have failed. In her presence I am the guilty one. To become innocent I must be away from her. I need to be innocent to live. She must be put out of my life. She is being put out. I am slipping away, covertly, to live for once without blame.

He finds a grocery deliveries van driver. Pay: £7 10s. You may receive, of course, he informs the applicant, a certain number of tips – the grocers concerned are in the West End. You got nothing that pays a bit better? asks the van driver. He calculates now that in London the wife may well earn more than he. Mr Corker looks at his books again. He looks up. How well do you know London? Not much, says the van driver, not much, but I'd pick up the routes quick enough. I've got a good sense of direction. Mr Corker says: Purley. Do you know Purley? Alec is repeating the phrase *You are killing me, William*, to himself. He has repeated it so many times that the meaning has worn very thin and the sound of the phrase has become like the noise of a machine. It seems to Alec that the man who has *You are killing me, William*, screamed at him is the same as the man who walks about in his pyjamas, talks through the lavatory door and says Damn Again when the shop bell goes. The screech over the telephone has confirmed that Corker is the *Old Bugger*. Alec can tick it for there will be rows along the stone landing here like there are rows on all the stone landings in Clapham. But this tick is not conclusive; everything depends on brother and sister not making it up and Corker really moving to Clapham. Even in Banstead they are temporarily like Clapham when they quarrel. Or Balmoral, says Alec to amuse himself. They specialize in rows in Clapham. I wish you were bloody well dead, Irene. Alec rehearses the come-back. Bloody well dead, Irene. Then you'll be sorry, William, you'll be sorry when I'm dead. Alec hears the voice, female, plaintive and yet dominating. Then he challenges himself as to whether *Having Jackie* means rows. You'll be sorry, Alec, you'll be sorry when I'm dead. He can't hear it in Jackie's voice. The voice goes with a moustache. Alec has never before thought of Irene as Corker's wife. She just lived in the same house, or rather he lived in her house because it was too big for her. Now she sounds like a wife. *You are killing me, William*, sounds wifely. He again sees the two figures slapping the sopping fish between them. The red-head of a few minutes ago would be a real fighter, Alec assesses. Nails, and tufts of hair. But as Alec remembers her complete with darkest nylons and pneumatic bosom, he also remembers what until now he had entirely forgotten: that Irene is an invalid. He has seen her. She looked like Death Warmed Up and she wore a massive beer-coloured necklace. He glances at Corker taking the van driver on a tour of London. We've got a job on our books there at Purley, Mr Corker is saying, a small furniture firm. Irene talks like a wife but isn't. She fights, but Corker, with his growing bald patch which Alec can always see, can't fight back because she's an invalid at death's door. Nine pounds a week but no overtime rates, Mr Corker says. The phrase that Alec has been repeating suddenly reassembles itself to contain an undreamt-of meaning. William *is* killing her. Three facts impress Alec. If she is an invalid, surrounded by medicine bottles, poisoning is very simple. If she is at death's door, Corker is doing no more than opening it for her. If she has a wifely hold over him and yet is no wife at all, how else can he escape her to emerge as the *Old Bugger*? Alec looks at the bald patch as he has never done before. Beneath the pale scalp the dome of the skull, within the dome the man's thoughts – all so ordinary that anything is possible. The fact that Corker may be killing his sister does not shock Alec: if he knew for certain that Corker was killing her, he might feel differently: as it is, he just may be and in Alec's experience anyone may be about to do anything. What does shock him is that for nearly two years Corker and he have kept up the pretence that Corker is exempt. The truth is that Corker is a *May-Be-Old-Bugger*. What are the hours? the van driver asks. Mr Corker says: they say that's up to you. The van driver says: What? Mr Corker says: they say as soon you've done the deliveries you're free, the quicker you get them done the sooner you get home. The van driver says: dicey I should think. Words within say: *I'm not sure now I want it.* Mr Corker says: Why not go and see them? The van driver says all right. Mr Corker types on a light-green Interview Card. The van driver asks himself: Is he ashamed? Or is he inconsolable? He then glances down at MrCorker's boots under the desk, and visualizes them under a woman's bed in a room in a street somewhere in London where you can drive a van for twelve hours a day and get no overtime. The light-green card is handed to him. He folds it in half despite its stiffness and puts it into the same pocket as he put the folded newspaper cutting. Mr Corker tells him to come back another day if he does not get the job, but says this in such a tone as to imply that he trusts the van driver won't be so foolish as to turn it down. The van driver gets to his feet. Will you please see Mr Immonds out, Mr Corker asks Alec. This is a code. Whenever Mr Corker says this, it means that a client has made him suspicious. He may have looked at the clock twice, he may have been found smelling a flower in the Waiting-Room, he may have been evasive in his answers. Whatever the reason, Alec has to follow the client to the top of the stairway and see him definitely down it. The two of them stand at the top of the stone stairway. From below comes the noise of London traffic regular as that of the sea. They smile at one another, because each with his own interpretation is now amused by the elderly man in the grey suit still sitting at his desk in the Inner Office. Hope you find something, says Alec. Thanks, says the van driver and goes down the steps two at a time. I'm not sure now I want it, not sure now. Alec watches him descend, not because he cares about Corker's instructions but because he is enjoying the realization that between these two men, the one descending the stairway and the one at his desk in the Inner Office, he is an equal.

Mr Corker in the chair behind his desk has his eyes shut when Alec re-enters the room. Alec continues writing out the show-case cards. Mr Corker neither moves nor says a word. The gas fire burns. Alec's pen scratches a little. Then Mr Corker sighs, a sad but also impatient sigh. You know, says Alec, I've been thinking I'd like you to meet my girl friend some time. I should be very happy to do so Alec, says Mr Corker, what's her name? Jackie, says Alec.

Alec looks at his watch. In twenty minutes it will be time to make coffee. And by after coffee, he always reckons, the longest part of the morning is over. Then, today being Monday, he'll go after the lunch hour to the *Advertiser* and since Jackie's shop is almost on the way, he'll go in to see her. The sensation which is almost a pain in his penis is still there. His lower ribs ache too. He wonders whether she has a similar sensation inside her. She said it never hurt at all when he went into her the first time. There is no such thing as *Unhaving-Jackie*. They were both creatures of the same necessity. Alec senses this necessity but does not name it. He remembers how each sought their opposite, at first half seeing and only locally, and then how they took their opposite and left it and took it and left it – each time more largely – and took it and took it until at a moment when their sight and arms could encompass the whole universe, the opposites became identical, their names forgotten, their seeking over, their sex unknowable. Mr Corker also looks at his watch. It is a gold watch on a gold chain which he keeps in a leather pouch in his waistcoat pocket. It was his father's watch. He looks from the watch to the clock on the mantelpiece which was his mother's to check that both are keeping proper time. Why don't you bring your young lady to my little talk tonight? he says to Alec. Is it tonight? says Alec. Of course it is, says Mr Corker. The one on Vienna? says Alec. Vienna, repeats Mr Corker, yes, Vienna, City of the Blue Danube. He closes his eyes and squeezes the end of his nose. Imagine we are there, he says, I've gone on business and I've taken you with me. We are walking down Karntner Street which is near the great Opera House, we have changed our money – we ought to get about seventy schillings to the pound – there are wonderful shops all round us, coffee houses and pastry makers and tailors and wine merchants and everything is of the best quality and very clean, and do you know where we are going? We are going to Dehmels. Have you ever heard of Dehmels? Alec shakes his head. At Dehmels you eat the best ice-cream in the world and you drink a little glass of Kummel. The inside is all pink and blue and crystal candelabra hang from the ceiling. In the days of the Emperors the aristocrats used to go to Dehmels for their ice-creams and to say hello to each other. And *it* hasn't changed, it's still the same. And with everything they serve, they bring you a glass of iced water. The telephone interrupts. Mr Corker frowns. You answer it, he tells Alec. It turns out to be the Coach and Horses where there has been a misunderstanding about a waitress. Mr Corker picks up the phone. You promised! bawls the manager of the Coach and Horses. We did our utmost, says Mr Corker. We have only one now! shouts the manager. We are sorry, says Mr Corker. Alec watches Corker perform as he has watched him many times before. He is performing *Suffering-the Last-Straw*. Between words, he smiles and looks comically up at the ceiling. Too bad, says Mr Corker. We were relying on you, says the manager, and now the lunches will be served cold. Cold, says Mr Corker, Buffet. No! Damn you! shouts the manager, the hot lunches will be cold by the time they reach the customers in the dining-room with only one waitress to serve! We'll do our very best, says Mr Corker, but you know what it is these days: you can trust nobody no more. Miss – Miss Sutcliffe promised us faithfully she'd be coming to you today. It's too bad when people let you down like that. Can you or can you not supply us with the staff we ask you for? says the Coach and Horses. Mr Corker taps the arm of his chair and grins as a man does when examining a tooth in a mirror. We'll do our utmost, he says. Alec wonders what the *May-Be-Old-Bugger* really does in Vienna, apart from drinking iced water. He also wonders what Vienna is like. Which of the rules that apply here apply there? Its being so far away is disagreeable, for so much can become unlearnt on the way there, one might arrive like a kid. But the fact that Vienna is far away from London is also promising; what is impossible in London may be possible there. Alec stares at Corker as though to balance the advantages and disadvantages. We are desperate, says the Coach and Horses. Just give me time to think, says Mr Corker, a little peace. He puts his hand to his forehead. Alec ticks another performance: *The Mind at Work*. The tick no longer means that the piece has been fitted into an overall pattern which is spelling out an answer. Now the tick only means that the piece as a piece is a familiar bit of the mysterious *May-Be-Old-Bugger*. I have it, says Mr Corker, just the lady for you. Hornby's the name. Hornby. Yes. Like the trains. You know, the clockwork ones. She was at the Dutch House in Thornton Heath. Yes, she has very good ones. We have seen them ourselves, yes. Not at all. A privilege. We'll phone her tooter sweet. Good-bye. Good-bye. Mr Corker puts the receiver down and scribbles a note on the memo pad which he has chosen because it has sayings printed on the top of each page. At the top of the present page is: Out of strength came forth sweetness. What were we talking about? asks Mr Corker, when we were interrupted? Alec, comparing his chances of survival with Corker's, says Vienna. How old were you when you first visited it? My first visit, says Corker, wasn't till 1950, but even then it was like going back to a place I'd been to before, and that was because of our nanny when we were children. She was Viennese you see. Her name was Liesel. I was her favourite and she used to talk and talk and talk to me about Wien, as it's called. Money and having nannies is an advantage, thinks Alec. I was very fond of her, very fond indeed, but she left us when I was nine and went back there. Perhaps she's still alive, says Alec, wondering whether the advantage still counts. I made many inquiries, says Mr Corker, but you see her name Muller is a very common one and I don't remember her address. Muller means Miller. When you go to Vienna, says Alec, what do you do? Do! says Mr Corker. I live! says Mr Corker. The Viennese have the secret of how to live. They are the most cultivated people in the world. You don't have to *do* anything. Everything's there all around you. You can go to the art museum, you can go to the Belvedere and sit in the gardens where Marie Theresa walked, you can take an excursion to the Vienna Woods, at night you can go up to Grinzing and drink wine and listen to music, if you came you could dance, everyone does, or just look down at the city below and the hills all round. It's the city of music too. Mozart and Beethoven lived there. I've been to Mozart's house, you know. And it's cheap. It's much cheaper than London. Much.

I don't mind telling you I've thought of a plan before now, but we weren't free before, like we are now. Mr Corker shuts his mouth tight but at the same time smiles at Alec, so that his expression is rather like that of the monkey who will speak no evil. Alec says nothing. We're going to make some big changes, says Mr Corker. Corker's of Clapham – why not Corker's of the Continent? All these young girls that come over to work and learn the language, don't they need an agency, well, don't they? And there's a steady turnover of them because they never want to stay long, they get homesick or into trouble or they don't like the food. We'd begin off with a branch in Vienna, then we'd open one in Scandinavia, then in Italy, then in Germany and then in Spain too, because in Spain wages are very low which is a great advantage. Corker's of the Continent! Overseas Vacancies! What would you say to managing here by yourself? Mr Corker looks at Alec. *Having Jackie* in the whole place, crosses Alec's mind. I'd need a bit of help, says Alec. And I'd take Vienna, says Mr Corker. Conducting with one hand, he hums a tune Alec does not recognize. When he has stopped, he says: Who knows? Alec asks: Have you got somebody in Vienna? Mr Corker looks so pleased at being asked this question that Alec believes he must want to tell a secret. To help me, you mean? asks Mr Corker. Yes. Well, says Mr Corker, I think I could find several. Several? says Alec. Mr Corker smiles and looks even more pleased. Not like you think, he says. Like what then? says Alec. Mr Corker seems not to hear. There is silence for a moment, until Mr. Corker says: We must be patient and plan ahead, step by step. The first step is to move in here. I've often thought to myself how Vienna – Wien as it's really called – isn't just a beautiful city, it's a way of life. In Wien some things are important and some aren't. They have a phrase you know – the Wiener Art, which means the Viennese way of doing things. Now to my mind if it's an art, you ought to be able to practise it anywhere, like the art of photography. I'll admit Clapham isn't as suitable for either photography or Wiener Art as some places in the world, but we've got to make a beginning somewhere. It's a beginning, and I don't mind taking a bet with you that in a few weeks you won't recognize it, Alec. It's going to be our own little Vienna, our own little place for practising Wiener Art. Alec is disappointed that the conversation has returned to Clapham. Why not get a housekeeper from Vienna? he asks. We must wait and see, says Mr Corker severely. There's always the financial side to consider. It's always the same with you young people, you think money makes itself. Why does the old bugger talk about it all if he thinks he can't afford it? That's not true, Alec says out loud, we've all had to work at home. Will you get me Miss Hornby on the phone please, says Mr Corker. Whilst Alec looks up her number and dials it, he marks it as *Funny* how Corker seems to want to tell him something but daren't. Mr Corker introduces himself to Miss Hornby. Miss Hornby, we have at last been able to find the job for you. Oh have you really? she whispers. We have indeed, says Mr Corker, and furthermore we have noted your special requirements, which frankly is why we are so pleased to have the chance of offering you the job now. Do tell me, Miss Hornby stretches her voice, where can it be? At the Coach and Horses, Miss Hornby, the Coach and Horses. Oh! she is disappointed. We know the manager well, says Mr Corker, he's a charming man. Oh dear, but I've been there before, says she, it's not a new place. Surely, says Mr Corker gently, it was a little while ago you were there and it has changed hands since then. You should just see the kitchens at the Coach and Horses! cries the lady still to be persuaded. My dear, says Mr Corker, it is entirely up to you whether or not you see your way to filling this vacancy and if you should decide it is not for you, you know, we trust, we shall do our utmost to find you something else approaching nearer to your requirements, but if here we may offer a little advice from the benefit of years of experience, do remember that no job is ideal and that everything depends on what you make it. The Coach and Horses is the busiest public house in Morden and serves approximately a hundred lunches a day, a hundred lunches must bring in approximately £3 in tips and we have ascertained that there is only one other waitress serving, which is why the wages as such are a secondary consideration although they will, we have reason to believe, pay what you are asking, for the real money, as we never tire of pointing out, is under the plates. You're so kind, says Miss Hornby. We cannot, of course, says Mr Corker, guarantee that others will not soon be after so attractive a vacancy but should you be interested we did gain from the manager an assurance that he will keep the vacancy open for you and you alone until tea-time. After all that trouble, says Miss Hornby, and all that you have done I do appreciate it ever so much and quite candidly I think the least I can do is to trot along to the Coach and Horses and see what I can see. I'll put my finery on and catch a bus right now. Well, says Mr Corker, we hope you'll see your way to being happy there. Thank you again, says Miss Hornby. After a few moments' silence Alec says: If you want a hand with anything when you move in, just ask me. That's very kind of you, Alec, says Mr Corker. Not at all, says Alec, perhaps one day I'll ask you for something. We'll help each other, says Mr Corker, Mutual Aid, they call it. How do you think I'd get on in Vienna? asks Alec. You'd love it, says Mr Corker, just love it.

(Whilst Alec is making coffee in the kitchen, Mr Corker interviews an old man. His shirt is without collar or stud. He has said that he was once a seaman.)

Confused and not wanting to be difficult and being willing to undertake any job for the doing of which he inspires enough confidence to be paid a few shillings, he says: Anything. Come, Mr Hodges, says Mr Corker, if we offered you a job as a head waiter you'd be lost, wouldn't you, you wouldn't know what to do, you don't even know how to carry a tray or serve a bottle of wine, do you? The old man is not in the least put out by this. Indeed as he thinks back on the expedients to which he has been forced, he wishes there were more things he had not done, and so he answers Mr Corker by saying: I've done most fucking things. Mr Corker takes his spectacles off. Mr Hodges, we will not tolerate bad language on these premises.

I often say that I do not understand the need for it but I know this to be untrue. I even know that I like the word fucking, but I like to use it myself in my own way. It is a word – and there are others too – which has grown up with me. I have always known, ever since I first discovered it, what it means and where I should keep it. I keep this word to myself. Sometimes it helps me to find my way, but I would not dream of using it to give directions to others. And when it is used by somebody else, it becomes a different word, it is no longer the one that has grown up with me, it is no longer like Sister or Bath or Bankrupt – all words which I know so well that when I walk they walk with me, and which I could recognize in the darkest silence without them ever being uttered; when it is used by somebody else, it ceases to be mine, and, worse still, it is disfigured, all the pretty attributes I have hung upon it are torn away in one brutal pronouncement and he, the speaker, bends it to his own foul purpose. How foul is easy to guess just by looking at him. He has taken fucking away from me and shat upon it. And I know too that his shit is not good shit, it is not like mine, for this man has never taken care of himself, never kept himself clean, and he has eaten things which I would never eat. Everything apparently confirms this: my position, my background, my principles, my life to date, my plans for the future. He could no more live as I intend to than could a dog. He is an ignorant, stupid, inarticulate, lazy, drunken, dishonest, foul-mouthed, penniless, probably lousy, soon to be senile, undeserving vagrant. He could not even in his best moments have ever aspired to the life I intend to lead. He is in a different class. His mother and father were probably hawkers, if he had a father who could be named. Yet I

48

know too that if I fell ill and could no longer run the business, and if this building was burned down, and if Irene refused to help, and if there was trouble, I should find myself beside him, without it being my fault. And then after a little while I would have no choice but to eat what he eats, so that my shit would be like his too. I know this but I do not know how to explain it. And, worse, I do not know how to admit the possibility that his condition may not be his fault either. I see the possibility sitting there, present but unreal, like the idea of my own death. But the possibility remains outside myself. There is no room for it in the knowledge I have. Indeed the possibility represents the opposite of any knowledge that I am capable of acquiring. It represents my ignorance. Like death, so also my possible ignorance of this vagrant. On occasions like this I know how much I do not know, and therefore sometimes when a client comes into the office it is as though I was watching somebody dying. I am made ignorant, or I am reminded of my ignorance, and the ignorance is profound, so profound that I suffer a kind of vertigo. This is not a physical vertigo, but a moral vertigo. In the face of it I resolve to be good. If I cannot know and yet if somewhere the issue involves a decision – and both death and the vagrant do this – then I must rely upon my virtue. I resolve to live a good life. (This resolution even passes through my mind as a thought.) I know that the meaning of being good has grown up with me just like the word fucking, but I have never thought of them both at the same time. To be good has been to be moderate and honest and hardworking and careful and kind and not always to think of oneself but to consider others, and to give more than to take, and never to envy or slander and to set a good example in all these things. To be good has been to practise all that the vagrant has not practised: for he is intemperate, sly, indolent, selfish, extravagant, bitter. But my resolve to be good is the result of my uneasiness, my vertigo in face of my profound ignorance. And I know of my profound ignorance because of the possibility of this vagrant being innocent. If he is innocent, and I resolve to practise all that he has not: What am I? I know this question, I know it well, but I never ask it. The answer I knew once, before I knew the question. I only know the answer now as part of my past knowledge. The answer has not grown up with me like the word fucking and the meaning of being good. It is an old answer. Before my first job but after Mother had told me about Father, I knew what I was destined to be. Whenever I listened to music I saw my destiny. The scenes changed from week to week, but the destiny was always the same. It was my destiny never to betray my trust, to save others at the risk of my own life, to respect the truth when all around denied it, to pursue what was right regardless of the cost, and to die a hero's death. My desire to be worthy of the acknowledgement of all good men, my desire to be welcomed at the end of the ordeal, my desire to contribute something undeniable, was far more precious to me than life itself. To the accompaniment of music I pictured my life as a Catherine wheel: bright in the dark, complete as a circle, golden in colour, brief. The sight of a lit Catherine wheel would bring tears to my eyes: all over so quickly, I knew. In a year or two I began to forget my destiny; there was nobody to remind me of it. This was not because I was any the less proud of it, but it was because I could not see what preliminary steps I should take. I worked at the sock firm. I helped to keep Mother. Later I joined the Medical Corps and was sent to France. I could find no heroes such as I had imagined, only men swearing and screaming and losing their reason. I found then that I was an idealist. That is the answer I know I once knew to the question which came after the answer. The new question: What am I? The old answer: A Fucking Idealist.

Words like that are quite unnecessary, says Mr Corker. What are your references? The old man thinks he said preferences.

Nothing too far away, he replies, and then looks about the room as though, given a little goodwill, a job might be found here and now. For the old man no job lasts more than a few hours and most jobs are something that has to be cleaned up. Have you any references to your general character? repeats Mr Corker. I'm as good as your next man, says the old man laying one hand on the desk as a token of ability. The knuckles are like pebbles in a shrunken skin sleeve. We've got nothing at the moment, Mr Hodges. The old man remembers the constant insult. You got a bloody window full of jobs down there, I don't believe you, he says. Mr Corker takes off his spectacles again. They are jobs for younger people, Mr Hodges. Despite the sense of what he is saying, Mr Corker's tone of voice is now that used for speaking to a child. A little gardening job? wheedles the old man. Mr Corker shakes his head. Now it's spring, says the old man, gardens need things done. Mr Hodges, we cannot discuss any job at all with you unless you pay a fee and you haven't got that fee. The old man screws his head round and up to look at The Authority from below and to appeal once more. Don't you know of a little gardening job? We do not. With all the suddenness of a fall the old man slides off his chair. As he slides off it, he moves sideways and stands up. The speed of this movement is like a ferret's. Bugger that, he shouts and is gone. Silently Mr Corker follows him out and from above watches him descend the stone stairway. Splay-legged and splay-armed he descends slowly like a man drowning. Mr Corker returns to the Inner Office and wipes the seat of the client's chair with a special cloth.

(The woman who now enters Mr Corker's office is the daughter of a vicar whose living is near Portsmouth. Her lover, who is nicknamed Wolf, is the leader of a housebreaking gang operating in South London. Amongst the gang and their associates she is known as Velvet. She has come to the office to reconnoitre. Wolf has been informed that Mr Corker keeps money in the safe rather than banking it; Wolf has also foreseen that Mr Corker's books containing details of all the large residential houses in the area might be of considerable use to him.)

Do I intrude? Come in, Madam. The Madam is normally reserved, according to *Office Day* practice, for employers. The lady is well spoken, well dressed, well mannered. She wears a smart little hat in the morning. Mr Corker stands up, passes his dirty coffee cup to Alec and opens the window a fraction more that the lady may perfume unsullied air. Unnecessary though she knows it to be, she is nervous. But she is also well trained. She takes off her gloves and puts her handbag on the desk with gestures designed to convey that competence which belongs to good class: that competence which gives to all who are looking for it the assurance that this woman will always be neat, even when manning the stockades, that her baths will always be clean, that her bed is always made when she slides into it, that her dentist is an indisputably good one, that she can come prettily out of the kitchen and make a middle-aged admirer calculate that if he had only married her he would have been offered a Partnership, that she understands how to get on both with New Boys and Prefects and has a better head than most men for figures which is to say money. The assurances are wasted on Alec. He considers her as he might a woman being interviewed on the telly about a dog show. He puts her age at 30. How can we help you? asks Mr Corker. She replies that, as a matter of fact, she is looking for a post as an hotel receptionist. He inquires gently whether she has had any experience. A good deal, she says, cutting the words sharply to make them sound like an understatement. She gives the name of Yvonne Browning. Yvonne is a French name, Mr Corker says, I love France. There is a pause because she was not expecting him to say anything so silly. Do you go there for your holidays? she asks quickly to fill the pause. Whenever I can afford it, says Mr Corker. She nods at him, smiling. And Browning the poet, he reflects out loud. It's a very pleasing name if I may say so. The word pleasing amuses her. She invented the name walking down the street, by taking Yvonne from a hairdressers and Browning from a removals firm. She studies the face opposite her, the mouth which has just said very pleasing. The mouth is soft, like the mouth of a fish that has no teeth, but, unlike a fish, if the mouth were opened wide, the scream would be only too audible. The eyes behind the spectacles are also soft and seem so protected by their lenses that they give the impression of being focused on ghosts or fairies. The nose is very large with hairs coming from the nostrils. The ears look curiously unworn, like a curate's. The face as a whole irritates her. And her irritation is increased by the fact that she must smile and make her voice encouraging, for her job will be much easier if he talks of his own accord and she just follows. Well, thank you, she says, though I must admit I can't claim any credit for it. I'm not so sure, says Mr Corker, his eyes on a fairy, we all have to live up to our names and I'm sure you do too. He begins to ask her about her training. She went, she tells him, to a Secretarial College, then adds: For my sins. Why? asks Mr Corker. It was like school all over again, she says. What irritates her is his unawareness. The last thing she wishes to do is to destroy this unawareness, yet she has consciously to stop herself shouting instead of speaking in a normal voice. He is not only – and fortunately – unaware of even the remote possibility of her being here for the reason that she is, he is also unaware of everything that operates around him. There is not a moment of her life in which he could believe. And this amounts to a kind of insult. Necessary as it is for her to convince him that she is Miss Browning, applying for a job as a hotel receptionist, it is a blow to her pride when she succeeds. I can't understand it, Mr Corker is saying, I simply can't understand why education cannot be made more enjoyable. She knows that if she tried to tell him about being Velvet he would understand nothing. He has been spared everything that has happened to her. His big smooth forehead and his soft mouth are like advertisements for the soft woolly vests that have always kept him warm. I have a little theory of my own about education, he says. She can easily imagine how his face would crumple if she simply looked at him hard and said quite softly but distinctly: Uncle, you've made a failure of your life, haven't you? My theory, he says, is that children should teach one another, the seventeen-year-olds should teach the fifteen-year-olds, and the fifteen-year-olds the thirteen-year-olds, and so on and so on until you have the sevens or the nines teaching the infants; it'll come in the end I'm sure, children will be self-educating. As she listens and parts her dry lips, she reminds herself that any schoolchild could teach him a thing or two – if it was allowed to, if it wasn't told to hold its tongue. Do you think we could turn the fire down just a little? she asks. Of course, says Mr Corker. Whilst he bends down to do it, she looks at the bald top of his head and shivers. All skulls are similar. That the difference between one and another should be so dear! And that way, says Mr Corker smiling, none of the children would ever be bored! But would they learn anything? she asks. The shiver leads to a premonition. The fear in her demands of her intelligence: is all this too good to be true? She re-examines him. Children are quick learners, he is saying, and in my experience there is nothing like having to tell somebody else to make you learn the facts yourself. It crosses her mind, in the guise of a joke, that the whole business is a cover and he is working for somebody else. But his smile reassures her. It is too daft, and too much like an uncle's.

I know without it occurring to me that if I had married, if I had become the man I might, I could by now have a daughter like the one sitting so presentably and nicely in front of me.

Mr Corker inquires whether she has worked as a receptionist before and if so might he ask where. She will make it all happen as far away as possible from this oppressive cluttered little office. In Bangor, she says, and Bristol and (why not?) Dublin. Mr Corker says: It looks as if you like travelling. Travelling's my passion too. Is it? she says. And for a fraction of a second she believes her own lie. She has worked in Bangor and Bristol and Dublin, and the sea and the wind beside and around these cities have tangled her hair and browned her forehead and blown a tear in her eye so that now in this oppressive cluttered little office, with the old-fashioned Chubb safe, she is proud of the taste of salt on her lips. She continues the conversation: Have you been to many countries then? Mr Corker begins to count them on his fingers. I've been to Finland, Iceland, Denmark, Holland, Belgium, France – the last counted on the little finger with the little bandage round it – Germany, Spain, Austria, Yugoslavia, Greece, that makes eleven, doesn't it? She is imprinting the office on her memory. This is not strictly necessary, for the situation is a simple one, but she does it for her own sake so that later she can better imagine Wolf here. This year I'm going to Calabria, says Mr Corker, I've just got Norman Douglas's book out of the library, I wonder if you know it? She shakes her head using the expression that originated from the child pretending not to know the story in order to persuade Uncle to tell it again. But in this case she is not pretending about never having heard of Calabria or Norman Douglas. I think he must have been very Bohemian, says Mr Corker, quite a Bohemian, but he gives some useful hints about Calabria. Where is Calabria? she wonders. The name doesn't suggest the uncle opposite, doesn't set a scene in which she can picture him screaming like a child who has seen a ghost, or in which she can picture him happily playing bezique over sherry. When he gets to Calabria he won't know what to do with himself. Then, for the first time since she sat down, a happy thought occurs to her: perhaps she and Wolf will go to Calabria instead of him. I begin planning each year's trip, says Mr Corker, quite soon after I get back from the year before's, reading it all up and deciding exactly where to go, and booking well in advance, you can't do it too soon. When do you plan to go this year? she asks. When the weather is cooler in September but I'm doing all the booking and arrangements this week. You just can't plan these things too well ahead, says Mr Corker. I think, she says, it's very enterprising of you to do all these things by yourself, going off into the wilds. Mr Corker rubs his chin and smiles. To Velvet Calabria sounds like an island with restaurants by the sea and dancing in rooms on stilts above the water and countless bushes with flowers upon them and bronzed men in canoes and white curtains billowing in their open bedroom window. You have your references with you, Miss Browning? Oh how silly of me, I didn't realize you would want them, I thought just the hotel. The question was foreseen and she has rehearsed even the trace of agitation in her voice. Doesn't matter at all, says Mr Corker, it's a pure formality on our part, purest formality. Now tell me what you want. Oh God, oh Calabria, how easily she can handle him! She must ask for a job he hasn't got, she must skip over the whole cluttered little firm in one stride. Something in the country, she says, Surrey preferably. She has said the last two words, she knows it, with exactly the same intonation as the young wife of some company director instructing her estate agents to find a week-end cottage, the figure in mind being somewhere approximately around £10,000. Surrey, preferably. She can't resist saying it again. Mr Corker responds. There are some perfectly lovely places in Surrey, aren't there? he says. Calabria here we come. Let me see now, says Mr Corker, let me see. The telephone rings. She hesitates. So does Mr Corker. Alec answers and finds that it is an inquiry about a barman. Mr Corker performs in front of Miss Browning, smiling all the while as though he were arranging the details of his own happiness. Hotel Staff Male is consulted and two notes taken. Hotel Vacancies Male is referred to. Prefix HE 3702/60 is selected. The time is fixed. The task done. Mr Corker rubs his hands together. Alec is disapproving. He has been counting up the charges against Miss Browning. There is her hat, there is her voice, there is the way she makes signs with her hands when she talks, there is what she says which she never means, there is the way she never really listens to what Corker says, there is her lipstick like blood, there is the snooty way she sits as though she was frightened something might fall down from between her legs. He can picture her business man with a bowler and a drooping hand. He believes her class must fuck in a different way, with Aids to help them. What a fascinating job you have! she says, I can't think how you know where to find everything. Mr Corker proceeds to explain the system to her.

I know that my gifts have been wasted, but I do not know how it could have been otherwise. As for what I think: I think and say that I have built up a very nice little business and I make magical plans for the future. I imagine how the business might take flight like a golden goose above Arabia and transport me with it. Even considering my knowledge I cannot altogether discount this possibility. My knowledge tends to lead me to the conclusion that miracles do exist, that a man's life can be completely transformed. Perhaps fate is just an accident, but the important point is that it is beyond anybody's control. It happens to them. It can still happen to me. It is possible that my fate is still to be decided. Why should I not therefore get pleasure from the happy ending I read into my life? But I do know that my gifts have been wasted. I have not wasted them. On the contrary I have used them as carefully and frugally as possible and have been able to benefit from them, building up my little business and being my own boss and earning my own living so that I have never been short of anything that really matters, no, it is not I who have wasted my gifts and it is not I who have suffered as a result, it is my gifts themselves that have remained discontented and it is life that has wasted them. I do not even regret this, for I recognize that it was either I or they who had to go under. Life demands sacrifices, and in a certain way I am even proud that I have chosen in the way I have. I feel this pride and I also feel the gifts nagging when I explain my Books and describe my System. These thirty books, not to mention the old ones discarded, are a life's work. That's what I say as a joke. And after I've made the joke I think it is not so untrue. But what I know is different. I know that they are not a life's work but a work's life. My life is not in them. They are a work's life because I and I alone have filled them with my handwriting, and that has taken 50,000 hours. I know I could have done better. I do not know how. I explain that I have had 100,000 people on my books, and I say that this requires some organizing, and I claim that not everybody by a long chalk could devise a system of indexing like mine: the Corker System. But I know that as the books get filled and the number of books increases, more and more of the information, so neatly sorted and arranged, becomes obsolete. Whenever an employer takes on an employee, I am paid my fee. The best moment of the week is when I total up what I have taken. Not for one moment would I deny the pleasure of demanding and receiving my fees. But whenever an employer takes on an employee I also have to record this fact in my books. This is done by rubber-stamping the date and the word *Filled* over all the details of the vacancy. I had the stamp, which is a large one with a decorated capital F, specially made. It is part of my System and I am proud of it, but I know that every time I use it, I add to the discontent of my gifts. This is why I often bang the stamp on to the page harder than is necessary. My gifts always want to go on adding and adding to what they have already done, so that their achievement, as I grow older, can become cumulative. I cannot agree with this demand: it is like a till demanding that it should never be cleared and never set back to nought. I know that it is the fascination of figures mounting, mounting to infinity that has ruined many men, beginning with Father. I know that one must think as well as live within one's means. Nevertheless I have now reached the stage where I shall offer my gifts a little more freedom. The woman who might be my daughter smiles at me in confirmation. My gifts can have photographs to take and arrange, and more Talks to give, and

Charts showing the History of Clapham to make. My gifts will have a dark-room to work in, new albums to fill and sheets of best quality paper for the Charts. And I myself will no longer check my thoughts when above this office I read in the evening and allow myself to imagine that the chapters, howsoever fantastic, are in part about me. I know that the Books of my Business are the proof that I have the means and therefore the right to be a little more myself. They are what I would show if challenged. But I do not think this. What I think is: The business is doing well enough for me to afford to make the change.

Velvet listens and watches. He is the little uncle who offered her a seat when she first entered the Inner Office. He is the little uncle who has a pearl tiepin stuck in him, and a gold watch-chain round him and ears like a curate. He is the little uncle who is now telling her all that she needs to know about the books which serve his cluttered little business but some of which could also be put to a different use in a quite different line of business. I'd never have thought there was so much to it, she says. You know, I have a saying, says Mr Corker, Plan Your Work and Work Your Plan. If you can do that, it's quite simple, really quite simple. His talking about simplicity begins to make her uneasy. It is always simple until the last moment. He is the little uncle and he knows nothing but he survives because he is protected. Only Wolf can ever make her completely forget the unevenness of the odds. Often, when she is alone at night, they appal her. She lies in her bed and knows that their time can only be ended. Everything is reversed – as though she were hanging from the ceiling with her head towards the floor, strung up by her feet – every success then brings the end nearer, every hope becomes a fear, every chance a trap. It is in these moments that she recognizes how undeviating is her hatred of all who oppose Wolf. This morning she is not yet appalled. But the soft mouth that doesn't scream, the soft eyes going softer when he explains his system, the soft clouds all round him the other side of the desk have another meaning which until now she has ignored. They are signs of unawareness, but they are also badges of survival. He still has a better chance of getting to Calabria than she and Wolf will ever have. How long have you been doing it? she says. Let me see, says Mr Corker, we have been here for seventeen years and before that we were in Kennington for five, which makes twenty-two, yes twenty-two years. Two-thirds of my lifetime! She says this because she is thinking about how their time can only be ended. Of course it's grown a lot, explains Mr Corker. In Kennington we just had one back room and now we've got two whole floors. Two floors? she exclaims. Yes indeed, two floors, we have the floor upstairs too you see. Why – have you got more offices upstairs? No, not at the moment, we're storing things there, but we have plans for it, we're full of plans. We're in a very advantageous position. Very advantageous. Why, demands Alec, does Corker tell her? Why does he creep? Her businessman doesn't know Vienna like he does. The *May-Be-Old-Bugger* has no reason to creep. Velvet's doubts, pointless and groundless as she declares them to be, increase. We may branch out in all kinds of directions, says Mr Corker. The little uncle has no need to defend himself; he will be defended. But we'll never leave here, continues Mr Corker, never. We're established here, you see, and even supposing I went abroad – to start an overseas branch – my assistant would continue here. Mr Corker indicates Alec and smiles. Alec assures himself that the whole thing is a pretence. The *May-Be-Old-Bugger* is acting again, and he only brings Alec in because they said they would help each other, and he had said Mutual Aid, and he had been more pleased than he had shown at Alec's offer of help. Alec acts as though he hasn't heard, because he does not want to have to smile at the drawling woman under the little hat. Behind the survivor, Velvet sees the whole organized mass of the punishers. He has millions of helping hands. The hands pass money from one to the other. But if threatened by an interloper the hands join and, forming a circle, close in to strangle. Suddenly she understands something: the Uncle is not alone: the Uncle is not even himself. *He is nothing,* are the words that occur to her. *He is nothing.* Really? she says. It's very important, says Mr Corker, I'll give you an example, you may have noticed there's a bus stop just outside our door, do you know what the conductors call out when they stop here? They call out CORKER'S OF CLAPHAM. That's what being established means! Everyone knows where we are. Everyone knows where to find us. The 'we' the old fool uses is in reality a threat. He is nothing. The 'we' is all. She grows aware of the whole Inner Office, even that part of the room which is behind her. The gas fire is squeaking. The rug is worn and musty. The clock may be worth £50. The window is mean and two dark tables stand on the floor, immovable like the decks of boats whose keels are on the bottom and whose holds are full of earth. There are dead papers on the shelves. There is a photograph of a cemetery on the wall. It is a morgue of an office she is in, and across the floor of it, which smells, she fears, of mice, sprawls her Wolf, trapped with the warm blood of him turning cold and his sweet breath smothered. She is stricken as she smiles and says: Yes they always say don't they that goodwill is the best asset of all? She fears that Wolf will cease to exist as Wolf. They, the old man's 'we' 'we', will confine him and break him. The streets and the rooms will be as though he had never planned and leapt and risked or even existed. And they, the old man's 'we' 'we', will ensure that he is rendered and kept powerless like a dead stone is, and this is the worst for a man to grow cold like a stone at night through being able to do nothing. And quite separately she fears her own loss, she fears the separation from her man, the limb from her taken as in the time before anaesthetics. Indeed a satisfied clientele is the best advertisement I know, declares Mr Corker. She checks herself. She tells herself that it is only the meanness and futility of the cluttered little office that is depressing her. The brave and the beautiful – unless in Calabria – never have the settings they deserve. That is their complaint. The cunning of her Wolf knows no bounds. And the complaint they are going to make in this little office should be a very easy complaint to make and take only twenty minutes. But you should stop me, says Mr Corker, I'm talking too much. It's most interesting, she says. You want a post at a high-class country hotel, preferably in Surrey, says Mr Corker. I dare say, she says, I'm asking for the moon. No, Miss Browning, says Mr Corker, you're asking for the best and why shouldn't you have the best? Mr Corker consults his books. We have nothing at the moment in a really first-class place but we do get them in quite often. If you're not in too much of a hurry we'll certainly find something for you, Miss Browning. Only a few weeks ago the Black Swan at Hazlemere were wanting a tip-top receptionist. It would have been ideal for you, ideal. And Hazlemere of course is a real beauty spot. I expect you know it? Oh very well, she lies. She lies now to propitiate him. The little uncle by the extent of his unawareness and the nature of his soft-ness and the degree of his fishy stupidity can only ever avoid being disappointed, can only ever have his pleasure granted, by being lied to. There are old men who go in search of little girls, as she has good reason to remember, found at the age of thirteen by her father's organist. There are others who like the little uncle with his 'we' 'we' go in search of little lies. If she makes him happy, it may bring Wolf luck. Then you must know Hindhead and the pretty view from the top, says Mr Corker keenly. Oh very well, she lies again, I was there only last month. The unscreaming mouth smiles. Isn't that funny? he says, because so was I. It was, half a moment, yes, it must have been the, yes, the second Sunday in the month. That would make it about the twelfth? she asks. Surely yes, he says. Then it must have been the exact same day, she declares. A glorious spring day! he adds. The little uncle now consults his diary to confirm the truth of their good fortune. Yes, Sunday, March 13th, Mr Corker says, that was it. We climbed to the top in the afternoon, he recollects. So did we, she says. And then we had a delicious cream tea with scones at the Copper Kettle. I don't eat cream, she says, it's too fattening. Mr Corker looks at her gallantly. If I may say so, Miss Browning, you shouldn't worry. The extent of his pleasure surprises her. It is now as though they were discussing not something thought to have happened four weeks ago, but a proposed plan for the next week-end. If she were to say: Take me to Hindhead, and if next Sunday she walked through the bloody gorse with him and climbed the hill and put some damned heather in his buttonhole and poured out the tea like mother and allowed him to kiss her good-bye, he would not at the end of the day, she imagines, be more delighted than he appears to be now. It's a small world, she says. And a strange one, he adds. How so? she asks, a little disconcerted. Do you know, says Mr Corker, there are people who drive up to the top of Hindhead and when they've got there just sit in their cars and read their newspapers. We saw dozens like that. Just imagine it. Velvet will give him further pleasure. What a waste! she says. It's more than that, says Mr Corker, there's only one word for it – it's *lunatic*. He places such emphasis on the last word that both Alec and Miss Browning are forced to acknowledge it. It sounded like the cry of a parrot. I ask you, what's a beauty spot for if it isn't for looking at? continues Mr Corker. They've put up wooden benches there so that you can sit and look in comfort. You can see five counties from there. And then people go all the way up there to read their newspapers. I simply can't understand it. Velvet can guess what she ought to say now. It has become like a game and like a game it can be relinquished at will, but for the moment it fascinates her. All her small girl's concentration is directed towards keeping it up and not allowing anyone to take the game away from her. And if she fails and is reprimanded she will say: I was only playing! The name of the game that goes through her mind is: *Fair exchange no robbery.* She will give Mr Corker disproportionate pleasure in exchange for all that he is about to lose. But it's not everyone, Velvet hears herself saying it, it's not everyone can appreciate beauty like you obviously do, Mr Corker. He accepts the compliment without commenting directly upon it.

His eyes become a little wetter. Yes, I like to see things, he explains. And above all I like to take photographs. I've taken photographs in every country I've been to. He pauses and hesitates. He looks at Miss Browning in some doubt. He adjusts his spectacles with his hand. You know what? he says, I'll give you an invitation to my illustrated lecture tonight. That's very kind of you, she says, I'd love to come but what time is it? It begins at 8 p.m. She nods. You'll have better things to do, Miss Browning. May I ask what you are lecturing about? Vienna, City of the Blue Danube. And where will it take place? At St Thomas's Church Hall, we call it the Victoria Hall and it's in Victoria Road next to the fire station. I'll give you this – it has a little map on the back. Don't take any notice of the other side. It was for a jumble sale. But only if you have nothing better to do. Thank you so very much, she says, have you any idea how long it will go on for? Until about 10 p.m., but there's a break for tea and biscuits in the middle. Thank you again, she says, I'll certainly try to come. Sweet Jesus of Calabria, thinks Velvet. And I'll see that a place is kept for you, Miss Browning, just in case. She can have, Alec believes, no intention whatsoever of coming to the lecture. Women like her do not go to illustrated lectures at the Victoria Hall. Why does she play with him? Why does the *May-Be-Old-Bugger* fall for it? He may know about Vienna, but he knows nothing about her type. He is as innocent as a child. And suddenly Alec feels passionately that he and the old man behind the other desk are united because they are both moving out, are both enlarging their lives, are both questioning why they should be excluded from anywhere. *Why-Not-Us?* unites them, Corker behind his desk and Alec, Jackie's lover, behind his desk. Corker may be cunning or timid, he may have a chance or he may be hopeless, he may know more than he pretends or he may know nothing, but he is trying. Alec speaks to Miss Browning inside his shut mouth: Not so fast my classy little bitch. You've still got me to reckon with. Lay off that man or I'll spill something in your face. Who do you think you are anyway? You'd climb up a monkey if he looked smart enough and arrived in a taxi. Ai sey taacksee taacksee buy me a newh hat darhlinge. I bet you count in your head when you're being fucked. Stop lying to that man. He may be a sucker but he's trying. And he's not trying to do what you do. Lay off that man. He's trying. And I don't want him discouraged. He's trying, so lay off. That is most kind of you, says Miss Browning. Not at all, Mr Corker says, the pleasure is ours. It's very rare these days to meet a kindred spirit. When she hears the little uncle say this Velvet knows that she has done all she can for her Wolf. It is rather, isn't it? she says. If you would just give us your address, Mr Corker asks, so that we can let you know as soon as we hear of a job for you. He hands her a buff-coloured card to fill in. Velvet immediately realizes what to do. The small girl explains she was only playing. The adult woman stands up, and as she does so she picks up her white gloves, her bag and the buff-coloured card. I can't thank you enough, she says, but now I've really wasted enough of your time. I'll fill in this card and post it straight back to you. She holds out the gloved hand so that it may be shaken. Mr Corker takes it gallantly. Hope to see you tonight, she says, and, with a little knowing wave of the white-gloved hand which as a gesture might conceivably and hopefully be confused with that of dispatching an aerial kiss, is gone. Yale on front door, mica job. Second Yale on Inner Office door. Chubb safe. Keys perhaps in very top drawer of large desk. Otherwise transportable. Employers' Books marked, to left of swivel chair. Stored furniture above, no tenant. Out tonight from 7.45 to 10.15. Take clock. Too old to struggle. Old enough to be father. Let Wolf be all right. If only all our clients were like that! says Mr Corker. She won't come tonight, says Alec, I ask you, can you see her in the Victoria Hall? Well what about the Albert Hall? says Mr Corker and, patting his chest, laughs, as though pleased with himself.

The office, the old woman decides, is neglected. Neglect is not a thing in itself that she dislikes; it is the persistence of neglect which she takes arms against. Neglect in itself is often the point from which she starts. Good morning, she says, you don't know me from Adam, sir, I'm sure. Alec recognizes her as old Bandy Brandy. But I do know you, she says. She is dressed in black with a black straw hat. She has black laced shoes. Her face is sharp like a very small hound's. Her hands, thin and nimble, have been lent a curiously ambiguous character by age. They look frail in one sense so that it is easy to imagine something being wrenched from their grasp, easy to imagine the fingers being broken. Yet in another sense the same thinness suggests an unsentimental and almost ruthless dexterity. They are hands which could wring a chicken's neck in a trice and skin a kidney in one. Alec remembers: What makes Bandy Brandy Randy? The Curate's Handy! I worked for the late Father Bean at St Thomas's, she says, and once you came there one evening for a bite. She snaps her mouth shut on the word 'bite' with considerable ferocity. I remember now, says Mr Corker, you were his housekeeper? For fifteen years, she says in a voice to emphasize the present interval of abeyance. It's silly of me but I'm afraid I can't quite recall your name. Miss Brand, she replies. She considers herself Miss Brand rather than Bertha Brand because she thus emphasizes her standing as a servant. *Miss Brand* is the summons to her work here on earth. It was a very sad business, says Mr Corker. He takes a buff-coloured card to write her name on. She has a humble respect for cards: cards are the means of government. I was with him to the end, she says, and he didn't suffer. Mr Corker closes his eyes for a fraction of a second. Then he continues writing on the buff-coloured card. Alec ticks *The End* under *Having Jackie.* Only spinsters get like that. I'm glad to hear it, says Mr Corker. The way he says this confirms her impression that he is definitely her kind of gentleman. He speaks gently. He clearly has problems on his mind. His collar is slightly frayed and his nails are clean. It is the boy by the window who makes her uneasy. You want another post as a housekeeper? asks Mr Corker. The boy represents all those who have no proper respect. The boy's mother, in Miss Brand's opinion, fails in her duty to both her children and her parish, a failure not to be excused by the convenience of her being a widow. The older boys drink too much so that it is no wonder to Miss Brand that there are nowadays more and more accidents on the railways, the older boys being railwaymen, whilst this one is sly and big-headed and out at all hours so that it would be no second wonder to her if he ended up a delinquent. Alec marks *Why-Not-Us?* as the opposite of Bandy Brandy. Bandy Brandy is *The End*. *Why-Not-Us?* is a beginning. Everything is about to change. A great deal has already changed. He is *Having Jackie* – his penis stirs at the name; Corker is the *May-Be-Old-Bugger* who has planned to get shot of his sister – one way or another – and to lead a life where it will be very nice, according to the Viennese art. Only the room and what the two of them are meant to be doing in it has not changed yet. But even this is about to change. They only continue now in the old ways because they haven't yet received the official order to stop, but the official order will come any minute. Any time now Corker will ask Alec to do something he's never done before, Alec is sure of it. And after that, nothing will be the same again, not even for Corker. Soon they will look back upon *Office Day* and ask themselves: How did we ever do it? Alec is not at all certain about his own exact place in the new scheme of things, but this does not matter to him. It is the very idea that anything may happen which now makes him enthusiastic. It is as though the future has become the present, as though he were living with opportunities instead of calculating what they might be. The noise of the traffic which comes through the window sounds different. Alec used to think of the traffic as passing them by and he counted the hours till he could join it and leave his desk. He saw the desk like a school desk which outlives those who sit at it, or like a seat on a train which supports traveller after traveller but is never affected by where it is: to sit down at the desk meant leaving wherever one wanted to be. Now the Inner Office seems no more than a compartment of the street below, the desk no more than a piece of furniture, and the traffic a proof that things are happening to other people too. He is impatient to see Jackie, more impatient than usual, but this is because he has so much to tell her, because today so much has happened. Perhaps Alec would have felt something like this even if nothing in *Office Day* had changed; after love it often becomes urgent for lovers to share events which neither of them would have noticed before. As it is, Alec has no need to distinguish between this after-effect of love and the actual dramas of the morning. Everything for him belongs to *Having Jackie*, even Corker's future. And so, although he is quite aware of the differences between himself and his employer, the warmth and the sense of freedom assured by *Having Jackie* colour his view of the new Corker. The new Corker will be happier, the new Corker will fuss less, the new Corker will be in a better position to help Alec, the new Corker will be a change. There's a change in the weather, hums Alec, a change in the sea. Yes, says Miss Brand, I do. How many hours a day? asks Mr Corker. Oh no, says Miss Brand, I'm not a char, I'm not going to go *out* to work, I've never been *out* to work in my life, I can't consider anything unless I live in. If I keep house, I keep house, and I don't mind telling you I was trained the hard way with coal fires and grates and holystoned doorsteps and real silver to polish and in those days no one would dream of sending sheets to the laundry like they do today, they don't know the meaning of work today they don't, they're bone idle. Miss Brand snaps her mouth on the word 'bone' as she did on the word 'bite'. I was twelve when I first went into service, she says.

I know the house she thinks she can keep. I know the smell of the linen cupboard where the heat of the pipes almost takes the breath away. I know the smell of the red stair carpet, which has the same smell as the stuffed tiger which was said to come from Bengal. I know the smell of the newly cleaned silver like calamine lotion that is used to soothe irritations of the skin. I know the sound of the tiny spitting on the iron and the sound of toast being scraped and the sound of the bath running and the sound of a meal on a tray and the sound of the front door being opened. Mother, I also know, would have approved of this woman. But I do not think this far back. I think: let me be good.

And how old are you, Miss Brand? asks Mr Corker. I am exactly sixty-four. Sixty-four, she repeats, and over fifty years of it in service. This is not a complaint, for Miss Brand no longer compares herself with other women. Indeed certain sensations in her mind, experienced occasionally as she falls asleep in the hard bed on which she always insists, allow her to find more in common between herself and one of the elements than between herself and most other people. Sometimes it is the element of water with which she feels a drawing sympathy, the very weight of her limbs then tugging at the centre to which they are anchored as the current breaks over them, nags them with spray and gathers all its drawing power to plead with them to break adrift and be eddied away in the purifying stream of no man. At other times, when her scalp is dry or the white skin of the inside of her upper arm has been irritated by scraping or her varicose veins agitate against the cotton, which now feels like chicken-wire, of her stockings, it is the element of fire with which she feels a sisterly connexion, that same no-man's-fire which turns to ashes, sterilizes and consumes all. Sometimes too when she enters a room to clean it, she knows that the wind also cleans and polishes. The difference, which Miss Brand never forgets, between herself and one of her sister elements is that the elements work effortlessly, performing their function by simply existing, whereas she works with feet which she must shoe, with eyes into which she must put drops, with hands which are worn. But I still keep a house spotless, she says. I'm sure you do, Miss Brand, says Mr Corker.

I know that it is the consequences of not being good which frighten me. All these consequences are unknown to me. I do not know how they follow the wrong done. Nor do I know the stages by which the wrongful pleasure is said to turn to ashes in the mouth. What did the tramp who was in here first do to set him on the road to ruin? And after the first step are there not ways of avoiding the full consequences of the wrong done? Would it not be possible for me to lie my way out? I know as certainly as I can do that there is only one final truth: It is me that it happens to. All the rest should be able to be lied about or bargained over. It cannot be a question of falling like a man out of an aeroplane. There must surely be time to come to an arrangement. My difficulty is my ignorance, my difficulty is all that I have not done. I know that it is now as though I am trying to emerge from a second – or is it a third, or fourth or fifth? – childhood only to find this familiar, shrunken woman in black opposite me. I know why she is familiar. It has nothing to do with my once having had supper at the Vicarage. This woman could have been a servant in any of the houses I have lived in. She is what is called a good woman.

I can think straightway, says Mr Corker, of a post we have at Epsom, a retired printer and his wife, the printer used to print — No Sir, interrupts Miss Brand, I couldn't, not to save my life. One woman, one house, I've always said it and I've always stuck to it. Women fight, they can't help it, it's in their bad blood. But you would be the only woman, says Mr Corker, they have no other staff. You said they were a married couple, sir, if I'm not mistaken, says Miss Brand. You see I've always worked for single gentlemen, sir. The last two were churchmen, but they weren't all. I'd change if I could, sir, but I can't now, I'm too old. It would upset me. As Miss Brand admits this she folds her hands in her lap and looks down at her feet as though praying. Alec can see the hatpin with the head the size of a black marble that skewers her hat to her bun. The stiffer of her two legs is straight out in front of her. There is a moment's silence in the Inner Office. Alec thinks: It is her fault she is old. He thinks this as an excuse, for she has put him in a false position: somehow she has turned her age into a stick and somehow she has forced him to beat her with that stick until now he begins to beat her just because she allows herself to be a victim. The bloody witch, thinks Alec. What are you asking, Miss Brand? asks Mr Corker. The late Father Bean, she says ignoring Mr Corker's question, he used to say to me, Miss Brand, he used to say, I don't know where I should be without you. You were a friend of his, sir, she says, so I don't mind telling you it wasn't always easy, but I looked after him right to the end, I looked after him as if he was my own brother. Miss Brand admires those who need her because, by allowing her to look after and take over the needs of their bodies, they are freed for those higher pursuits to which she could never presume and to which their minds are naturally attuned. I mended all his clothes for him, I did all his washing for him and towards the end I shaved him. Miss Brand calls herself a housekeeper even to herself, but she knows that she is a body keeper. During the last few months, the tall dark rooms of the vicarage became under her care outward organs of the late vicar's physical being. What Father Bean's glands performed within, Miss Brand contrived to perform without. She is a shy woman to herself and her fantasies are reserved. But once, muttering as she washed a satin tablecloth over which for the second morning running the sick man, increasingly sloppy in the control of his hands, had spilt a full cup of coffee, she found herself facing a fancy in her mind the meaning of which, though she desisted from putting it into words, was unmistakable: what master eats, I defecate. I'm sure, says Mr Corker, that Father Bean was a very lucky man to have somebody like you. The praise pleases her because it indicates that Mr Corker is getting nearer to appreciating the extent of what she is prepared to do. I see it as my duty, she says, to try to make my gentlemen a little happy and if, heaven forbid, it comes to it, to ease their going a little. We've all been put on earth to do something, haven't we? Alec pretends to cough and the noise makes both Miss Brand and Mr Corker look at him. Alec has never dared to do this before in the middle of an interview. It is an innovation to celebrate the new Corker and to defy the spell of the old witch. Also, if he coughs, he doesn't have to call her *The End* again. Quite so, says Mr Corker.

I know now that it would be possible for me to have a Mrs. McBryde as housekeeper: that I could live as I have never lived as yet. It is just not too late. But to become what I have never been frightens me, being what I am. I know that there will be no way back, the consequences of my new actions – actions which I can only make as timidly at first as a child – will block the path behind me and I will never again be able to return to the safety of which I am so weary. Danger does not in itself attract me, far from it, danger is a direct threat to the one truth remaining true: it is me that it happens to. I hate danger, it is a kind of insult, a brushing aside of my credentials as a man capable of enjoying himself, doing no harm to anybody, wanting to live and to learn, glad to share his thoughts. I am not weary of my safety because it is safe. I am weary of my safety because I no longer gain any assurance from it. It no longer cradles me. It no longer gives me the sense that I have somewhere where I belong. My safety – if that is what it really is – has brought me to the point of believing that my life is bound to be safe barring accidents, revolutions, lunatics, burglars. The safety I enjoy extends in every direction to become a flat park. There are no surprises and I can see from any one point all the regular walks of my life: from the gabled house at Banstead to the station where I meet Eddie and Giles, from Clapham Junction past my bank to here, from here to the Mitre when there is a Lodge meeting, from the butcher where I buy the meat for Irene to the greengrocer where I buy the apples for my lunch, from the Public Library past the municipal flower beds to my doctor's waiting-room or the insurance office, from the woman at the corner who sells the evening papers to the shop where I buy photographical materials wholesale, from the cinema to the request bus stop in Arkwright Road, on Sundays from West Winds to the Golf Club and from the Golf Club to the car sale-rooms. I can name all the good people I speak to, beginning with Irene at the front door, Harry Gould who is always just behind me on the way to the station, Eddie and Giles, Mr Robinson at the bank, on masonic evenings Fellow Craft Saunders, Fellow Craft Whatham, Master Mason Crawley, Entered Apprentice Glover, Mr Bowness the butcher, Elsie as she is always called at the greengrocer's, Mr Tidmarsh at the library, Dr Brown, Mr Dunkerly of the Equity and Law, Maggie the newspaper seller, John Arden the photographer, Mrs Bleeton manageress of the Odeon, Major Trumper at the Club and, at the New Haven Garage, Manager E. Duffield to whom I have never actually spoken but whose name I read every week printed on a card which is balanced on an easel that stands between the new cars, costing more than I can afford. Such is the safe, flat park in which I live. I know that for some time past a question has presented itself. Is the flat park in fact so safe? The profound doubt which this question raises in me occasionally finds expression in my thoughts. I think: It is funny to think that a Mahommedan can have six wives and yet be doing no wrong. I think: It is funny to think that if I'd been born in China I might have died by now of starvation. I think: Wouldn't it be much simpler if we did away with money altogether. I think: I think I'd have liked to have been a Roman, especially with those lovely tiled baths, big as a room, where they lay in hot water and philosophized. I know that I have begun to fear that the flat park is dangerous. It encourages a sense of false security. In the flat park time has no meaning for it seems to be safe and the good people stay the same good people, but the danger is that before I realize it my life will be over, and when I die, the safety of living in

73

the flat park will not even be questioned, for it is a recognized fact that a safe life, having excluded all the dangers, ends in death. I am weary of my safety because I begin to know that I am no longer safe and because I do not want to die as I am, when I die I want to be different, I want to be less ignorant of the consequences of not being good. (I know that it is unlikely that heaven or hell exist, but I never deny them in my thoughts just in case it should be unlucky, and hell should prove the danger into which I would then fall.) I have seen the trap. Father died after he had been declared bankrupt. But I do not need to break the law. I do not need mistresses and secret trips to Paris and crates of whisky and bets on horses and dinners with actresses. The not being good which I know I want is modest, natural – I dare to know that it is natural – and almost safe. It may in truth be much safer than the flat park. I want a woman to whom I am not bound. Whether we do the fucking depends on how strict she is: in itself I doubt if it is essential. I want a McBryde to be with. Somebody who is kind, somebody who listens, somebody who rewards me, somebody who looks after my comfort, somebody who teases me, somebody who runs my bath, somebody who laughs too much, somebody who has warm hands, somebody who is not thin, somebody who, because it is her job and because we have a little arrangement but not because she is good, surrounds me with her care so that I may at last be forgotten by Irene, Harry Gould, Eddie, Giles and all the good people I know, somebody I can disappear with. I want a home of my own where I am not alone and where I can do anything. I know that I am a natural man. I know it. But none of this have I planned or thought about. Be careful, is what I think.

Quite so, says Mr Corker again, now what are you asking, Miss Brand? Three pounds ten all found, she whispers. Miss Brand is aware that she could, the times being what they are, ask for twice this amount. But Miss Brand has one constant fear: it is not of death: it is of failing to find a gentleman to work for and being sent to a Home. Her asking for an unusually low wage puts her into a special category, it turns her into a kind of charity and she believes that if she is a kind of charity herself, she is in a better position to fight the charity she dreads. There is no logic in this any more than there is in her habit of always turning her head away when she passes the Old People's Home, and she can feel her heart beating faster and pinheads of sweat coming out on her palms and between her fingers, as might happen to a young girl walking at night through a graveyard. There is no logic but there is a great deal of obstinacy. All her life she has known what charity is, for she was brought up in an orphanage. It was there that she learned to scrub, sew, pray and hate other women. And now the fear of ending her life in the same way as she was introduced to it, the fear of the institution which is deaf and blind, is large enough to make her ignore the pain in her leg and be determined to work until she drops. One of the lessons taught her in the orphanage was: God has a reason for everything. Now she comforts herself by thinking that if she is looking after somebody, God can have no reason for forcing her to be looked after, and the higher the aspirations of the gentleman whom she looks after and the more straitened his circumstances, the less likely it is that God will fail to see the special value of her work or be able to find another woman to replace her. She trusts that in the sight of God asking for only three pounds ten makes her indispensable. I have all my uniforms and aprons, she adds. Three pounds ten, repeats Mr Corker in a voice that in no way admits the modesty of the wage: it is as though he has found the voice he was using fifteen years ago when three pounds ten was as much as anybody was prepared to pay for a housekeeper. And you'd be free straightaway, Miss Brand? The half-promise is not lost on her. She tells herself that she always did think Mr Corker was the gentleman to help her. O yes indeed, she says, I could start tomorrow. I've nothing else to do you see. Where are you staying at the moment? asks Mr Corker. I'm still at the vicarage for one more week. The new vicar, I expect you've met him, he's a married man, he told me I could stay for a fortnight if I was looking for somewhere else. And that was last week, so I've got till the end of this week to find something. Ever since he told me I've had all my things packed ready to go, and I'm not going to stay a minute longer than I must. I didn't like his tone at all – and he's very low church too. Now let me see, he said to me, let me see, Miss Brand, I don't see why we shouldn't fit you in here for a fortnight, and that was all the thanks I got after fifteen years – Mr Corker interrupts her. Do you enjoy cooking? he asks. Well what a funny question, says Miss Brand, I don't know I'm sure, but I can cook a good meal, I've often been told that. A cheese soufflé, says Mr Corker, what about a cheese soufflé? Miss Brand looks at Mr Corker as though he had confessed to some childish fear. You don't want to worry your head about things like that, she says imagining that a cheese soufflé is some kind of macaroni cheese, I've always been complimented on my cooking, always. Mr Corker lowers his eyes and touches the brass top of the inkwell. Miss Brand, he says, there's a gentleman I know who may well be interested, he's looking for a housekeeper straighta-way and he's a single gentleman too. Miss Brand smiles and puts up a hand to ensure that her black straw hat is straight. Whereabouts does he live? She whispers the question as she whispered three pounds ten. Very near here, says Mr Corker and touches the end of his nose, of course I can't tell you defi-nitely. He shrugs his shoulders. He may have found somebody else. Could I go and see the gentleman now? asks Miss Brand, I've nothing else to do you see. I'm afraid, says Mr Corker, he won't be there. Is he out at work all day then? asks Miss Brand. Mr Corker leans back in his chair and rests the tips of his fingers on the bevelled edge of his mahogany desk. Let me be frank with you, Miss Brand, it is possible, it isn't certain by any means, but it is possible even probable that I shall be needing a housekeeper myself. You, sir, says Miss Brand. Yes, says Mr Corker. No, thinks Alec, no, he has gone mad or he is laying some trap, the new Corker isn't really going to live here hagridden by this old witch. He remembers the second line: What makes Bandy Brandy fiddle? The curate's middle. The schoolboy rhyme no longer makes him laugh, nor even smile. It seems to him now to be obscene, as obscene as Corker's suggestion that she might install herself here. *Office Day* was preferable to this. He vehemently wishes that Corker had made no new plans, that he had remained as he was: better that Corker was exempt than that this woman should work in the same place for the same man as himself. Do you live far away? asks Miss Brand. As she looks at the man in the grey suit three feet away from her, she tries to estimate how long it would take for her to get used to him. She pictures him in the future in the same way as an old nurse pictures in her memory babies she has looked after, and she uses the same expression to herself: one of mine. I shall probably be living here, says Mr Corker, as I told you it isn't certain by any means, it depends on many things, but if I should find I need a housekeeper can I take it that you'd be willing? You can, says Miss Brand who is happier than she has been since she knew that Father Bean would die and he asked her to witness his will and apologized for not being able to leave her more than fifty pounds, it's not as though we don't know each other is it? You were a friend of the late Father's. Mr Corker opens a drawer, does nothing in it, shuts it and then says: Tell me, Miss Brand, are you nervous? Do you mind being left alone at night? The questions strike her as slightly improper. It is the kind of question that a soppy boy hanging round the kitchen door might ask of a maid. It reveals an improper concern about her. But the Home would be a thousand times more improper. Not at all, she says. And you are in good health, Miss Brand? You don't suffer from insomnia? What's that? she says. Sleeplessness, explains Mr Corker. No, no, she lies, my legs give me trouble that's all but I'm used to them. Good, good, says Mr Corker, and the money is three pounds ten and one half day a week. I never, says Miss Brand, go out in the evenings, I always like to be home by the time it's dark, but yes, sir, one afternoon a week and of course time for church on Sundays. Mr Corker leans forward like a cross-examiner. If I'm not mistaken, he says, the late Father Bean was a teetotaller. O yes, he was, confirms Miss Brand, he never took a drop, there wasn't a drop in the house all the time I was there, I can vouch for that. And you yourself, Miss Brand, are you teetotal too? Mr Corker is playing in the corner of his mouth with one finger. I don't like it myself, says Miss Brand. Then she suddenly sees the doubtful expression on Mr Corker's face and not knowing whether the doubt is because she has gone too far or not far enough she uses her stock phrase: But my gentlemen's ideas are their own, I never interfere, never. Quite so, Miss Brand, so you don't object to drink in the house? She looks at the face with the big nose and the soft eyes and the grey hair a little too long by the pink ears and wonders if it is the face of a drunkard. There is a softness round the gills which worries her. Her attitude isn't a straightforward moral one. She believes that weakness can suddenly appear in anybody like a disease. We tried to save him from his weakness, she would say: or, We couldn't stop him, it was his weakness and in the end it killed him. A man's weakness, for Miss Brand, is like a galloping consumption. What is worrying her about Mr Corker's gills is not the abstract moral principle involved, but the possibility that Mr Corker may, as a result of drink, give up his higher pursuits, cease to be the Master eating, and become just another body defecating like her own. I wouldn't dream of presuming, she says. Good, good, says Mr Corker, now as I told you it may not be necessary, I may not need a housekeeper at all, but I promise we'll let you know within forty-eight hours. I see, says Miss Brand, I haven't anything else to do you see, except for the other gentleman you were speaking about, the gentleman who's at work all day – I don't like going out at night but I could go and see him this evening. Mr Corker laughs and brushes his hair down by his ears. Alec stares at the back of his head and marks: *Ninny.* That was just my little joke, says Mr Corker. Excuse me, sir, says Miss

Brand frowning in her confusion, you mean the other gentleman was really you all the time, sir? That's right, says Mr Corker. So you'll be in touch with me? says Miss Brand. That's right, says Mr Corker. The woman gets to her feet, clumsily. Her legs feel like spade handles that she has to walk with. She looks round the Inner Office and is reminded that Alec has been listening all the time. It could do with a clean, she says, shall I have a look at the other rooms while I'm here? She wants to estimate her duties and discover her hiding-place where she will be safe from the women of the Home. I think not yet, says Mr Corker, next time. He shows her out. She limps down the stone corridor with that rhythm which, common to all lame people, suggests that since she is so slow, she is always on her feet. Mr Corker watches her a moment and returns. As soon as she comes through the door Alec says: I've known her since I was a kid. Yes, says Mr Corker vaguely. And I'm telling you, says Alec, she's mad, she's bonkers. You said that other one was mad, the red-head, well, if you think she's mad, you've got a surprise coming with this one, do you know what she does at night, she fills up bucket after bucket of cold water and then waits up by the window to fling them over the cats when they start, she's a mad old spinster, mean as hell, and I'm talking out of turn and it's none of my business and if you tell me to get out I'll go, but she's a real menace and if you'd lived here and you heard all the stories about her and you saw her scrounging round the shops trying to get something for nothing and then in church too on Sundays, a mate of mine tells me she stays standing up when everybody else kneels down, if you knew about her – you'd never have her, honest you wouldn't. Mr Corker replies: We haven't decided yet, Alec, we must wait and see. But, says Alec, but I don't get why you ever considered her, there must be millions of housekeepers better than her. She's an old spinster and she's ill and she ought to be looked after somewhere in a Home. There aren't *millions* of housekeepers as you say who only want three pounds ten, says Mr Corker.

Part Two

Corker as Lancelot

I

At half past two the same afternoon the boy and the elderly man are standing in the room directly above the Inner Office and Waiting-Room. Three flights down, the front door on to the street is shut. Nobody walking past can see the notice which says: You Will Want The Jobs We Have. Come Up. Mr Corker has closed his business for the afternoon, and has asked Alec to help him move and arrange some of the furniture upstairs. The furniture, stacked to the ceiling, fills three-quarters of the room. Mr Corker has taken his grey tweed jacket off and has put on a long brown overall which he has kept for years in the kitchen cupboard for just such an eventuality. In the overall he looks rather like a man serving in a little hardware shop. Alec, just back from the *Advertiser* and his lunch hour, is still wearing his leather jacket. It is cold in the room and there is a cold smell: the smell of mothballs and wood and fabric long left to settle.

Alec has seen Jackie in the florist's shop. At first he just looked at her through the plate-glass window, his heart beating faster and his hands in his pockets. She was clipping white paper round a large bunch of daffodils for a big woman in a fur hat. Beside her Jackie looked very small, small and perfect in Alec's eyes. Recently she had taken to putting her hair up and even through the shop window Alec could see the back of her neck, with its slight dip in the middle, the same shape and almost the same size as his tongue, as though his tongue in some season when he

81

hadn't missed it had lain there like a turtle in the sand. If he licked the back of her neck there, the fair hairs which were too short to be gathered into the great sweep upwards and which now curled and hung loose would go straight and slightly darker and stick to her skin. All three assistants in the shop had to wear the same green dresses with Lipsons embroidered on them where they would have worn their medals had they been soldiers. Underneath the Lipsons on Jackie's green dress was her left breast. Last night her bra had been the last garment she took off. When she took off her bra she was complete. Alec stood there in the High Street apparently looking at the hyacinths arranged on a bank of shelves, but in fact letting himself be amazed by the value of his secret. She wore a green dress with Lipsons on it, and neither the manageress nor the other assistant (who was middle-aged with glasses) nor any of the men in the street, nor the fat tobacconist next door, knew or could imagine what she had looked like then, after she had taken her bra off. The difference between their ignorance and his secret, the difference between appearances and the truth, had never before seemed to him so strange. It's a kind of dressing up, he thought, wearing clothes, and all the time you wear them you act as though you were in a play, but nobody sees it as a play except Jackie and him; most act all the time, pretending like Corker, pretending like the manageress drinking a cup of tea, pretending like the woman in the fur hat. Alec looked down the street at the shop windows and the shop signs above them and the shoppers and the bus coming towards him, and his hand, the five fingers of his right hand, wanted to reassure him that the pretence was pretence by holding her breast again. He had often had his hand in her blouse before last night, but her breasts had felt different before, like something under water before, with his hand beneath the sea before: but last night her breasts were in the room like the vase and the records and her new shoes. The woman in the fur hat came out of the shop and Alec went in. The other assist-ant, the old one with glasses, came up to him. Then Jackie turned round and saw him. Jackie had said he must never come into the shop because the manageress would bawl her out then. You can come to Corker's any time you like, he replied, I don't take any nonsense from him. But she hadn't come. It's all right, Miss Baxter, Jackie said sweetly, I've finished my lunch. Miss Baxter went behind the cacti and the rubber plants back to her sandwich. The manageress dolefully eyed the young couple over the rim of her teacup. To his surprise Alec felt himself blushing as he said: I wondered if you had any violets. Jackie was trying to do two things simultaneously with her face, and make both imperceptible. She wanted to smile at him and she wanted to shake her head to warn him not to say anything indiscreet. Over here, she said and tripped like an air hostess to the far window. There a jar full of sprays of beech leaves painted silver and blue hid them from the scrutiny of the manageress. Jackie now did three things simultaneously with her face, but this time, being hidden, openly and shamelessly. Half closing her eyes and pouting her mouth out, she made a face to kiss him, to whistle in surprise, and to give him another warning, a shoo to keep quiet. Alec looked down at the Lipsons which was curved with the curve of her breast. She showed him a bunch of violets, holding it just under the Lipsons. They're lovely, said Alec, how much are they? His voice sounded to him like a voice in a play. Eighteen pence, she said. It was only now that Alec saw the joke about paying. He would have to pay with the half-crown that Jackie had given him at six o'clock that morning to get a cup of coffee with because he had been short. The half-crown was in his hand in his pocket. He tried hard and quickly to think of something he could say out loud. All he could think of was: Do they grow in the woods? But he decided that that would sound funny and unnatural. He just stood there, half-closing his eyes and grinning. Jackie was far more composed and could judge exactly how much she was revealing. When the manageress could see, she treated him like a customer. When they were hidden she behaved as she might have done yesterday morning in similar circumstances: she treated him like a secret admirer. But on no account would she reveal in the shop – even to him – the secret of what had happened and changed between them last night. This was a point of honour for her. In a sense it was the supreme test to date of the art of deportment which she had been teaching herself, and constantly learning in the street, in the cinema, on the telly, from her friends, ever since she was eight, nine years ago. You want to put them in water soon, Jackie said. Alec made a crude kissing shape with his mouth. He wanted to remind her of all that in the shop she was determined not to admit. She wanted to wait. He wanted to pull her towards him there and then and prove again the sweetness of the truth for which he also had been preparing himself, over ten years or so, by means of jokes, stories, books of pictures, boasts, scuffles on the common, dreams. Will they keep till tonight? he asked in the voice which he could hear too distinctly. They'll keep for ages and ages, she said and she looked straight into his eyes for the first time since he had come into the shop, if you look after them properly. He fetched the half-crown out of his pocket. It's yours, he whispered as he gave it to her. They had only slept for about two hours because at five she had got up to go down to the kitchen to make his breakfast and he had had tea and an egg and he had repeatedly pulled the white dressing-gown off her shoulders to see her breasts once more and just when he was going and she was cold in the hall with the bicycle in it, he had remembered he had no money and she had run upstairs and got half a crown from her handbag and so vividly did he remember her coming down those stairs with her hair all loose and her legs coming and going in the opening of her dressing-gown and her handing him the coin, and so delighted was he in the florist's shop that underneath the green dress and the swept-up hair style and the Lipsons this was the same newly discovered, newly made-perfect girl, his own Jackie to whom he was now giving back the half-crown, that only after she had tripped half-way across the shop to the till did he realize that it was the shop he was paying for the violets and that between them he and Jackie had actually lost eighteen pence. The till rang in celebration. When she gave him the change, he seized her fingers and held them hard. She glanced over her shoulder. The manageress had gone out to the back. Miss Baxter was still eating behind the rubber plants. She let him have her hand but she kept it well into her body, near her sex. In his other hand he held the violets. Within a second, however, she freed herself. I hope she likes them, she said in a loud voice and with a little sarcasm so as to make it convincing. At last Alec knew what to say, knew how to carry it off. Why, they could act to deceive anybody, he thought proudly, they were a team, he and Jackie. Well, he said by the door, if she doesn't, I'll ask for my money back! and then he laughed. When he was outside, he looked back but Jackie had her back to him and was talking to Miss Baxter. He glanced down at her legs to assess them from a distance. Even if he didn't know her at all, he would still think they were a pair in a million.

Now, says Mr Corker, we need a plan, that's what we need isn't it?

What's this room for? asks Alec.

This'll be my bedroom or the housekeeper's, there's a choice between this one and the back room.

The back room will be quieter won't it?

But this one is bigger. Mr Corker walks over to the door and across the landing to the top back room. His boots creak on the bare, grey wooden floorboards. The two of them stand in the doorway looking at the room which is quite empty except for a full-length mirror propped against the wall opposite the window. One of the sashcords of the window is broken and hangs down. In the grate of the little fireplace is a faded, yellow newspaper. From the ceiling hangs a lamp bowl. Alec tries the switch.

It works, he says, surprised.

I know it works, says Mr Corker, and the water works too. He opens the third door on the landing and goes into the bath-room and turns on the bath taps to show Alec. The bath has been chipped and the black marks on the bottom look like moths. The water from one of the taps is a rusty brown. The moths do not move as the water covers them.

And the boiler, says Mr Corker.

Yes? says Alec.

I came and lit it two Sundays ago, just to see. You want to get everything prepared first when you're making a move, that's the secret. I'd have got the furniture done if I could but I couldn't.

The water from the taps is still rushing up to the far end of the bath, being turned there and then running down to whirl around the plug hole and disappear.

On his way back to the office from Jackie's shop Alec had passed a baker's. He was wishing he had been able to tell Jackie about Corker's morning. He wanted to hear it being told, he wanted it turned into a story, so that it could become exaggerated and altered. He wanted to describe Corker as hopeless and mad. In a story Corker became a joke, even his name was a joke in a story. When Corker turned on Alec angrily, Alec could show by the way he told that part of the story how little he minded; when Corker talked about going to Vienna or making Alec a manager, he could show in that part how funny it was; when Corker's sister screamed *You Are Killing Me, William*, he could make it sound blood-curdling; and when Corker announced he was going to have Bandy Brandy as a housekeeper, he could imply in the telling that this was bound to have happened. In a story Corker became the *Old Bugger*, there was no *May-Be* about it. Outside the baker's was a van of cakes and buns which two men were unloading, carrying the trays on their heads. Alec stopped to watch. What fascinated him was how they negotiated the wide trays through the narrow door, just by turning their shoulders. Before he had gone to Corker's he had been offered a job as a baker's deliveryman and the firm had guaranteed to teach him to drive. As it turned out one of his brothers' friends taught him on a tractor in a building merchant's yard. Whilst he stood there, leaning against a letter-box, watching the men going in with the trays and the shoppers ambling by, a dreamy idea occurred to him. He remembered Jackie's shop where he had just been. He remembered Jackie who is so small beside him. And he made Jackie and the shop even smaller, so small that they were like toys, and he put the shop with the people in it and the street outside on to a bun tray and he himself walked down the street with the shop, just as it was at that moment, on the bun tray on his head. He smiled at the spectacle. What he liked about it was that this way he would have Jackie with him all the time. As he continued his walk back to the office, he continued to examine the idea of Jackie still being with him, whilst at the same time serving customers with flowers in the shop. He no longer thought of her as something new that had happened but as something new that was going to happen. Half the day had already passed. Her mother was back in her house, and the bedroom had been tidied. Soon it would be the evening and they would have a snack together and he would make her laugh about Corker and then they might go to the Talk so that he could show her what Corker was really like. The feeling of the healing scar in his penis had disappeared. It could grow once more, and very soon, somehow, somewhere, they'd fuck again. All this Alec marked as *Where-We-Like* and ticked it under *Having Jackie*. As he ticked it, he jumped in the air to grab at an overhanging branch of a tree in the garden of the Old People's Home. He missed it and laughed. But when he arrived back at the office, *Where-We-Like* made him try to see Corker differently. He pretended he was already telling Jackie about him. He pretended Jackie was hidden there in the office watching them both. He began to want to exploit Corker, to produce him.

Compensating by the tone of his voice for the impertinence of the question, Alec asks: Why didn't you then?

Mr Corker turns off the taps and smiles. The best-laid plans of mice and men, he says, that was a best-seller once, the man who wrote it must have made millions.

Alec tries again. What went wrong? he asks.

Mr Corker looks at him quite gravely and stands with his back to the bath, holding the lapels of his brown overall as though he were a preacher wearing a cassock. You're very young still, he says, and I don't know how much you know. I don't know that I want to tell you very much either. But there's one thing I will tell you. I've put up with a lot.

I'm sorry, says Alec, already made a little ashamed of his questioning.

And now I've had enough, says Mr Corker. I'm not going to wait any longer.

When will you move in properly? asks Alec.

I have moved in, says Mr Corker.

Yes but I mean when will you stay here?

I'm staying here.

Please be serious, Mr Corker.

I am being serious.

When will you live here? When will you sleep here?

From now on.

Tonight?

Naturally, says Mr Corker.

But where? says Alec.

In the usual place, says Mr Corker, where you sleep, in the usual place – that's a bed.

Mr Corker leads the way back to the front room and points at a few bed springs that are visible right at the back. There's my bed, he says.

I see, says Alec, amazed at how they are going to spend the afternoon.

Mr Corker examines one of the hangings thrown over a chest of drawers. It's in perfect condition, he says, no moths at all, I'll take you on a little bet, we won't find a moth in the place.

I can smell the mothballs all right, says Alec.

I've taken proper care of these things, says Mr Corker. Which is more than they do in those depositories. My sister had a piano in store and when she took it out, it was ruined, pure neglect, criminal neglect you could say, but do you think they'd pay? I reckon it was cheaper in the long run for me to look after these things myself.

It must be quite a weight on the floor, says Alec banging the floor to test it with the heel of his shoe.

I don't know about the floor, says Mr Corker. He goes over to one of the windows and looks out. He is well above the tops of the buses. The people crossing the road look very small and yet at the same time certain of what they are doing. Level with the floor below there hangs the sign which says Corker's of Clapham. The letters are black on khaki. The sign is swinging slightly in the wind. London! says Mr Corker, London!

Alec gazes up at the mahogany-coloured barricade with the bulbous legs of upended chairs and tables pointing like guns in every direction. Is it very valuable, all this stuff? he asks.

Mr Corker turns round to peer at the barricade through his glasses as though the question had made him decide to check that nothing was missing. One or two pieces are worth something, he says, and then there's the sentimental value. This is all part of the furniture I was brought up with. It has sentimental value.

The telephone rings downstairs in the Inner Office. Let it ring, says Mr Corker harshly, let it ring. He pulls at the lapels of his overcoat. We're shut for the afternoon, we want no interruption.

Alec picks up two dining-room chairs by their legs, one in each hand. I'll put these in the back room and we'll clear some space. The chairs are upholstered with woven pictures on their backs. As he puts them down in the back room, Alec notices that one of the pictures is of a girl in a wood with a deer. It smells of mothball crystals with a smell like that of the disinfectant used in lavatories. The girl, Alec decides, looks as though she was made of china. He goes back for another two. They all smell the same.

I don't want you to run any risks, says Mr Corker, be careful not to strain yourself. What we can't move we'll leave.

Alec laughs and lifts a chair high up until its back touches the ceiling. Mr Corker looks worried. Please don't take any risks, he repeats.

Seven chairs, says Alec picking up the last.

One must have got lost, says Mr Corker.

Shall we take the table now? asks Alec.

Will it go through the door?

On its side it will.

They prepare to pick up the table, which is round.

Careful not to scratch it, says Mr Corker.

It's scratched already a bit.

It's very old, this table.

Yes, says Alec.

Well, my father didn't buy it new. I'd say it was a hundred years old, at least.

That's not so very old, says Alec.

Well, it's older than me, says Mr Corker, and it's older than I shall ever be, I hope.

I've got a mate who's a french polisher, says Alec, he wouldn't charge you much if I told him, and he'd bring it up as good as new.

That's very kind of you, Alec.

They put it on its side and ease it towards the door. Alec does all the manœuvring. They get it through the door by twisting it through the space at the top of the staircase. In the back room they stand it upright and Mr Corker starts placing the chairs round it. Alec had stacked the chairs in pairs, one upside down on another.

King Arthur, says Mr Corker, did you ever learn about him at school?

Just the name I remember, that's all.

And the sword Excalibur, says Mr Corker, placing the seventh chair in position.

What was that?

It was a kind of magic sword, which only a true king could have. In the beginning it was stuck in a stone at the side of a church and nobody could pull it out. When Arthur arrived there, he pulled it out without realizing what it meant – he didn't know it would prove he was the true king of England. He was just a young knight that nobody had heard of. And then when he was King of England, he made the Knights of the Round Table. Mr Corker looks down at his hands resting on his own table. When we were children we used to call this the Round Table and I used to be Sir Lancelot.

What did he do?

Sir Lancelot, says Mr Corker in a sing-song voice, Sir Lancelot, whom Arthur loved most dearly of all, Sir Lancelot the valiant. Sir Lancelot! whose heart was full of the best intentions, he wanted everything to be good, his dearest desire was to be a true knight, but he was human, that is to say he was the victim of circumstances. He never intended the pain he caused. Mr Corker blinks through his glasses.

But what did he do so bad? asks Alec.

He broke up the Knights of the Round Table and he killed Arthur.

He kills him with that sword! says Alec.

Goodness no, says Mr Corker. He didn't kill him himself at all but he was responsible for killing him. It was one of his men who killed him. It's a long, long story.

What happens? says Alec for whom the connexion between Corker and the repentance of a killer is still just possible enough to be interesting.

Mr Corker sits on one of the chairs with a woven picture on its back and lays his hands loosely on the table, in a gesture of submission to the story he is remembering. Occasionally he glances towards the gilt mirror leaning against the wall. In it he can see the sky through the window. Sir Lancelot, he says, is a kind of foundling. His mother and father were a king and queen but they had to flee their country. When we were children there weren't millions of refugees like there have been recently, a refugee was quite a rarity in those days, and I used to think how terrible it must be to leave your home and all the things you own and your friends and be chased night and day through forests and fields to another country where nobody knows you and everybody is suspicious because of what you look like, and especially if you'd once been a king. Anyway the king died of a broken heart by the side of the road. I forget what happened to his mother but she disappears, and Lancelot was stolen by a fairy of the Lake and then taken to the beautiful Lady of the Lake who brought him up. He never knew who his real parents were. It's a very delicate idea, isn't it? The Lady of the Lake! I've often thought of it on my travels and tried to visualize the Lady of Lake Como or the Lady of Lake Windermere, there's a beautiful little lake in France near Switzerland where you can almost see the Lady of the Lake behind the rushes and in the mist. A very delicate idea. Mr Corker pauses.

Alec is leaning against the wall by the fireplace with the old newspaper in it. Mr Corker still has his hands on the round table whose top has many stains on it, the colour of black cherries. The room is cold but Mr Corker doesn't appear to notice. There was a film, says Alec, called the Lady of the Lake, with Bogart in it, I think.

You could never make a film of King Arthur, says Mr Corker, you couldn't do it. It's too much to do with feelings, don't you know. If you just showed the events it just wouldn't be the same. I mean how could you show Sir Lancelot going into a trance after he's seen the Grail? He's in a trance for as many days as he's lived years in sin, that's what the story tells.

But what did he do? repeats Alec, what did he do? Was it all to do with killing Arthur?

He was the Queen's secret lover, says Mr Corker solemnly.

And so? says Alec.

You can't imagine it, says Mr Corker. It was different when we were children. Sir Lancelot loves the Queen, really loves her. Just to see her smile makes his day for him. He goes on pilgrimages for her and he fights in tournaments. Mr Corker makes an appreciative noise in his throat as though at a story somebody else is telling. We used to stage tournaments and fight with golden rod for our lances. Bernard liked to be Sir Galahad, I can see him now in the garden house in his knickerbockers. He was always wanting to be wounded, Bernard was. And then he was wounded four times, before he was killed in the Great War. I've often thought of that, I have, and how there may be a connexion between what children play and what happens to us when we grow up. It was the same with my sister. She liked to be Elaine. She kept on saying: I want to be rescued, I've been cast into a fortress, o where has my true knight gone? And if she wasn't rescued, she'd start crying. She had two long pigtails, Irene did in those days, and she was always accusing us of pulling them. Funny to think of that. It was so different in those days, children today just wouldn't believe it. When guests came to the house we didn't just stroll in and lie on the furniture and ask questions like they do now. We had our set pieces each one of us. I played the piano. Irene had a favourite bit of Tennyson she used to give as recitation – how does it begin? It's about Elaine. Something, something

> As a tiny helpless innocent bird
> That has but one plain passage of a few notes
> Will sing it o'er and o'er
> For all an April morning till the ear
> Wearies to hear it, so the simple maid
> Went half the night repeating Must I die?

As Mr Corker recites he holds his index finger up and beats a vague kind of time with it like an old music teacher.

> And then to right she'd turn and now to left
> And something something something
> Him or Death she muttered Death or Him.

I can see her now, she used to hang her head on one side and then on the other, and she had the same high voice as she still has now, very piercing. Mr Corker stops and looks up at Alec. But I forget what I was saying, what was I saying? Oh yes. About the games we played. That's a little theory of mine – according to my theory games are a sort of practice for later life – if anybody was clever enough you could tell what was going to happen to a child when he grows up just by watching him play. My sister, don't you know, always loved the tragic even as a child. Just as I said. Him or Death she muttered Death or Him. You see what I mean? Mr Corker looks up at Alec again. It's all a kind of practice.

What did you practise? asks Alec. Because the bath water has been drawn off, there is the noise of the water tank refilling. The water tank is above the room they are talking in.

What did I practise? I can't say, I'm sure. Perhaps it made a difference my being the eldest. I was always the one to be held responsible.

Did Lancelot come to a sticky end?

In the end he becomes a monk I think and the Queen, his Guinevere, she goes into a nunnery, but that's after King Arthur's been killed.

Was he caught being the Queen's lover, I mean beforehand, did Arthur catch him?

Yes, says Mr Corker, he was, and that was a terrible blow for King Arthur, for a long time he just couldn't believe it, because Sir Lancelot was his favourite knight.

When you were Lancelot, says Alec, keen now as a cross-examining counsel, who was the Queen?

Mr Corker smiles as at an old, favourite joke. She was secret, he says, that was the whole point of the story after all. She was a secret. Nobody knew who Sir Lancelot was in love with. He goes about doing his knightly feats – jousting it was called in those days, because it's all true you know, the story of Arthur, and you can go to the places where it happened – Glastonbury and Malmesbury and Tintagel – he goes jousting and he kills giants and he rescues maidens and he fights the king's enemies and all the time in his heart of hearts, secretly, he is thinking of Guinevere. But nobody knows it. That's why I would never let my sister be Guinevere. Guinevere had to be a secret. Only I knew who she was and I would never, never betray her. Never.

In the story, does she have a baby? asks Alec.

No, nothing like that, says Mr Corker, it was the age of chivalry, remember, we were very innocent then too. I'll give you an instance. At number nine Priory Road – it was a big house where we lived then – there was a big geyser in the bathroom and one night when the maid was having a bath it exploded and I rushed out to see because of the noise. My father was already standing in the doorway but through his legs I could see the maid lying without a stitch on her on the bathroom floor, and that was the first time, the very first time, I knew what the difference was. Mr Corker smiles weakly.

Was she dead?

No I don't think so, there wasn't any blood, but they never told us what happened to her. She was sent away, I think. And my father said he couldn't afford any more earthquakes. He often said things like that which we didn't understand at the time. I can see him now sitting at this table here and all of us quiet as mice while he ate. When he spoke, he spoke very loud. Well Liesel, he would say, are you tired of other people's children yet? Mr Corker imitates his father's voice by making his own several tones gruffer: he also draws his lips in, which, whether intentionally or not, gives an effect of toothlessness. He didn't understand our games at all, and he made jokes about the Round Table although again we never quite knew then if they were jokes or not. Will you pass the grail, Mother? he used to shout when he wanted a dish passed. After he'd ate his food he'd lean back in his chair – one of these very chairs here, they're the same chairs – and he'd push the plates away from him and light his cigar and say, Well Lancelot, where's your horse? I didn't know what to say. But then he'd say: Got a horse myself today. And Mother would get up from the table because she disapproved of gambling. But afterwards Mother would read to us, up in the Nursery, and Liesel would sit there too darning our clothes or sewing something. Mr Corker pauses, puts his hands on the table to push his chair back and says much more loudly than before: A long time ago that was and a lot of water has passed under the bridge since then. I think we were happier in those days than children are today. We appreciated what we had much more. There was none of this saying all the time, I must have this, I must have that.

We didn't have much, says Alec, remembering the years just after the war and his father working as a shunter.

But you expect much more, says Corker, that's the difference, you want so much more compared to when we were children. You—

Again the telephone rings. Again Mr Corker says: leave it, we're shut for the afternoon. But he gets up from the table and, smiling at Alec, says: Back to work. And never finishes his comparison of the generations.

The next thing to move, for it stands in the way to the bed, is a chest of drawers. It is a cumbersome piece of heavy reddish wood. On top of it is a pale yellow silk lampshade which is torn in places. Beside the lampshade are some china dishes.

Gee! what's this? says Alec, is this that grail?

A vegetable dish, says Mr Corker.

You could wash in it! And look at that one.

That would be for a joint.

It's all jumbo size, says Alec.

Jumbo?

Yes, jumbo – big, bigger, biggest! People must have had a hell of a time moving things in those days! I mean look at that wardrobe – you could live in it, it's like a bloody shed!

Alec says bloody deliberately. It is not that he wishes to provoke Corker. On the contrary, he wants to reassure him and

96

even encourage him by stressing that now, *Office Day* over, they are on equal terms.

A bloody shed, repeats Mr Corker in his *Funny* voice, is surely a slaughterhouse. Then he picks up the silk lampshade and holds it above his head. Ladies wore hats like this once, he says. You couldn't go to tea without a hat in those days. A lady wasn't respectable without a hat. It just wasn't done.

They put the dishes on top of a book-case, and with difficulty push the chest of drawers a few inches towards the door. We'll have to lift her, says Alec.

Mr Corker starts opening the drawers. Empty, he says, empty. He opens one, shuts it again quickly without saying anything, and doesn't bother to investigate the others.

It's easiest, says Alec, if you take a grip at the bottom. They both bend down so that they can no longer see one another. Mr Corker cautiously slips his fingers underneath. Ready, he calls out. Both bent double, like men waiting at leapfrog, they carry the chest very slowly towards the door.

Is it too heavy? says Alec.

No, says Mr Corker after a pause.

It'd be easier if we lifted her higher, says Alec.

Let's stop, says Mr Corker.

They straighten up and see each other. Alec notices that Corker is pinker. If we could walk upright it'd be a lot easier.

Mr Corker is examining his hands very closely as though looking for a splinter.

Anything the matter?

No, says Mr Corker, but it's a very sharp edge, you want to be careful not to catch yourself.

They bend down once more.

Higher, shouts Alec, higher!

The chest of drawers rises unsteadily. Mr Corker's nose is pressed hard against one end. They shuffle a few steps; Mr Corker forward, Alec backward.

O.K., says Alec.

Then the chest begins to lean over towards the left, to tilt. Mr Corker's fingers are slipping. It's slipping, he shouts, slipping! Look out! He jumps back and the chest thuds to the floor as if it had come through the ceiling above.

Christ! says Alec.

They both look at the chest. It is far too solid to be broken. But one of the drawers has come out and lies on its side. Once inside the drawer but now for one fraction of a second on the grey unpolished floorboards is a dead fox. In several places its brown fur is matted and limp and appears stuck to its skin, as is the nature of fur when it is made wet or has been seized and held in a mouth. It is a mangy dead fox and if it were not now sprawled over the grey floorboards which are so worn and grazed that their surface is covered with a kind of grey wool of splinters, its fur, even where it is unmarked, would seem to have scarcely any gloss at all. One of its hind legs, limp, is caught under the drawer which has fallen out of the chest. Its front legs are splayed sideways and outwards in the crucified position in which trappers nail their skins to a wall to dry. Its eyes, with amber irises, are fixed open, suggesting that death was instantaneous and that their stare is as empty as was the silence that immediately followed, and, in retrospect, actually seemed to surround, the thud, the blow, as the chest hit the floor. Under its mouth, running the length of its gullet but on the outside of the throat, there is dark blood, so viscous that it looks solid like the dark red sugar that forms round the core wounds of baked apples.

My fault, shouts Mr Corker, my fault! He is holding one hand in the other as if the held one were hurt.

Are you hurt? asks Alec.

It caught my hand. Mr Corker is still shouting unnaturally loudly. Alec observes the sweat all across his large, plain forehead.

Let me see, says Alec.

Just nipped it, says Mr Corker, feeling with his unhurt hand behind his back so as to sit down on the arm of a leather armchair.

Alec looks at the hurt hand. There is a triangular piece of flesh the size of an apple pip missing on one knuckle.

My mother's fur, says Mr Corker, I didn't know it was there, I had no idea. His voice is gradually becoming quieter. You're all right are you? he continues, what a crash! it could have been a terrible accident, you might have been killed, we might both have been crushed, a horrible accident. As Mr Corker's voice becomes calmer, the sense of what he says becomes wilder. It could have been the end of both of us and it was my fault, it was all my fault, my fault. He keeps the hurt hand up near his mouth. It must have brought the ceiling down in the Waiting-Room. O Dear. What a wretched thing. Go and see what the damage is Alec will you?

Alec rights the chest of drawers and slides the drawer back in. He leaves the fox fur on top of the chest. Its clip was the blood. Then he goes downstairs to see.

There is a crack from the light fitting to above one of the windows, but Alec tends to believe that it has always been there. He cannot remember having actually looked at the Waiting-Room ceiling before. He knows the floor much better because he sweeps it every morning. In one place on the linoleum there is a scattering of round pock-marks, each about the size of an air-gun pellet; he has often wondered what caused them and has debated with himself whether they could have been caused by drops of some hot liquid or molten metal. *The pimple marks and yet not burns* is the thought to the rhythm of which he has often swept under the chairs. Whether, however, the crack across the ceiling was or was not there before, he will certainly tell Corker that it is old. Alec is glad to be by himself if only for a moment. Corker is beginning to become a problem. This problem has nothing to do with the physical difficulties of the job in hand. Alec is already quite resigned to having to shift everything himself until he can get Corker's bed out. It is the man himself who concerns him. This morning it was, by comparison, much simpler. Then

Corker was transformed before his eyes into the *May-Be-Old-Bugger*. All he had to do was to overcome his initial surprise and then agree that even Corker was a man like another. Of course he was plump and short-sighted and had been brought up in a different class, and was gullible, and had travelled and read a lot, and knew Vienna and was old, and was hen-pecked by his sister whom he might be poisoning, and was able to speak foreign languages, and perhaps was a virgin yet far more likely wasn't but was always embarrassed, and was suspicious and mean as hell to most people, and talked like a dreamer, and was a snob, and could not be trusted to react in any certain way if told about Jackie, and was a man who liked him, Alec. But this morning even Corker was a man like another, and there were times when Alec wanted to cheer and times when he wanted to groan. When he ticked *Why-Not-Us?* he wanted to cheer. When he named *The End* he wanted to groan. Now, Corker is no longer a man like another. He is the man Alec is helping. Imperceptibly at any one moment, yet continuously, Alec is being turned into an accomplice. Alec knows that he cannot blame Corker for this. He has listened to Corker talking many times before and it was never like listening to a confession. He has done many jobs for Corker which have had little connexion with being a junior clerk, but they have never amounted to helping Corker. Yet Corker himself has not made any new demands. The difference is that it is today and not another day. It is Corker's Today that is making demands. Corker himself seems helpless, which is one reason why Alec cannot refuse to help him. He does not resent having to help him. What he resents is that he cannot trust Corker not to make a mistake. Corker, he knows, may well do something ignorant or stupid, just as this morning he considered taking Bandy Brandy as a housekeeper. And the difference between now and this morning is that the consequences of Corker's mistakes will now affect him in a different way. This morning he wasn't helping Corker. This morning Corker could in no way, howsoever small, involve Alec in a defeat: now he can. Alec, as he sprawls in a chair in the Waiting-Room still gazing at the crack in the ceiling, is not worried by this possibility as such. He is simply glad to be alone for a few seconds, alone with the premonition of which he has been vaguely aware since Corker began talking about Lancelot. The premonition is all contained in the word *Help*, and it is this word that Alec gently repeats to himself whilst gazing at the ceiling. He pictures Corker's face: the large, plain forehead, the big nose, the moist eyes, the grey hair over the ears, the mouth like that of a child waiting for a spoon of jam. By the expression on the face he can tell that Corker has made his mistake. It is similar to the expression on his face when the chest fell, and, in a curious way perhaps due to some interaction of the senses, this imaginary expression is also connected in Alec's mind with a thud. Confronted with Corker's face like this, Alec fears for Corker's safety and calls out *Help*. Yet no sooner has he called out *Help* than it occurs to him that he is calling for Help not for Corker but for himself.

I say, Alec, is it all right? shouts Mr Corker down the stairs.

Perfect! shouts Alec.

The ceiling! shouts Mr Corker.

Not a crack! shouts Alec.

Could you bring the first-aid box with you? shouts Mr Corker.

Where is it? shouts Alec.

In the left-hand drawer of the table with the cards on it, shouts Mr Corker.

The instructions are like an employer's instructions. Alec gets up and walks over to the window to look out. As an employee he can no longer be in a hurry. He watches a woman cross the road. He can't see her face, but he guesses from the sharp little way in which she moves her legs that she's a girl. He ticks *Where-We-Like* and then changes it to *Where-We-Bloody-Well-Like*. He needs it strong this afternoon. In the Inner Office he discovers that the drawer is locked. It was once a rule of *Office Day* that all drawers should be locked whenever there was nobody in the room.

It's locked! he shouts disagreeably, and then, following his own message, goes upstairs. Mr Corker has a lamp in one hand. Round his hurt hand he has tied a handkerchief. There are little, irregularly shaped spots of blood on it. The fox has disappeared.

Well that was lucky! says Mr Corker. All's well that ends well, eh? The colour has come back into his face. Did you get the first-aid box?

No, it's locked. I shouted.

Stupid of me, says Mr Corker, of course. He puts the lamp down and finds the key-ring in his pocket. It's either this one or this one, he says. In the left-hand drawer, it's an old cigar-box with a red cross painted on it. Regulation issue in the First World War. You've seen it before haven't you?

No, says Alec.

Then this must be the first little accident since you've been with us! says Mr Corker.

With *you*, says Alec trying to make it sound singular.

I always keep it stocked up, just in case, says Mr Corker.

Mr Corker unbinds the handkerchief and says again: Just nipped it. Again Alec looks at the triangular piece of flesh missing from the knuckle, the missing piece about the size of an apple pip. Above the knuckle and below it, Mr Corker's fingers sprout straggly black hairs. Just a spot of iodine and some sticky plaster, says Mr Corker as he sits down again on the arm of the armchair.

The iodine'll sting, says Alec.

It's nothing, says Mr Corker. Do you know I've seen men who shot their own fingers off. Dozens of them.

I only said it would sting, says Alec and goes downstairs with the keys in his hand. On the key-ring there are a dozen keys of different types and sizes. The two that Mr Corker selected the boy keeps separate. They are quite small, these two keys, no larger than the keys once used for winding up toy animals. The first one which Alec tries fits but does not turn the lock. He remembers clearly that Corker said the left-hand drawer. Nevertheless he takes the key out and instead of trying the second key, tries the same one in the right-hand drawer. His motives for doing this are vague and mixed. There is the impulse which works so mechnically that it can hardly be called a motive but which derives from a lazy, physical hope for response. The key did not fit the first drawer and since it is still between his fingers and since it is only a question of moving the hand one foot to the right, why not try it in the second drawer where, if it fits, something will have happened, a response will have been found, without yet making the effort of changing keys? This is the idlest motive. The most conscious one is one of mild defiance. Alec resents Corker's untrustworthiness, he resents having to help a man who, he now believes, is so liable to make a fool of them both, and this resentment is increased by the fact that nominally Corker can still give him instructions. Look in the left-hand drawer, Corker instructs: and Alec answers, I'll look in the right if I want to. The motive which is probably the most profound is his curiosity. Who is Corker? his curiosity demands. Until today the question could never have arisen. Corker was then the sum total of all that could be ticked under *Office Day*, and to seek yet further items for ticking when there were already so many, so repetitively and tediously amassed, would have seemed a waste of time. Now with *Office Day* abandoned and Alec forced to help him, Corker has become a stranger. Alec's curiosity is not without self-interest. Who is Corker? He needs to know. The key turns and Alec pulls out the drawer half-way. In the front are the stubs of old receipt books. Alec does not hesitate. He flicks through one to check it. The date is 1948. In those days the Registration Fee was only half a crown. Corker's handwriting was exactly the same. Farther back is a pile of used blue-black carbon paper. Alec slips his hand underneath to see if there is anything else. There is and it is hard. He lifts the carbon paper to the front and pulls the drawer farther out. He stares at the revolver. It is black and as long as a large King Dick spanner. When he picks it up, he finds it surprisingly heavy. On the barrel is written Webley and Scott and then the number: 647925. There are cartridges in each of the five chambers visible. He tries to turn the cylinder so that he can see the sixth, last chamber. It won't turn. He lays the revolver on top of the carbon paper and feels again with his hand at the back of the drawer. He finds an old De Reszke cigarette tin. He opens it. There are eleven more cartridges inside, arranged as neatly as the pipes of a minute organ. *Help*, thinks Alec. He takes up the revolver and holds it at arm's length as though he were going to fire it at a figure standing in the doorway, but he is careful to pull with his finger on the trigger guard instead of the trigger. *Help*, he thinks again. Then he presses harder with his finger at the end of his outstretched arm and closes one eye. He has never fired a revolver. He plays with his index finger, straightening it and then pulling with it. He remembers Corker's finger with the little triangular bit of flesh, no bigger than an apple pip, missing from the knuckle. *Help*, he thinks yet again. Then he thinks: It's a *Killing Machine* I have in my hand. There is a noise on the floor above. He asks himself why Corker should keep it, and if he keeps it why he should keep it loaded. He answers himself that Corker has kept it since the First World War and that he has it in the office in case of burglars. But the gun still goes on staying in Alec's hand whilst he grips it, and if the sixth chamber is loaded and if he slips his finger inside the trigger guard and if Corker appears now in the doorway, Corker will be dead. *Help* thinks Alec. Then he pictures Corker's face again. It is the same face as last time. It is not the face of Corker, shot. It is the face of Corker with the gun in his hand. If it is a burglar Corker will shoot him. That is what he keeps the *Killing Machine* for. Alec slips his finger inside the trigger guard and lets the trigger touch his finger. There is now only the thinness of tissue paper between the silent Inner Office where he stands, arm outstretched, with Corker's revolver in his hand, and the *Killing Machine* killing whoever gets in its way. Instead of letting the trigger touch his finger he now actually moves his finger against the trigger. Corker will appear. There will be knocks on the door below. There will be a bitter smell in the room. Will a secret have been let out? *Help* thinks Alec.

What are you doing? shouts Mr Corker.

The familiar voice, unexpected at that moment, startles Alec and his finger jerks hard against the trigger. There is a fraction of a second when with the speed of light Alec knows what he has done and is appalled because he never meant to. Then he realizes that it did not fire, that there was not even a click.

Nothing, he shouts.

I'll come down and get it myself, shouts Mr Corker.

I've got it! I've got it! shouts Alec.

(The following concerns Mr Corker whilst he waits upstairs in the front room after Alec has gone down for the second time to find the First-Aid Box. Mr Corker has slipped off the armchair into the seat so that his legs now dangle over the arm and his head rests on the other arm. He cannot sit in the chair in a normal position because the front of the chair is still wedged against the sideboard. His eyes are shut.)

Corker thinks: Something I said made him cross. He was quite rude about what I was telling him about the Blighty ones. It's always the same thing – if you give an inch, he takes a mile.

Corker knows: I have been telling him lies, ever since lunch I have been telling lies. This lying is not altogether deliberate on my part. My memories are lies, yet they are, when all has been said and done, my memories. So I do not know how I can talk about the past and not lie. It is true that I want to impress Alec and so sometimes I embellish even the lies that are my memories. For instance: many men shot their hands off in the war. I saw one man who had shot his hand off. I told Alec I had seen many so that he should not believe I was making a fuss about my finger. I know that I want to impress Alec particularly today.

Corker thinks: He's taking advantage of me.

Corker makes believe: He walks out on me on today of all days. He is down by the front door now. He is leaving me in the lurch.

Corker thinks: Funny how I can't help being fond of him too. And that's the trouble I daresay – I've spoilt him. A nice mess I'd be in if he did leave me in the lurch now.

A voice screams: Abandoned again! Again!

Corker makes believe: Sir Lancelot for his sins is put to shame and lies defeated in the wood. On the ground he groans but no man pays him heed. He heard their voices: 'Tis the end of Lancelot, they said.

Corker thinks: I can hear them saying it – He's gone to pieces, *aged* you know, ever since he left his sister . . .

Corker makes believe: Which saying grieved Sir Lancelot sorely, and especially when he brought to mind the high hopes and noble endeavour with which he had set out apace that morn.

Corker knows: I am old as I lie here. This is the worst moment of the day yet. Perhaps now I shall fail to carry out my plan. There is so much yet to be done and it is possible that I haven't the strength necessary. As I grow older there is always an old person beside me. It isn't me yet, this old person, but quite often I have to stop and attend to it and this uses up precious time and energy so that the real task in hand suffers as a result. I call the old person *it*, because it isn't *me* yet and to think of it as *him* is intolerable. I would hate to be so intimate with another old man, and after all, this old person, this *it*, is always there. I know it. And I know too that this is what makes me dependent on Alec. It isn't only because he's moving all the furniture and because he is downstairs fetching the first-aid box; it is also because he is young. The old person is overawed by his youth and so it leaves me alone.

Corker makes believe: Sir Lancelot growing weak from his wounds, raised himself up and addressed himself to his squire: Straightway bring water and dressings, prithee, for I bleed.

Corker thinks: If everything collapsed at once!

Corker makes believe: The squire departed but it seemed to Sir Lancelot as he lay in the darkening wood that never had he clapped eyes on one whose mien revealed so much unwillingness to do as he was bid. He would as lief have me die as bestir himself! sighed the wounded knight. And a great sadness came upon him.

Corker knows: There are stupidities and inevitable mistakes which must be accepted as unquestioningly as the law of gravity. If I throw myself out of the window, I fall to the street. If I act as though mistakes are not inevitable, if I pretend to myself that stupidities are unnecessary, I will fall just as certainly as from the window, but this time through the dark into the blackness, until I reach the bottom. It would be useless after I'd begun to fall to complain that it was all the result of a stupidity. When I begin to fall nothing can stop me except the bottom. This is why life is so dangerous. We are surrounded by stupidities we must accept as though they made sense and by mistakes we must count on being made. No appeal to justice or truth can ever save a faller: all that can save him is being forewarned: he must know that the stupidity is certain, that injustice is bound to be done, that the truth waits to be travestied. For these reasons men do not tell their wives how much they earn: people are seldom foolish enough to explain how the power of their secret passion (whatever it may be) is irresistible: death is never mentioned even at a funeral: no man asks for the money he thinks he's worth, and it is impossible for me to say to Alec: Let us be quite frank with each other, you are young and beginning and I am old and beginning again, if we shared our experiences we would both benefit, we have each spent more time with the other during the last two years than with any other single person, it's a pity we don't know one another, and today I feel it especially, for today is one of the hardest of my life.

Corker thinks: Why is Alec so long? Is it true he's walked out on us?

Corker makes believe: Sir Lancelot lay him down in the wood wherein many had died of their wounds and reckoned his solitude: a state he knew full well.

Corker thinks: I'll be alone here tonight.

A voice screams: I want to disappear!

Corker knows: Tonight I must face the fact that I've chosen to come here. There will be no fire, no cooked meal, no voice and Alec, who is always here when I am here, will be at home or with his girl. I know that I would like to know whether they do the fucking. He's big enough. It will be silent. I will hear only the gruff noises of my own actions. When I turned the bath taps on this afternoon I knew how they would sound when there was nobody else here, when I was alone. I have chosen it. I want to be forgotten because to be forgotten is like being given a second chance. Only Alec is young enough to be able to change his mind without first having to forget me. I know that, but I do not know how I can make him change his mind in the way I want.

Corker thinks: It's all my history, this furniture. It's historic.

Corker makes believe: And behold Sir Lancelot saw a vision. His young squire mounted on a fair horse, well saddled and bridled, rode into the clearing of wood wherein Sir Lancelot lay bleeding with none to do dole for him. And the squire full young and tender of age dismounted and addressed Sir Lancelot in this manner: Master, I beseech you make me a knight, for I have served you well and this way, by my body's oath, you shall have my allegiance for ever. All this in vision Sir Lancelot saw as he lay in the darkening wood.

Corker thinks: Promise him a share in the business one day, why not? It would be an incentive for him, something for him to work for and prepare for. He could take over when I have to stop.

A voice screams: My son! My son!

Corker thinks: Better than the idea of a second branch. Always provided he really worked for it. He's still got a lot to learn. But I can teach him and there'll be more and more that he can do here. Of course he's still very young.

Corker knows: Alec is growing older. We are growing older together, Alec the clerk, and I his employer in the business I have made. As he grows older his age becomes less and less important. As I grow older I become less and less important. When he was younger, when he came here straight from school, he used to listen to me more. As he grows my influence over him diminishes. Soon we shall face each other as equals, he and I. But I know that I fear that when that happens, it will be to say good-bye.

Corker makes believe: Sir Lancelot pondered the meaning of his vision but could find no just answer. Then anon an old man made his way through that dark wood. This old man was a hermit, wise in affairs. I pray you, said the good Sir Lancelot, tell me a vision that befell me this very day. Say on, said the hermit. Then he told him of how his squire mounted on a fair horse came to beseech him to make him a knight. Sir, said the hermit, I will tell you a part now and the other deal later. The squire riding a fair horse betokeneth that the squire grows dissatisfied and thirsts for greater glory. Then Sir Lancelot desired the hermit's counsel. Lo, Sir Lancelot, said the good man, grant him . . .

Corker thinks: A ten shilling a week rise.

Corker makes believe: And the hermit having spake these words made to depart.

Corker thinks: Is it too much?

Corker knows: To offer Alec more money is not to get nearer to him.

Corker thinks: You can't expect gratitude – but he's bright enough to know when he's well off.

Corker makes believe: Sir Lancelot cried upon the hermit: If it please you, keep no secret from me and say now the other deal you have withheld. Alas, said the good man, it cannot please thine ear to hear it. It is right necessary to hear the truth, declared Sir Lancelot, speak out. Then the hermit in black clothing said: the squire's beseeching to be made a knight signifieth that his time has come and thine is done.

A voice screams: Don't leave me.

Corker thinks: Must have dozed off for a second. Perhaps ten bob is not enough, but we can't afford more.

Corker shouts out loud: What are you doing?

Corker knows: He is fiddling around in the Inner Office. He is touching the things I have collected and saved over the years. Alec always behaves as an intruder and that is what I like so much about him. He leaves the door open and flings up the window – not literally, but in the sense that I know, in the sense that he has previously had nothing to do with what he finds here. If he came from Paris or Vienna he wouldn't be more of a foreigner than he is – to all this, to all the business downstairs and to all the domestic history that surrounds me here. The fox didn't bring him back to Mother's funeral that I couldn't mourn at. The lamp is not Liesel's for him. If he had been the right age and had been in love with Liesel he would have taken her away out of all this. It is funny and comforting to know that even now it would not be beyond the bounds of possibility for him and me to be in love with the same woman. She would not be in love with me, of course. But still in face of her we would stand side by side.

Corker thinks: Let him choose the housekeeper – then he'd stay.

Corker knows: I hate this stuff that surrounds me. It is prison furniture. I intended to transform it. But now I know I cannot do it singlehanded.

Corker thinks: He's only a boy, it's not practical.

Corker knows: I am only an old man and it's not practical.

Nothing, shouts Alec from the Inner Office.

Corker thinks: The boy's a fool.

Corker shouts out loud: I'll come down and get it myself.

I've got it, I've got it, shouts Alec.

Corker makes believe: Sir Lancelot that was hurt awaited the return of his squire with soft ointments to salve his wounds. And when he did hear him approach he was overjoyed to be no more alone.

2

The telephone rings for the fifth time. Let it ring, shouts Mr Corker, we're shut for the afternoon. Mr Corker has said the same every time it has rung. Each time he has said it as though Alec were just about to pick up the receiver; whereas, in fact, Alec has been moving a chest or listening to Mr Corker talk or crawling over a table. It is an injunction that Mr Corker apparently feels obliged to make for superstitious reasons. This time Alec is sitting on top of the large wardrobe, his head touching the ceiling. Mr Corker is on the landing, wheeling a tea-trolley into the back room.

The back room is now full of furniture. Folded curtains have been piled on the round table. Lamps lie on cushions. Pictures lean against the skirting boards. The armchair has another armchair on top of it, with its castors in the air. A book-case with glass doors lies on its back, its glass facing the ceiling. There is not a square yard of floor space left. Mr Corker has decided to take the front room as his own, and so, without bothering to stack the pieces, Alec has moved as much as he can into the back room in order to clear the front. Mr Corker has taken the handkerchief off his finger and now only has an Elastoplast round it.

The telephone continues to ring and Mr Corker, having dumped the tea-trolley, hurries back. He repeats again: Let it ring.

I'm not answering it, says Alec.

Only interrupt us, says Mr Corker, when we are getting on so well. Can you see the blue carpet up there?

Yes, I've got it.

Good boy, says Mr Corker, we're getting on like a house on fire, we really are.

Can you take it from me? says Alec.

Mr Corker stands by the side of the wardrobe. The wardrobe is a good ten feet high. Alec, kneeling on top of it, slides a thick roll of carpet over the edge into Mr Corker's upstretched, open arms. Alec is careful to keep a good grip of his end lest it knocks Mr Corker over. As Mr Corker embraces the roll it slips down between his arms and his body. Then it touches the floor and Alec lets go. It stands twelve feet high. Mr Corker still holds it upright. His gesture is like a child's when a child tries to see if he can get his arms round a tree.

Can you lie it down? says Alec.

Mr Corker moves awkwardly to one side, still holding the roll but trying now to support it as one supports a helpless man being lowered on to a stretcher on the ground. He holds it until it is at an angle of about 60 degrees. Then it topples over, brushing Mr Corker's nose as it does so. As it thumps on the floor, it bends in the middle like a kangaroo's tail.

Like a house on fire! says Mr Corker apparently unperturbed. Alec dangles his stockinged feet over the side of the wardrobe and jumps lightly to the ground. He has taken his tie and leather jacket off, his trousers are dirty, and his large hands dark grey all over with dust.

And you've done everything, says Mr Corker. He is now on his hands and knees fiddling with the string tied round the carpet roll, and he looks up at Alec with a smile.

That's all right, says Alec.

Ever since he came back with the first-aid box Alec has answered everything pleasantly but briefly. He has made no remarks of his own. The work to be done has been a relief for it has meant thinking about the job in hand instead of speculating about Mr Corker. As soon as he had stuck the plaster on the finger, Mr Corker had turned to him and said: I hope you are happy working for us, Alec. Alec didn't know what to say. In the end he said: Well, today's like a day off isn't it? Then Mr Corker said: Alec, we must have a talk one of these days about the future. You must tell me what your plans are. We're going to make all kinds of changes, changes for the better, don't you know. For instance the first change is that we're going to offer you a rise of ten bob a week. At first Alec thought it was a joke and made a polite guffaw. I'm serious, says Mr Corker. But why? said Alec. If you don't want it, said Mr Corker, in a voice he usually kept for trying moments with difficult clients: a very precise voice as if the proceedings were being taken down by a slightly deaf reporter. Of course, said Alec, it just sounds funny that's all. We want you to be happy here, said Mr Corker, the main thing is to be happy. *Help!* thought Alec.

The telephone rings for the sixth time. Let it ring, shouts Mr Corker. Alec also gets down on his hands and knees to help unroll the carpet. With heads near the floor the telephone bell in the room below sounds more vibrant and urgent than before. It rings for over a minute and then stops abruptly in the middle of a ring.

Do you know, says Mr Corker, I remember the first telephone.

It sounded like somebody who really wanted — Alec almost says *you* but then out of consideration of Corker's feelings and the mystery of them, he says *us*.

The carpet smells of camphor and has been rolled up with sheets of newspapers laid all over it. It was invented by a man called Bell, isn't that queer? says Mr Corker.

It'll fit crossways, says Alec, then we can put the bed on it with its foot towards the window.

Mr Corker, on his knees, looks round the room. O.K., he says, you're boss. The way he says this reminds Alec of the way he said No Can Do to Mrs McBryde: it's as if he is pretending very inefficiently to be somebody he isn't. Perhaps it was when he was pretending, thinks Alec, that he loaded the gun.

When they have unrolled the carpet, its edges and corners curl up, to reveal the canvas-like grain of its underneath. It's been tied up for ten years or more, says Mr Corker, it'll take a bit of time to flatten out, but it's in beautiful condition, isn't it, just feel it, feel what they call the pile. Mr Corker is picking up the old newspapers, crumpling them and dumping the lot outside the door on the stone landing. He does this, bent double in his brown overall, with a feverish show of activity. Alec reminds himself that if it were still *Office Day* Corker would be folding every newspaper separately.

As soon as he has picked up the last piece of newspaper, Mr Corker stands as far away as possible in the corner, and looks down at the carpet with his head slightly inclined and his eyes screwed up. It is the customary posture for looking at paintings in museums. The room is mostly cleared; only one sector of the barricade is left where wardrobe, sideboard and beds are; the carpet covers nearly one half of the floor. Against the grey floor-boards in the mean light from the uncurtained and unwashed windows, the richness of the carpet's blue is quite unexpected, like the blue of bluebells in a scrub of derelict winter trees. That's a proper bedroom carpet that is, says Mr Corker, there's the right and wrong carpet for every room you know, a dining-room carpet, for instance, you couldn't put this carpet in a dining-room, a dining-room carpet should be darker and much more elaborate and much less blue, you want reds in a dining-room, greens in a drawing-room and blues in a bedroom, it's a proper bedroom carpet this. We're getting on like a house on fire, we really are.

Alec is already studying the structure of the heavy iron bedstead next to the wardrobe, and trying to work out how to assemble it. It'll be more like a bedroom, he says, when we've got this up.

The head and foot of the bed have massive iron legs on castors, and dozens of brass-coloured bars, the larger of which are crowned with white china knobs with posies of flowers painted upon them. Leaning one on top of the other, these two end-pieces look like the side of a cage on wheels; the springs of the bedframe itself are deep and made of very coarse, thick wire, the ringlets of a hideous, rusty metal giantess. *Soft-as-silk-Jackie-where-we-bloody-well-like*, acknowledges Alec.

I'd call it a Royal Blue, says Mr Corker, when I was in the hosiery trade we had thirty-four different shades of blue, and we had to be able to recognize every one. Then, either because Mr Corker is remembering his own youth or because he has noticed that Alec is unresponsive, he changes the subject and asks: This girl friend of yours, Alec, what does she work at?

In a shop, says Alec.

A hairdresser, is she?

Just an ordinary shop-girl, says Alec and bangs with his fist at one of the springs. Shall we have a go? he adds.

Are you tired, Alec?

Not at all.

You must bring her here one day, when we've got it all nice, says Mr Corker, now that we're going to turn it into a home here, I want you to feel quite at home.

Thank you, says Alec.

There is a knock, three floors down, on the front door.

Go and look out of the window, says Mr Corker quickly, there's a good boy.

Alec goes across to the window.

Don't let them see you, says Mr Corker.

Alec notices all the agitation that is in his voice.

We're shut, says Mr Corker, who is it?

A woman.

Who?

How should I know?

Has she got a stick?

Not as I can see.

Is she looking up?

Yes.

Keep back then.

Could it be, Alec asks himself, that it was when he loaded the gun that he wasn't pretending?

Tell me when she's not looking, says Mr Corker.

She's writing something on a piece of paper.

Mr Corker tiptoes to the window and cautiously looks out. All right, he says, she must be a client.

Alec decides that even Corker must be aware of how he is betraying himself. He ticks *Help!* under *Poor Bugger*, because there's no *May-Be* left.

I didn't want a scene you see, says Mr Corker.

Of course, says Alec. Then he says, more kindly: Let's get this bed done. He carts the head over to the wall which the blue carpet is touching, leans it there and very quietly, as though he would prefer Corker not to hear, adds: At least there'll be a place to kip then.

She's gone, says Mr Corker, still by the window.

Can you give me a hand with the springs? says Alec.

Yes, yes, what do you want me to do?

You take that side and we carry her towards the window and lay her on the carpet, it's quite heavy so hold it at the bottom.

They place the bedframe gently on the carpet. Looking down through the springs on to the blue, the blue goes dowdy.

Now, says Alec, we've got to fit this into the head there. We lift it up, just this end, and then you get that knob into that hole. We must both get in together else it won't fit.

They lift the bed up, Mr Corker with two hands, Alec with one so that he can have a hand free to tilt the headpiece.

Are you in? hisses Alec.

Nearly.

Hurry.

I'm in! I'm in!

Good.

They stand back to see what they have achieved. The head-piece, at right angles to the frame, now tilts forward from the wall.

The foot next, says Alec.

He wheels the second side of the cage over from the wardrobe.

This'll be trickier, he says, seeing we've got to hold the foot up whilst we do it.

Couldn't we lean it against something? asks Mr Corker.

No, says Alec, the best way is I'll get underneath and lift up, you hold the foot and guide the knobs in.

Mr Corker holds the foot from the side, like a man opening a gate to let a woman through.

Jesus! exclaims Alec, you want to face the thing.

Mr Corker comes round to the centre of the foot, holding the top rail with both hands all the time. Alec crawls under the bed at the other end and then lifts the bedstead up on his back. He arrives on all fours at Mr Corker's feet.

Can you get the knobs in?

Nearly.

Mr Corker hangs over the top rail to try to see what he's doing.

It's not straight! shouts Alec.

How? whispers Mr Corker.

Go about two inches to the right, says Alec.

Your right? asks Mr Corker.

My bloody right! says Alec. The springs are wriggling into the flesh of his shoulders.

Is that nearer? says Mr Corker.

Worse, says Alec.

I'm sorry, says Mr Corker.

Leave it, says Alec, I'm going to let it down.

He crawls out from the other end. Could you get underneath? he says.

I'll try, says Mr Corker still holding on to the rail.

I'll lift it up for you, says Alec.

Alec goes into the back room and comes back with a heavy green curtain over his arm. This'll protect your back, he says, put the foot down, lay it flat on the floor, and if you get on your hands and knees, I'll lift this end for you to get under.

Alec drapes the folded curtain over Mr Corker's back and then lifts the bed. All right, he says.

Mr Corker crawls forward.

I'll lower it very gently, says Alec, so you can shout if it's too much. Tuck your head in though. Right down.

He lowers the bedstead. Too heavy? he says.

Part of the curtain has unfolded and fallen over Mr Corker's head and face. His voice is therefore somewhat muffled by the curtain.

I can manage, the voice says quickly. Mr Corker is now carrying his bed on his back.

Won't take a second, says Alec.

The telephone rings.

We're shut, gasps the voice from the green hood.

Done! shouts Alec and lifts the whole end of the bed up by the foot.

Mr Corker doesn't move.

The telephone stops.

You can come out! says Alec.

Mr Corker crawls to the side, still keeping his head right down underneath the green curtain and not realizing that he now has twelve inches clearance. When he is out from under the bed, Alec lowers it.

Am I clear? asks Mr Corker. Am I clear now?

Alec lifts the curtain off.

Mr Corker has his head so low that it is as if he is kissing the ground. One of his trousers is rucked up to disclose a white very smooth calf. At the back of his neck just below his hair, there is a scratch with a smear of rusty blood over it. Alec will never in his life be able to forget this glimpse of Corker. And he will never be able to explain, even to Jackie, why the memory hurts him

Mr Corker looks up quickly and then clambers to his feet. He puts his hand up to the back of his neck. Then he says: Now I know what it's like to be Job. Job is the old testament, don't you know. Job spelt just the same as job, J O B. He laughs. We're getting on with this J O B like a house on fire. We really are. Is my neck scratched?

Instead of saying Yes immediately, Alec examines Mr Corker's neck again as if he hadn't noticed it when Corker was on the ground. Already Alec is trying to forget that sight. A little, he says.

Never mind! says Mr Corker, now for the mattress!

I haven't seen a mattress, says Alec.

You couldn't, says Mr Corker, it's downstairs in the Reception-Room. He glances round at the bed as though suddenly he has remembered something. You know I was born in that bed, he says, I was.

Alec stares at the brass bars and the hideous ringlets and the painted china balls.

I'll show you the mattress, says Mr Corker.

Mr Corker descends the stairs first and Alec, following, sees the scratch on his neck for the third time. He knows why Corker is making no fuss about it, no fuss compared to the fuss he made about his knuckle. The *Poor Bugger* is getting more and more excited. *Office Day* is being left farther and farther behind. The truth is becoming wilder than any story he can tell Jackie. He, Alec, is now in control, Corker is beside himself.

The mattress is leaning against the book-shelf in the Reception-Room. It is a new one, vast and thick, and pale blue in colour and covered with polythene. There! says Mr Corker.

You take the front end, says Alec.

They negotiate the doorway and arrive at the foot of the narrow steep staircase.

Now for the ascent! says Mr Corker, pink in the face and with ruffled hair.

You lug it up behind you, says Alec, and I'll shove from below.

The ascent of Annapurna! says Mr Corker, it sounds like a woman doesn't it, but Everest and the Matterhorn sound like men don't they? Jungfrau's another woman, of course. Do you know what Jungfrau means in German? It means virgin.

Mr Corker is mounting the stairs backwards pulling the mattress towards him. Sometimes he pulls at the top towards his face, sometimes at the bottom between his legs. The mattress is hard to grip because of the Polythene which squeaks when it is hauled. Alec, behind, is pushing the thing away, keeping it at arm's length.

Heave away! puffs Mr Corker, believing now in seamen. He heaves so hard in one of his top pulls that the mattress actually lurches up against his face and presses against his mouth.

Got it in the mouth then! he says.

Alec gives the mattress a harder shove from below. He wants to see what the *Poor Bugger* will do next. He wants him further humiliated. Alec can only choose between wanting this or being powerless to prevent it. This is why he wants it.

The mattress buffets Mr Corker's face.

Up she rises! he says.

Alec shoves.

Mr Corker retreats up another step, holding on to the mattress now to prevent himself falling over backwards. Then he suddenly sits. The mattress falls squeaking on to his shoulder. Let's have a little rest, he says.

Like dancing with a fat lady, says Alec.

More like getting a drunk one to bed, says Mr Corker.

Alec laughs. They both look over the banisters down to the stone entrance below. They can see the banisters going all the way down, snaking.

And she's fucking heavy. It is Mr Corker who says this. He says it in a distinct but high voice, as if he were trying to maintain the note of Alec's laugh. After he has spoken, the words flutter down into the silence like pieces of paper fluttering down the stairwell to the stone entrance. Mr Corker puts his hand to his mouth testing it gently to see whether he bit his lip when the mattress smothered him. Alec eventually says: We're nearly there now.

Mr Corker, returning to the use of his normal voice, says: We're getting on like a house on fire. We really are.

When they begin again Alec no longer tries to push the mattress into Corker's face: on the contrary, he does his utmost to take all the weight himself so that all Corker has to do is to guide it. Alec lifts and as he lifts he imagines himself, for the second time today, carrying an unusual load. This time it is a vast blue Polythene cushion – he can smell the airless sweetness of the Polythene – on top of which lies a kicking, struggling baby: but the baby wears bifocal spectacles, has grey hair, is growing bald and is wearing a brown overall like a smock. He is carrying a baby on a cushion up the stairs. Here he must get round the corner, where each stair is cut like a triangular piece of cake, without letting the baby fall off, for if it fell it would fall right down to the stone entrance thirty feet below.

The mattress gets wedged between the wall and the banisters on the corner. The baby disappears and Mr Corker reappears. Alec pushes but the mattress just yields. Mr Corker sits on the top of the stairs and tugs. When it slips free, Mr Corker pulls it on top of himself on the landing floor. We've done it, he says, done it.

After they have at last placed the mattress on the bed, Mr Corker hurries across the landing to the back room and comes back with a little bedside table. Then he fetches two cushions and a lamp. He puts the cushions where the pillows would be at the head of the bed and the lamp on the table. He plugs the lamp into a point at the bottom of the wall and switches it on. He looks at the effect. In one corner of the room there is the remains of the stacked furniture. On the blue carpet stands the blue-mattressed double bed. Beside the bed is the pink lamp. Otherwise the room is empty and the light is beginning to fade. The blue of the blue carpet is now like blue paint. Through the uncurtained window a red neon sign is visible. It says *Water*. The reflection of the pink lamp can also be seen in the window. Now, says Mr Corker, I've got somewhere to sleep tonight and we're going to stop.

Have you got any blankets? asks Alec.

Blankets and sheets and pillow cases, says Mr Corker, all in the kitchen cupboard.

I'll go and make a cup of tea, says Alec.

I just don't know what I'd do without you, says Mr Corker, and, sitting on the bed, leans back until he is lying. I'm not as young as I was, Alec, he says. His brown overall is spread out either side of him and Alec can see the top of his trousers pulled up by his braces until they're almost round his chest. Alec has often noticed this before. And so it seems to Alec that the habit of having his trousers pulled half-way up to his chin is all that remains of the old Corker.

Corker thinks: I am here, we've succeeded, nobody can stop me.

Corker knows: I am in a position such as I have never been in before, I have done something irrecoverable and now I must wait for the consequences. It is desperation that has temporarily halted my ageing. I shall stay desperate.

A voice screams: Back! Back!

Corker thinks: Bit by bit I shall make it as I want. I want to put the long mirror over the fireplace there. One of the emperors had mirrors all round his bed so he could see his mistress better. Mirror glass is so dear these days, that's the difficulty. So dear you can't afford to look – I could make a joke of this. *Mirrors are so expensive nowadays that a man can't afford to look at himself.* At this rate we'll get mirrors with slot machines. Put in a penny for a ten-second look. Put in a couple of bob to see yourself at your best. Put in five, to see yourself young again. I could use this idea in the lecture. Looking glass, looking glass hanging on the wall. Who is the fairest of them all?

Corker makes believe: McBryde.

Corker thinks: It's funny to find it all again, the carpet, the bed, the dinner set.

Corker makes believe : There is an orange curtain across the doorway. I part it and enter. A beautiful woman stands there as though expecting me. She wears silver brace-lets that are almost white, and comes towards me, arms outstretched. Welcome, she says, we have been waiting for you for a thousand and one nights. You have travelled far and you must need refreshment. A bed has been prepared for you, a serving maid hired, a bath made ready. Nor have we wasted the many days and nights we have waited since first we expected you. In these cupboards is the cloth of many colours that we have woven for you. In those draw-ers is the linen we have embroidered. On those shelves are the plates and bowls we have decorated.

A voice screams : Back! Back! Back!

Corker makes believe : Master what is your wish now? Whatever it be, we shall grant it. I answer her in a clear voice in this very room lying on the bed that has been prepared. I wish to begin again.

Corker thinks : If at first you don't succeed . . .

Corker makes believe : You know he has quite an interesting little collection, has Corker. You should drop in at his place sometime and get him to show you his maps and silks – and his own photos too, you know, he's travelled over half the word. He's an interesting man to talk to, he is, one of the characters of Clapham – it's a cosy little place and he lives with his housekeeper.

Corker thinks : I must make up my mind about Miss Brand.

Corker makes believe : My brother walked out of my house and I never saw him again. It was a Monday morning. The shock of it nearly killed me. I did everything for William – and then to be thrown aside like an old coat that's worn out – that was the unkindest thing about it. The doctor said to me, he said, you've been through a very difficult time, Miss Corker, a woman less courageous than you—

Corker thinks : If she went to hospital I could collect my things from West Winds and I wouldn't have to see her.

The telephone rings.

Corker makes believe : Hello is that Corkers of Clapham? Mr William Corker? This is Burgh Heath Hospital here. Your sister, Mr Corker, is dangerously ill and has been asking for you. We imagined that in view of the gravity of her condition you'd probably like to come straightaway.

Corker shouts out : We're shut!

Corker makes believe : Unfortunately I have a business to run and it's simply out of the question.

Corker thinks : She's always used her illness.

Corker makes believe : Your sister has died, Mr Corker.

A voice screams : Back! Back!

Corker makes believe : He was funny all day he was, the day his sister died. I never saw him like it before, it was like he just let himself go. When we got the bed up, he flopped down on it like a drunk. I wouldn't be surprised if he was drunk.

Corker thinks : It must be past five. It's getting dark – I shall put the picture of the bird-bath on that wall. Wonder if there are any birds here. I'll try with some mutton fat.

Corker makes believe : Ladies and gentlemen and that includes I hope the gentleman from the Burgh Heath Hospital and Miss Irene Corker and Mr Alec Gooch. Ladies and gentlemen, the title of our little Talk tonight is Why Not? Some of the material is similar to that used in another little Talk I gave in this same hall and which was called Why I Did It. I am proud to be an Englishman (Cheers), I am proud of the country of my birth. And to be an Englishman is to be free. You have only to travel – as we shall travel tonight to Vienna – to discover how much foreigners admire the Englishman's liberty. England is a free country. And so I am claiming only one of my most elementary rights: the right to live in the place of my choice. I have worked all my life, first in the hosiery trade and then in my own little business which has now become Corker's of Clapham, has not this earned me the right to sleep in my own bed and to put that bed where I wish? I repeat – has it not?

Corker thinks : This Polythene may not be healthy.

Corker makes believe : I have been charged with deserting my sister and with being indifferent to her suffering as a cripple. But I ask you, friends, how many brothers are there who do not desert their sisters? On the contrary, I have refrained from deserting my sister for far longer than most brothers. I have lived in that miserable house of hers for twelve years. For twelve years I heard nothing at night but her noises. Nor am I indifferent to her suffering, for I have suffered it. The right of a man to be himself, the right of a man to find a way out of his suffering, the right of a man to live where and as he wishes – eager, curious, hopeful, experimental – the right of a man to say: I wish to begin again. (Prolonged cheers.)

Corker thinks : I hope Miss Browning comes tonight.

Corker makes believe : Ladies and Gentlemen, thank you, and now I have a little announcement to make. Miss Browning and I have decided to become Uncle and Niece.

Corker knows : I am desperate.

Corker makes believe : Bless O Lord the bed that I lie on.

The first thing Alec noticed in the kitchen were the violets in the tumbler on the windowsill. Then he lit the gas stove. The gas stove is an old-fashioned one. Each ring is a kind of miniature, perforated life-belt. Rusty flakes of cast-iron have flaked off the grid and fallen on to the tray underneath the grill. During the last ten years the stove has only been used for boiling a kettle or water in a saucepan for an egg. Mysteriously, since vegetables are never cooked in this kitchen, a cabbage-water smell clings to its walls and the wooden doors of the cupboards. A light hangs from the ceiling without a shade. In each corner of the ceiling there are cobwebs. In an hour Alec will give the violets back to Jackie, in an hour he will get to hell out of here. He doesn't really believe in the ten bob. It seems to him that if *Office Day* is ever to begin again, Corker and he will have to pretend that the day Corker kissed the floor never happened. And if they pretend it never happened, then Alec was never offered his rise. He goes across to the cracked draining board where the old brown teapot is always left to drain upside down. There he begins another line of reasoning for not believing in the ten bob. It begins: I can't help being sorry for the *Poor Bugger*. He pours the hot water into the pot to warm it. He is sorry for Corker because since lunch-time Corker has grown old and incapable. He imagines Corker in his dressing-gown tomorrow morning making his breakfast here – Alec himself is now putting two teaspoonfuls of tea into the pot – and the poor bugger won't get much of a breakfast. But more than anything else, he is sorry for Corker because of all that remains unforeseeable, unknown, unsaid. Alec isn't certain why Corker left his sister in such a hurry, or why she is dying, or why Corker said Fucking Heavy, or why he keeps a loaded revolver in his drawer, or why he says he'll have Bandy Brandy for a housekeeper, or why he is behaving like a drunk upstairs, but he is certain that Corker couldn't explain why either. Corker, it seems to Alec, is being hustled along as though there was a 100-m.p.h. gale behind him. It's a man-made gale that has got into a tunnel and Corker is being hustled through the cata-combs. The kettle, boiling, whistles. Alec has never seen a cata-comb but, as he pours from the kettle he can feel and hear the crusts of fur that have formed over the years inside (they weigh one side of the kettle down and they make a brittle tinkling noise) and these suggest to him the fleshless, encrusted, mineral and subterranean world which he uses as a metaphor to describe to himself what he imagines to be the nature of Corker's suffer-ing. He goes across to the cupboard. On one shelf a few odd cups and saucers and plates. On another shelf a packet of salt, some tea, a roll of biscuits and a small, almost empty pot of Marmite. On the lowest shelf are the sheets and pillow cases which Corker mentioned. Alec leaves the cups on the Marmite shelf and bends down to examine the sheets. If Corker explains nothing, Alec can search for himself. The sheets don't look new. Presumably Corker smuggled them out of West Winds. Did he also have a double-bed there? Behind the sheets he can now see two boxes. One is a white cardboard box with nothing written on it. He opens it. Inside is a bottle, about the size of a gin bottle. It is unopened. The label is in a foreign language but Alec reads the word Kummel and recognizes it as the kind of booze Corker was talking about in Vienna. The second box is golden coloured and has *Allure* written over it in an embossed, black and sloping script. Alec carefully sees whether this one will open too. It will. Inside is a tray of chocolates of different shapes and in different deep-coloured silver-papers. A few of the chocolates have been eaten and their deep-coloured cups left. Above the tray, resting against the inside of the lid, is a picture, like a gigantic cigarette card. It shows a woman lying naked on her back on a bed. She has dark hair and big eyes but no hair between her legs so that she must have been shaved. She is small and about the same size as Jackie. Her skin is very white – even the underneaths of her feet are white. It looks like a photograph but it is coloured and might be a painting. Underneath is written Maja Undressed. Alec looks down again at the chocolates and pointlessly starts counting how many have been eaten. Seven. He pictures Corker eating them in bed. Then he pictures him looking at the woman whilst he eats them. *Help!* he thinks, and shuts the box and puts them both back behind the folded sheets which are glossy with ironing. He takes the two cups to the table beside the gas stove. The milk is always kept in the wooden cupboard underneath the sink to keep it cool. On the windowsill above the sink are the violets. The lead waste-pipe U-bends through the cupboard. The difference between the milk that goes into the bottle and the waste water that goes through the pipe suggests to him the different histories of his penis and Corker's. He sighs and kicks the door shut with his foot. He renotices the violets and retraces their history. He asks himself why Corker can't be like other men, like other men but just older than some. He remembers Corker the baby on the blue cushion. He remembers Corker saying that Kummel is quite strong. It crosses his mind that he might open the bottle and put some in Corker's tea. As he gives him the cup, he will say: with love from Maja. Then the old man might fall asleep in a drunken stupor, muttering Maja! Maja! My love! The fucker, thinks Alec, the drunken fucker who knelt down on his knees to lick the floor. Alec pours the milk into the two cups. One is slightly cracked. He has jumbo-size vegetable dishes but no decent cups. When Alec pours the tea on top of the milk and it goes the familiar ginger-brown, he remembers Jackie making tea for breakfast this morning. Tea, tea, tea, tea, he thinks, and each tea represents somebody wanting a ginger-brown cupful, himself drinking tea in Jackie's mother's kitchen, his own mother, his brothers taking their tea cans to work, the cycling club when it's raining stopping at a caff, the boys hanging around the tea stall by the station at two in the morning. It is true that Corker also likes tea but Corker is different. Corker with his chocolate-box and round tables and fancy sentiments, and these all get dragged in when he drinks a cup and Alec has to sit there listening. Alec can't blame him for what he was born like. But he now sees the conclusion of the second line of reasoning for not believing in the ten bob: I can't help being sorry for the poor bugger but I can't say with him for ever, well, can I?

3

That was a nice cup of tea Alec, says Mr Corker, I've left my watch downstairs but it must be nearly six and that's time for you to go. Are you coming to my little Talk tonight? You said you'd bring your young lady if I'm not mistaken.

I'll try, says Alec.

I'd certainly be very pleased to meet her. I'm sure she's very charming.

You know the Kummel drink you were talking about in that ice-cream parlour, what's it made from?

Ice-cream parlour?

Yes, in Vienna.

Kummel, says Mr Corker, it's pronounced K*i*mmel you see. It's made from seeds, I think, caraway seeds – you know the little brown seeds you get in cakes, very aromatic they are. That's what Kummel's made from, and you come across it all over mid-Europe. I can't promise but I rather think I've got a little downstairs – would you like to have a little glass before you go, a little house-warming toast between the two of us, eh?

You don't want to open it specially for me, says Alec.

I think it's opened, says Mr Corker.

I see, says Alec, realizing that he has almost given himself away.

You have worked so hard, says Mr Corker, you deserve a drink.

If you don't mind, I'm in a bit of a hurry to get away tonight.

I insist, says Mr Corker, you can go straightaway now, but you must have a glass before you go. Let's go downstairs and see if we can find it.

At the door Mr Corker looks back at his bedroom. We're going to make it really nice, he says, but it's bound to take a bit of time.

Alec thinks: I wouldn't sleep here, not if you paid me, I wouldn't sleep here, not if I could bring Jackie too.

When they are on the stairs the telephone begins to ring.

It's after hours now, says Mr Corker, we're shut. It should be in the kitchen.

Alec puts the cups into the sink. The almost white stalks of the violets are bending a little and their purple heads pour downwards. The telephone continues to ring.

It will be very different when we get settled in, says Mr Corker, raising his voice. It will be a great advantage living on the premises then – so far as the telephone's concerned, I mean. We should get more business.

Mr Corker is searching along the bottom shelf of the cupboard. Alec rinses the cups. The bell goes on ringing and ringing.

Here we are, says Mr Corker. He opens the white box that Alec found. Kummel! You've never had it before?

No.

I thought it was open, says Mr Corker, but never mind, today's an occasion. He is shouting rather more loudly than strictly necessary to be heard against the ringing of the bell.

This one, you see, is from Bavaria. Mr Corker points out the name with his finger with the Elastoplast round it. It's strong, mark you. You don't want to have *too* much.

Alec wonders whether Corker will also offer him a chocolate and show him pictures of Maja. The telephone rings ceaselessly.

I'll tell you what, Mr Corker says, I'll go upstairs and find two liqueur glasses – I think I know where to find them – and you just go and lift the receiver off, then we can have our little toast in peace.

Mr Corker mounts the stairs once more. He looks tired. Alec goes along the stone landing, through the Waiting-Room towards the Inner Office. As he enters he recognizes that he is now in the same position as the imaginary intruder when he was aiming the revolver at the door and accidentally squeezed the trigger. It is dark in the room but he can just see his way between the desks and he deliberately refrains from switching the light on. What he is doing is meant to be secret. The small room is full of the ring of the telephone. To Alec it seems far louder than usual, as though the noise had accumulated since it began ringing. He lifts up the receiver. For an instant there is total silence. Then the noise of the voice begins at the other end. From the moment he entered the room Alec has known that he would listen if anything was said.

Hello, Hello, William. Answer me, William. I've been trying all the afternoon. I know it's you, William, because the office is shut now. You're going to be sorry when I'm dead, William.

I have something more to tell you; you're not going to get a penny, William. You're going to be very very sorry very soon, my boy. Poor Mother died before she knew, but I've always known you for what you are, you are a scoundrel, a filthy scoundrel . . . Alec places the receiver very gently on the blotter, and tiptoes to the door. As he passes the revolver-drawer, he puts out his hand and touches its handle. The voice is still talking but from this distance it has acquired its galvanized echo. You have stolen from me, William. Alec shuts the door of the Inner Office, quietly, with the gesture of an adult who leaves a bedroom where a small child is asleep.

Mr Corker is in the doorway of the kitchen with a small glass, shaped like the flower of a lily, in each hand. Each glass is full of the transparent Kummel. Mr Corker has not yet discarded his brown overall. Did you lift it off? he whispers.

Alec nods.

And?

Alec stares at him. Mr Corker's face has on it the exact expression that Alec foresaw when he first thought *Help!* Alec says nothing.

And was there – Mr Corker tentatively touches his chin – any trouble?

Alec shakes his head. Good, good, good, says Mr Corker. You certainly deserve a little drink.

No, Alec says, I must go. He bounds up the stairs three at a time to fetch his leather jacket. When he comes down Mr Corker is still standing there in the doorway with a glass in either hand. He is holding them very carefully because they are full to the brim and the slightest shake will spill them.

Sorry, Mr Corker, says Alec and charges down the next two flights to the stone entrance. He looks up but cannot say he has left the violets behind. He waves.

Mr Corker goes into the Reception-Room, carrying the two glasses of Kummel. There he drinks them because it is too difficult to pour them back into the bottle. Having drunk them quickly, he is able to imagine – as he would never normally be able to – the desirability of drinking a third; the third leads him to the fourth.

Corker knows : How disturbingly the moment of idleness descends! The moment of idleness in which all will-power gives up the ghost, and only a kind of sad equanimity remains. Drinking prolongs the moment. I am beside myself. I am just one among millions I know of in my moments of idleness. It is they who come in such moments – all the other men who I am not. Who I am not for as long as I persist, by avoiding the moment of idleness, in being myself. These moments are disturbing, yet somewhere hidden within them there is a promise which I never find. It is the hope of finding this promise that makes me drink another glass. I need that promise now that I am alone. I need it today more badly than I have ever needed it before. My thoughts never do me justice. My thoughts are like the suit I happen to be wearing. This very moment I know with unusual clarity that there is more to me, William Corker, than my thoughts. Drink stimulates to excess, but all the more reason therefore that I amount to more than a catalogue of my meagre thoughts. And to more than a catalogue of my actions. There is a me waiting to be liber-ated. There is a me that could be loved. There is a me that could embrace the world. Sometimes in the street I have collided with somebody and for a moment apprehended the warmth and smell of a life lived differently from mine, in a train I have woken up and seen outside the window a country beginning a new day – without us who have already passed; in the big stores at Christmas-time I have looked at the hundreds of people calculating what they can afford to give; in the Inner Office I notice often during interviews a pair of eyes looking at me dully, as though I were blocking their view. On all these occasions, I have glimpsed the world. Now, thanks to the Kummel, I have more than a glimpse. It is all around me.

Corker thinks : Alec has gone, he's walking away fast, out there with the lights. There's a saying about sitting in the dark – the dark is light enough. Anyway, it's to do with the dark. Some fish are luminous they say.

Corker knows : There are millions, there. The numbers which, in a moment of idleness, can demand recognition, are what make the moment so disturbing. Millions upon millions. They are all doing something. They shift, they carry, they assemble, they turn, they dismantle, they dig out, they bury, they strip, they coat, they screw, they nail, they build, they mine. Their energy, their stamina is what they possess. Their appetites seem to be demands for fuel. Yet despite their work, and although they do not talk at great length, they appear to have some secret understanding between them. Each knows the roads the others must follow. They obey a law which is mysterious to me. A man raises his bare arm and there is salt in his armpit but the reason for the movement remains a mystery. Two hands belonging to two different people suddenly clasp. They know what they are doing but I do not. They all look like the damned in hell to me. They bear so much and their noise is so discordant. Yet they are not in hell. It is the earth they are on. And if only their law was not a mystery for me, I would go out amongst them. I must join them for I am idle unto death. I must go out.

Corker makes believe : We are drunk.

Part Three

Corker's Flight

(Alec has brought Jackie to the Talk in order to show her Corker. He has told her most of what has happened during the day and has admitted that he is in two minds about continuing to work for Corker.

Miss Browning has seen Wolf. The raid on the office will take place at 9.15. Miss Browning has come to the Talk in case Mr Corker changes his plans and it becomes necessary to detain him. This at least is the reason she had given to herself. But if pressed she would admit that it reassures her to have him where she can see him. She is still unaccountably nervous.

Miss Brand has come since the vicarage is only four houses away and she maintains the hope that, despite the unfortunate questions, Mr Corker is still her kind of gentleman. The hope is so precious to her that she is prepared to overlook a great deal.)

Ladies and gentlemen, I believe that Mr William Corker needs no introduction to you of St Thomas's Social Club. Even myself, a newcomer, have heard about Mr Corker's famous journeys and beautiful slides. We are happy indeed to welcome you again, Mr Corker.

The new vicar, having whispered something to the welcome speaker, looks down at his notes.

Tonight Mr Corker's talk is entitled The Blue Danube.

The welcome speaker shakes his head and whispers something to the new vicar.

I beg your pardon. Tonight Mr Corker's talk is entitled: Vienna, City of the Blue Danube.

The interior of the Victoria Hall is wooden. The exterior is made of corrugated-iron, painted dark green. The main hall, as distinct from the pantry, the Ladies' Room and the store-room, will hold nearly eighty people if packed tightly. Tonight there are fourteen in the audience, apart from the vicar. There are four rows of chairs with hard wooden seats and cane backs. Most of the audience are sitting in the first two rows.

When the vicar sits down there is a little patter of claps. The vicar sits down in the front row and leans back with an obvious dumb-crambo gesture to indicate the anticipated pleasure of listening to the traveller home from the sea. Miss Brand is in the front row but several empty chairs separate her from the vicar. Next to the vicar are young Mr and Mrs Wheatley who arrange the Annual Dance and all the club's more ambitious activities. They are what Father Bean used to call live wires. He, Desmond, works in a music shop and she, Barbara, is an infant teacher. In the second row two old men sit together, then after a decent interval, three old women and finally old Dr Sargent. Dr Sargent always comes to Mr Corker's lectures. Nobody knows what he is a doctor of, but all know that he was once a missionary in China. Next to Dr Sargent, and chatting to him is the best-dressed woman in the hall, Miss Browing. She sits on the outside of the row, next to the gangway to the exit. In the third row are Alec and Jackie, holding hands deep in her lap, and a middle-aged woman with red hair who reminds Mr Corker of Mrs McBryde but who in fact is older and fatter. In the fourth row is a very fat woman who sits at the back at every St Thomas's gathering and helps to make the sandwiches.

Friends, says Mr Corker . . .

He always starts the same way, whispers Alec to Jackie. Alec can feel the clips of her suspender belt.

Tonight, friends, I want you all to come with me to the one-time capital of the Holy Roman Empire. . . . A city of music and wine and, if the vicar will forgive me, beautiful women.

My Dear Fellow, booms the vicar, of course my Dear Fellow.

Miss Brand wouldn't be surprised if the new vicar was one of those monsters – even though he is married.

A city where I lost my heart . . .

He's talking funny, whispers Alec. He's pissed.

Alec! whispers Jackie.

And to which I shall certainly return . . .

Mr Corker is wearing the same grey tweed suit, but he has brushed his hair. When brushed his hair tends to ruff, like a lion's mane. So now with his spectacles, his large forehead and the leonine hair either side of his head, he looks to most of his audience a true expert. In his hurt hand he holds a notebook with papers in it.

Vienna is a city in the arms of the Danube. The mighty Danube! Its population is over one million and a half and it consists of nearly eighty thousand buildings.

Dr Sargent is counting the names of Chinese cities: Cheng-tu-Fu, Nan-chang-Fu, Ngan-king-Fu, Hankow . . .

Mr Corker pauses to give the figures their full weight.

Vienna – or Wien as she is called – is surrounded by woods and hills on the slopes of which the vine grows. Whether there be a connexion between the vine and the Wien I just can't tell you. But there may be.

He's tight all right, says Alec, the filthy old bugger.

Jackie in protest lifts Alec's hand out of her lap and places it on his own knee. Be quiet do, she says.

Now I want you to hear how Wien impressed a Pope five hundred years ago. The Pope was Pius II and this is what he wrote to a friend: The dwelling houses of the citizens are large, richly bedecked and well built, everywhere there are glass windows and iron doors and frequently they keep song-birds and beautiful utensils. . . . As Mr Corker reads, he allows one of his hands to conjure up and sculpt from the empty air imaginary Viennese objects to match the old Pope's words. To somebody who couldn't hear the words it would seem that Mr Corker is cleverly playing with only one hand with a large invisible balloon. . . . When you enter somebody's house, you think you step into a prince's. The wine-cellars are so deep and extensive that they say there may be another Vienna underground. Mr Corker looks up from his notes. But there's no underground railway! he says.

Mr Wheatley laughs and glances at Babs to see whether she too is enjoying herself.

What lots of victuals are brought to town every day, you might fail to believe, continues Mr Corker in his Pope's voice, wagons full of eggs and crayfish arrive. And the vintage takes forty days, three hundred wagons loaded with grapes going to town twice or thrice a day. Imagine it! says Mr Corker in his own voice. Then the Pope's voice takes over: Most girls choose their men without their fathers knowing anything of it. Widows often get married before their one year of mourning is over. Enough! says Mr Corker and bangs on the table which is standing in front of the portable screen. Mr Corker always brings his own screen with him. The bang echoes through the corrugated-iron shed. If we go on listening to the Pope, you will think Wien is an immoral city – and nothing could be farther from the truth. Nothing! Mr Corker seizes the lapels of his jacket. Nothing!

Dr Sargent is now making another list which begins – Sodom, Gomorrah, Shanghai, Vienna . . .

Wien is a city of pleasure and of art. But pleasure is not, as they say in Rome, *ipso facto* immoral. If pleasure is immoral, then heaven is hell! Here quite distinctly Mr Corker hiccoughs. I beg your parson, sir.

The vicar reckons: Very lax my predecessor, very lax. My Dear Fellow! he says out loud.

The fattest woman at the back is impatient for him to get on with the pictures. She prefers sitting in the dark.

Mr Corker puts down his book and extemporizes. Wien combines pleasure with style, style with dignity, dignity with comfort. It is a city of happiness, is Wien. The Viennese understand how to live. Do you know what they say? They say the Viennese achieve by marriage what other countries do by fighting. He picks up his book and continues. In the city municipality of Vienna 60 per cent is woods and 13 per cent gardens and parks. However. To return, as they say in French, to our mutton. In Roman times Wien was called Vindobona. The modern city dates from 1221 – an easy date to remember that, one two, two one.

I rather like him, whispers Jackie, he's funny.

The Hapsburgs, the Royal Family of Wien, the builders of the Austro-Hungarian Empire, first came to the throne in 1282. And they lasted until 1918. There's still one Hapsburg left, but he's not on the throne any more. Austria is a republic now. The last of the Hapsburgs. What's his name? It'll come in a minute. The last of the Hapsburgs. Mr Corker hiccoughs again but this time he is able to disguise it better. Because at the same moment as he hiccoughs, he remembers the name, and so is able to turn the hiccough into *Yoptto!* That's it, Otto. An easy name to remember really O, T, T, O, like one two, two one.

Dr Sargent makes a list of the remaining Royal families: Our own, the Dutch, the Swedes, the Belgians. He picks at a nail because he can go no farther.

The fare to Vienna by rail is £38 return continues Mr Corker, but now on the magic carpet of dreams, let us all go together – for nothing.

He bows his head and solemnly walks to the back of his own audience. There on a table is his projector.

Less of an exhibition of himself in the dark, thinks the vicar.

Some of the pictures are in colour, says Mr Corker, and some aren't. He switches on the lamp in the projector to check that it is in the right position. It isn't, for half the projected rectangle of light misses the screen and falls on the far wall. He drags the table nearer to the front. The flex leading to the projector is pulled taut. He goes on dragging. The flex pulls the projector over with a clatter. Everyone in the hall turns round in their seats.

Its position should have been checked beforehand, thinks Mr Wheatley, no organization. Mr Wheatley has coined a slogan for St Thomas's Social Club Committee: God Needs Us Efficient.

Do hope the lens hasn't gone, mutters Mr Corker to himself.

Shall I give you a hand? booms the vicar, on his feet, a leader in a crisis.

I can manage, thank you, Father, says Mr Corker and then mutters: if the darned lens isn't broke. He stands the projector upright, plugs in the flex. It works. The same half rectangle of light misses the screen and hits the wall.

Mr Corker reappears in front of his audience. If the mountain can't go to Mohammed then Mohammed must go to the mountain. After this announcement, he disappears behind the screen which is on a tripod. His boots are visible underneath the screen. Jerkily the screen begins to move up, intercepting more and more of the rectangle of light. Mr Corker tries to peer round one side edge to see whether the screen is high enough yet. The screen leans over with him. He jerks it up higher. Nearly all his trousers are becoming visible beneath the screen.

It's all right now dear – says one of the old women.

The vicar frowns and uses the same phrase to himself: Altogether very lax.

Mr Corker screws the rods tight and re-emerges from behind the screen. He bows and tiptoes to the back of his audience as if they were already asleep. He switches out all the lights. Only the silver rectangle on the screen remains. It looks like a mirror, but one in which nobody can see themselves.

A STATUE OF MOZART'S MAGIC FLUTE

Mr Corker would like to say: You see the bottle in the advertisement. Just to the left of that is Frau Hartinger's house where I always stay. You see the couple walking behind the cars. Every day I walked along there, past the posters, on my way to and from Frau Hartinger's. At night it is very quiet in the little platz. All you hear are the jets of water playing in the fountain. Frau Hartinger says the Viennese water is the best in the world. I have often sat by myself on the edge of this fountain. After it has been hot for a few weeks the whole of Wien smells at night of dust. Outside there is this stone dust smell of the streets: inside Frau Hartinger's flat the smell of eau-de-Cologne and Turkish coffee. Sitting there, I have looked up at the lighted windows of apartment after apartment: sometimes a figure comes to the window to get a breath of fresh air: a man in his shirt: a woman after her bath. Above are the stars which it is so hard to believe are there in the daytime too. I have wondered whether there is not a parable there. Friends and Miss Browning whom I want to welcome specially, our actions, once over, are forgotten. It is only when their consequences affect us that we realize that nothing can disappear without a trace. Everything people have done is there all the time, inextinguishable as the stars. This is what I have felt sitting there on the fountain. And so I have said to myself: O World! And later I have tried to put it into words for Frau Hartinger. And Frau Hartinger has said: You English gentlemen are all the same, you and your little stars.

Mr Corker actually says: There are two statues in Wien devoted to the great composer and infant prodigy Mozart. One is in the Imperial Garden, which we shall come to later, and the other is this one. When Mozart was only six years old he played before the Emperor. One day he slipped on the polished floor and Marie Antoinette, who was later Queen of France, lifted him up; whereupon the little Mozart said: You are very kind. When I grow up I will marry you. The poster in the background is advertising a kind of fruit cordial.

Dr Sargent takes Miss Browning up to the statue and says, It's just like the Peter Pan statue in Regent's Park, isn't it? Miss

Browning, who doesn't even know that Dr Sargent has borrowed her, is in the car, which is parked behind, and Wolf is starting it to make a getaway. Miss Brand won't look at the statue itself for she doesn't like the way the girl is pressing herself against the boy's backside. Instead she crosses the street to study the fruit cordial bottle. Jackie climbs up the statue and stands where the girl is and the flautist becomes Alec. No one minds what you do in public if you're a statue, she thinks.

> *Mr Corker says:* The Magic Flute is one of Mozart's most famous operas. The story of the magic flute is like the old, old story of Orpheus. Orpheus invented the harp and he played on it so beautifully that he charmed the gods and the animals and even made the trees and rocks follow him wherever he went, and the rivers stop running whilst he crossed them. The magic flute was the same kind of thing.

Mr Wheatley has always maintained that the Magic Flute is the most perfect of the Mozartian operas. Alec is looking for the differences which aren't there. The city looks the same as any other. The same things are possible, the same things impossible. He looks up at the statue again. The couple don't move. They have been pushed up above the street against the sky. The same happened to him and Jackie. When his prick grew large and she was on it, they were forced upwards without choice. They became as unmistakable as this statue, as hard and definite against the grey, absorbent complexity of all the town around. They would stick up, the two of them, like that anywhere. Alec squeezes Jackie's fingers. Howdy! she whispers. Alec wonders why all the surroundings of them sticking up there, clean and hard as a statue, have to be as they are. Why, he wonders, can't they be somewhere different, where the things that are possible and impossible are not the same?

> *Mr Corker says:* Now, this was built in 1869. It took eight years
> to build. It was in this building that I actually heard another
> Mozart opera. An opera called Don Giovanni – which is all
> about the famous Spanish lady-killer.

It looks like a big building, just like any other big building,
but bigger than any in South London. Dr Sargent is counting
Mozart's operas. Mr Wheatley thinks of Don Giovanni purely
musically. Miss Browning has changed her mind about Calabria.
This Vienna would be better. She is shown to her seat in evening
dress. Wolf is wearing a tuxedo.

> *Mr Corker says:* It's funny to think all this was built just for a
> few people to sing in, don't it?

A STATUE OF SCHILLER

Silhouetted against the sky he appears to be a giant walking
across the roof of the building behind.

> *Mr Corker says:* I have not read any books by Schiller but he
> is a very famous poet in Germany and his dates were 1759
> to 1805.
> *Mr Corker would like to say:* Those leaves that are also silhou-
> etted against the sky remind me of the leaves I used to
> press in a book when we lived in Priory Road. The book
> was specially for pressing leaves and had kind of blotting-
> paper pages. I pressed flowers too and Liesel told me about
> the flowers she used to find at home – wild cyclamen and
> gentians. It is odd to imagine Liesel at dusk in this very
> square, perhaps even looking up at this very statue. I real-
> ise that I haven't told you much about Liesel – even less
> than I told you about Frau Hartinger – but it isn't really

necessary for you to know about her in order to understand what I mean. When they're lost, all loves haunt us
in the same way, and we long, like Schiller there on the
rooftops, to walk back over the miles and years that separate us to when all the details mattered and you could have
understood nothing unless I had told you about the sound
of Liesel's voice, and what her waist was like, and how she
used to pronounce *Willy* when she was pleased with me,
and the way she washed her hands. What is it that tears
people apart? Schiller in your overcoat as it goes dark:
What?

It's quite good as a photograph, says Alec to Jackie. The fire-
escape thing behind looks funny, says Jackie. Miss Brand finds
the silhouetted figure to be remarkably like the late Father Bean
when he walked down the aisle from the altar at the end of the
service. If they put a statue up to him, they ought to do it just
like that. Taking God's word into the great unknown, thinks
Dr Sargent as Schiller approaches the foliage which, if he were
moving, would hide him from sight within a couple of seconds.
Miss Browning, long since out of her backless evening dress,
nevertheless shivers: it is how she imagines a man going to be
topped.

> *Mr Corker says:* The artist who made this statue of Schiller
> was called Schilling – isn't that a coincidence? Schiller and
> Schilling.

THE IMPERIAL GARDENS AT DUSK

> *Mr Corker says:* This is another pretty little fountain among
> the flower beds. There are many fountains in Wien but not
> so many as in Rome. Those young ladies are lady students
> from Paris. They were all talking French. The colour is a
> little too blue because it was getting quite late.

144

Mr Corker would like to say: I have sat in these gardens and watched for a whole afternoon in the shade of a tree. I went there after a light lunch and I wore my alpaca jacket to stay cool. There was a haze of heat over the flower beds, almost like the fumes you can see rising from petrol and making everything you see through them undulate and shimmer: or perhaps it was the combination of the heat and the white wine I had for lunch. I dozed a bit and dreamt that my holiday was as endless as the heat. But most of the time I watched. I watched the sparrows bathing themselves in the dust. The children all wore sandals and ran along the white paths like they do over a beach to the the sea. The sea was the palace at the other end of the gardens. . . . In it, it was cool and dark and there were strange objects to look at. Women sat on the garden seats with their babies. I listened to languages I cannot understand being shouted and talked around me. Most of the voices were confidential and went on for a long time without interruption – the stories of lives, I thought to myself. And all the time there was the smell of the stocks and nothing moved except for the fountains and the children and those who were driving in the city and those who were working somewhere. It was then that I asked myself: Why do we suffer? And I replied to myself: It's senseless.

Mr Corker says: I like public gardens . . . I like watching the people in them. Why go to the cinema, I always say, when you can be in the fresh air and there's a free show in front of you all the time? It's senseless.

Miss Brand also likes public gardens, because she likes flowers and although she has never had a square yard of ground to call her own, she collects seedsmen's catalogues. In her heart of hearts she believes that heaven is made of flowers and that the ones which grow in the ground on the earth are the left-overs. As she walks through the Imperial Gardens, she forgets her limp and forgives Mr Corker all his shortcomings. She thinks of the garden around her as his, and although there is no garden to the flat above the office she feels convinced that she will be happy there. In the same way as flowers grow from seeds, the garden that now surrounds her has grown from one of Mr Corker's little pictures. In the flat she will find her own way through the pictures into the gardens of many foreign countries. Whenever she has completed her duties and the master's body is comfortable she will slip into a garden. The vicar looks askance at the five French girls who come from a Catholic country and whom a priest has prepared for confirmation and who will enter, exquisitely, the state of holy matrimony. In their printed frocks they are like flowers themselves and when this thought strikes the vicar, the word fragrance comes unbidden into his mind.

A STATUE OF GOETHE

Mr Corker says: Now this statue is at the entrance to the Imperial Gardens. Goethe was one of the twelve greatest minds in the world.

Dr Sargent is delighted to be given such an easy cue. He comes regularly to Mr Corker's lectures just because they can be so stimulating in this kind of way. He begins: Plato, Aquinas, Dante . . .

Mr Corker says: Goethe was a poet, a philosopher, a dramatist, a thinker. His dates were 1749–1832. Frau Hartinger – that is to say my charming hostess in Wien – always says: Goethe is a guide to everything. There is not a thing he did not say! I don't think she means that, of course, but when she is excited her English gets bad. What she means is that there is hardly a subject which Goethe did not think about. She is always quoting Goethe – I can hear her now. Herr Corker – (Mr Corker imitates her accent) – Herr Corker if only you could read German you would understand us so much more! And you would know how much we have suffered. In the war and when the Russians came! You have no idea. But when you have waited long, the arrival is different. That is what Goethe said. (Mr Corker resumes in his own voice.) Dante in Italy, Shakespeare in England, Goethe in Germany – that's how it is.

Mr Corker would like to say: Frau Hartinger also told me I had Goethe's nose. And I have looked at this statue to see if I can find any resemblance. Do you find any? To be honest I don't. But looking up at this statue and wondering about my nose I have asked myself what makes us so different, why is there so great a gap between what one man and another can achieve? I mean there is as much difference between Goethe and me as there is between me, on my way to a cup of coffee, and this motionless statue. Yet it is not beyond my imagination to be Goethe. It is only beyond my means

Mr Corker says: Wien is a city of thinkers. It's not like London, rush, rush, rush, rush all the time. In Wien, like Goethe here under the trees, you have a chance to think.

Miss Browning waits beneath Goethe who has the face of a Quarter Sessions Judge. He sits back, sums up, sentences. Even with the birdshit all over his coat, he is still a man of property. Nothing can ever cancel out the advantages he has enjoyed. When he said we, he meant we the winners. I'll meet you by the monument, Wolf has said, and so she waits. She walks up and down on her stiletto heels. Twelve steps to his Worship's right, twelve steps to his Worship's left. Men look at her and she looks back through them. Miss Browning offers Dr Sargent a cigarette, he shakes his head and she lights one. As she walks in one direction she imagines that when she turns she will see Wolf coming round the corner by the bushes at the end of the path, he is coming now she says to herself and since it is not yet time for her to turn round he will have passed the corner of the lawn and be near enough for her to see the expression of his mouth, when she does turn there is no Wolf but only some fool in a macintosh coming safely towards her, she wants now to imagine immediately that Wolf will arrive from the opposite direction and that indeed he is now behind her having just come round the corner by the tea stall but she disciplines herself and will not allow herself to imagine this until she has taken another ten paces, then she becomes sure that her instinct was right and her discipline unnecessary, that now he has passed the tea stall and is even nearer to her, but to prove how certain she is of this, she will not look round until she has reached the end of her turn, when she has reached the end and she does look round there is no Wolf but only some fool of a woman pushing a pram away, so, she imagines, she was right after all and he will be coming from the other direction, coming round the corner by the bushes which are now behind her so that soon he will be by the lawn and when she turns . . . The stone face of the winner is as still as ever before. It stares over her head, impassively, at the blank trees opposite. And Miss Browning thinks, looking at the face of the winner: He'll never come now, never. Dr Sargent is trying to decide between Nietzsche and Luther. Alec examines the stone face in the hope that it may tell him more about Frau Hartinger. Is this the face of a man who might appeal to a woman who was a friend of Maja's?

THE HOHER-MARKT

> *Mr Corker says:* History! Now we go back much farther – long before Mozart or Goethe. Back to the middle-ages when Wien was a bunched-up little town with a wall all round it and a moat. Before anything we know was born. You must use your imagination because I took this picture in the Hoher-Markt as it is today and today it's a fashion-able square with hairdressers and scent shops and offices.

148

But in the middle-ages it was the centre of Wien. And before that it was the centre of the Roman settlement of Vindobona. The great Roman philosopher and emperor Marcus Aurelius died here. Perhaps he died in this very square where it says Anchor Insurance Company. And just off this square under the Anchor clock the Romans may have had their baths. Just like nowadays we have cocktail parties – the Romans used to have bath parties.

It occurs to the vicar for the first time that he may be forced to cut the speaker short.

Mr Corker would like to say: With Mrs McBryde, whom I see sitting over there, I am going to give a bath-warming party and you are all invited. No dress! Ha! Ha! No dress at all. Of course I would prefer to give it with Miss Browning, but I know she's too busy.

Mr Corker says: As I was saying, here we have the centre of Wien in what were called the Dark Ages, six or seven hundred years ago. This square was the covered market place and besides buying and selling it was here that criminals were tried and the executions carried out. Imagine it! Meat and flagons of wine and fat monks with red faces and horses, but also cages and men on the gallows. In those days you could be hung for stealing a few apples, and you could be burnt as a witch for just looking at a man. Lives were two a penny then. There is, you see . . .

To everyone except Dr Sargent the Hoher-Markt looks like a part of Westminster. One of the old men wishes literally and not at all metaphorically that his wife might be burned as a witch today. A shiver goes down Jackie's spine. She is in the market of the Dark Ages. She does not imagine this or think it, for the fraction of a second is too short. It is as though her mind shivers it. The covered-in market is very crowded and it smells like the lion-house in the zoo. The noise is similar too. The noise of voices, echoing slightly because it is covered in, the noise of feet moving in a crowd, the noise of bars of metal or wood being banged and rattled, the roars of the animals – but here there is an important difference, for although the roars sound as though they were coming from animals, they are in fact coming from people, people in cages and people hanging from chains. Corker is there. He has the same face as Jackie saw before the lights went out, but he wears different clothes. It is hot in the market, as hot as Alec's hand on top of her hand because she has pushed hers underneath his to prevent his impatience getting the better of them. If you buy anything in the market you do not pay in money, but in drops from a bottle which are called *histories*. Corker is selling spills but unlike the other sellers he is talking quietly and poshly in the very same voice that he is using in the Victoria Hall. The spills are made of paper and he holds them in one hand like a bunch of straws. People are buying them from him and having bought them they set fire to them. The spills which Corker is selling – there is nobody else selling spills – are people's lives. All men and women have lives as well as heads and legs and bodies and tempers. And Corker is selling them. As he sells them he says very quietly: Lives two a penny, Lives two a penny. But because he says *pennies* instead of *histories*, Jackie suddenly realizes that she was mistaken: it is still happening today: the market has never shut: it always stays open. Everything dreadful that can befall her comes from it. The accident that can hurt Alec, the war that can kill them all, every blind force that wipes out sweet impatience for ever.

Mr Corker says: . . . such a thing as progress.

Are you cold, love? whispers Alec. No, no says Jackie and lifting her hand from underneath his presses his hand between the very tops of her thighs.

Mr Corker says: We have become more humane.

Jackie turns round in her chair to try to look at Corker in the dark. The light from the projector reflects off his glasses as he bends over it to read his notes. She sees also his smooth forehead. He is not funny any more.

STOCK IM EISEN

> *Mr Corker says:* Now this is a very funny object, quite near the old market – still in the old medieval part of the city. As you see it's a piece of wood with thousands of nails driven into it. I'm afraid it's not a very good photo. But there is a story behind it. In the middle-ages there was a tree at the corner of this crossroads and the trunk of the tree is the piece of wood you can still see. The nails were driven in by travelling apprentices – carpentry apprentices. In those days an apprentice, before he became a journeyman, went from one master to another. And the story goes that every carpentry apprentice who passed through Vienna on his way from his last place of employment to his next drove his nail into this tree for luck. In the end it killed the tree – but it's still there as a sight worth seeing. The *Stock Im Eisen* – means the wood clad in iron. If you were very fanciful you might say a tree wearing armour, just like the knights of the round table wore armour!

It crosses the vicar's mind that Mr Corker may be drinking in the dark in the hall at this moment.

> *Mr Corker would like to say:* Sir Lancelot is clad to fight for the honour of his Guinevere.

Alec borrows a hammer to drive his nail in. It is a long nail and he hammers it in with long swinging strokes. He is on his way.

The screen opens on to a shopping street which is wider than anything in Clapham, just as the sunlight is brighter. If Dr Sargent is not mistaken, Mr Corker was wrong about *stock*. Stock surely means stick not wood, as in *alpenstock*. Alec would like to give Jackie something unusual, something you can't buy in London. Before he connects he thinks why not ask Corker to bring something for her when he goes on his next trip. Then he remembers driving his nail in. Miss Browning checks the two clocks in the Graben: they both say twenty past three. Her own watch says 8.40. The red-headed woman who reminds Mr Corker of Mrs McBryde is thinking what a good schoolmaster Mr Corker would make. Mrs Wheatley would like a spring costume in navy blue and white.

> *Mr Corker says:* Now Graben means moat. Because in Roman times and medieval times the moat went round here: this was the edge of the city. You had the city wall and then you had the moat – to keep the enemy out. And over the moat you had a drawbridge – just like toy forts. I read somewhere that Austria means Eastern outpost. Beyond Wien which is in the East of Austria – at least twelve hours by train from Innsbruck – the infidels began. Wien was the last stop in Christendom.

And I will have everything ready for him when he comes home, having been out, repeats Miss Brand to herself.

> *Mr Corker says:* Quite early on, however, the city got bigger and the moat was filled in and houses were built on top of it. The man who did this was called Duke Leopold the Glorious.

What a man! Alec whispers to Jackie who has borrowed Alec to walk with in the sun, He filled all that moat in!

Mr Corker says: And today the Graben is one of the most beautiful corners of old Wien.

Mr Corker would like to say: Here I have felt myself in a civilization. I have had a sense of history and of the future. I have become aware of how men make life worth living. I bought the Kummel I've just been drinking here. But here you can buy everything, not only liqueurs. The clothes you need to satisfy the longing which is in us all to look distinguished: books of photographs infinitely better than mine: reproductions of great paintings which show us how we could live – with hangings and flowers and fruit and peacocks in the gardens and white linen and marble and beautiful pillars and urns and the Duchess of Alba: leather brief-cases in which the documents of men would be safe forever: ice-cream, the art of making which is understood in Wien alone: furniture as beautiful as miniature palaces.

Mr Corker says: There's hardly a thing in the world you can't buy in the shops round here. I'd say they've some of the most stylish shops in the world. And they're cheap too. That's one of the beauties of Wien. Its cheapness.

Mr Corker would like to say: Friends, I don't want all these things to be exclusive either. Not everybody has a liking for the same thing. There are those who prefer Mozart and those who prefer Bing Crosby. There are some who don't want to wear coats with astrakhan collars in the winter because they would rather wear ski-ing jackets. You would be like that, Alec. I myself would like the astrakhan collar. There are some who would like the ice-cream more than the paintings. You, Mrs McBryde, hiding in the corner there – you would like the ice-cream – and you should have it every day of your life. You, Father, might like the paintings more. Didn't you say, Alec, that your lady friend works in a florist? The flowers in Wien! The garlands they make there for weddings! When you both get married, the bride should be adorned in the Viennese fashion! I want everybody to have what they want!

Mr Corker says: And even the shops that are too dear are interesting to look at through the window.

Mr Corker would like to say: Miss Browning, for the pleasure you have given me in after all coming to Wien, allow me to thank you in my own way: a way we shall nevertheless be agreed about, seeing that we share the same tastes. Let us first walk the length of the Graben on the shady side of the street and I, if I may, will take your arm. We are part of this civilization we can feel around us. If we had been Greek, a sculptor might have put us on a frieze together. We are proud to be here. At the corner is a jewellers, if there is anything you like you shall have it. In our true civilization money has been abolished. Money is the root of all evil. And evil is everything that destroys civilization. If there is nothing in the jeweller's you like, let us go round the corner for there we shall find a scent shop – did I ever tell you my scheme for making a fortune by setting up a scent shop on the top of the St Bernard Pass? People always spend money on top of mountains. And next to the scent shop is a shop of musical instruments. What can you play, Miss Browning? Whatever you can play, you shall have. And if you need a Stradivarius, I will get it for you, for in our true civilization all must be given what they need, and money is a thing of the past. For myself I want almost nothing, a little glass to sip, something beautiful to see and somebody like you, Miss Browning, to talk to. Let us now promenade down the sunny side. You have no parasol? Then here we shall find one. Miss Browning, do not for one moment misunderstand me. My intentions are entirely honourable. I think of you quite purely. My only desire is to see you living a life worthy of your discrimination and taste. In the Graben we have the right setting. For here we can look around at everybody having what they want. And

whilst you are looking, I shall disappear for a moment and
buy you the best chocolates in the world.

Mr Corker says: You can buy the best chocolates in the world
here.

Jackie cannot forget the covered-in market. She senses that
from now on she will become more and more aware of danger.
This is the consequence of last night. Seventeen years old, she
recognizes that now she could become a widow. Lives two a
penny! whispered Corker. The best chocolates in the world. To
all the others in the street and to all those everywhere who can
order her around, it will for ever be, she is aware, a matter of
total indifference whether Alec is dead or alive. Ali Baba! she
whispers.

THE PLAGUE COLUMN

Miss Brand sees herself. Her kind of gentleman has taken a
photograph of her playing her part. It does not occur to her that
the old woman with shrunken breasts and toothless mouth is
more like her, because she is convinced that this old woman is a
sinner, which is why she is falling, struck down by god's wrath.
Miss Brand is the young woman, eyes upturned to heaven,
extending a helping hand. Miss Brand considers that by taking
this beautiful photograph Mr Corker has vindicated her and
proved that he can see beyond appearances.

Mr Corker would like to say: Why this slide now? In the sunlight
– death. Among the most stylish shops in the world – death.
Even between Miss Browning and me – death. Why can
nobody avoid it?

Mr Corker says: This is the most famous monument in Wien,
it is a landmark.

Mr Corker would like to say: Friends, I am 64 and when strolling
down the Graben I have looked up at this monument and

for me it has not commemorated the plague of 1679, it has reminded me of my own death before 1979. Alec, you will still be young, visiting places for the first time and I shall be nowhere, unvisitable, gone. I can already mourn for myself, but, strangely, it is no longer myself, for the dead lose their individuality and only very briefly can the living keep them separate, it is any man I mourn, men far abler than myself, an old man walking through snow, badly dressed, entirely concentrated on not slipping, Alec when your time comes and you stroll down the Graben and notice how the stone of this monument has been opened by the wind and cold which have made dust of it, men who knew this and were old when I was still a child in Priory Road, a man not born yet, all whom I have seen or known or can imagine, all who are somewhere in my mind I mourn. I would like to change everything that is irreversible and irredeemable. I know how absolute loss is.

Mr Corker says: If you want to meet somebody in the centre of Wien, you meet them by the Plague Column, like Swan and Edgars in Piccadilly.

Mr Corker would like to say: But, Friends, what can I do with my little business and a certain talent for taking photographs? I ask you what can I do, what can any of us do? There is God. There is you, there is myself, there is this monument to our mortality in the Graben. It is between us that it must be settled – or, rather, it is between us that we must find a way of accepting the fact that it will all be settled in the grave, regardless. The solution of God is at hand. I admit it. To you, Father, I may pretend to accept it. But I cannot. I know that I am too complicated for any God to understand.

Mr Corker says: It was erected in 1693 by the Emperor Leopold I because he made a vow to put up a monument to the glory of God if he ever survived the Plague which ravaged Wien in 1679. We can't know whether God liked it or not.

There are some titters. The vicar grips the seat of his chair. Well! he says out loud. He will have a word with Mr Corker in the tea break. If he hasn't sobered up, he'll cut the Talk short. He rehearses in his mind various ways in which he could do this. He also rehearses various sentences with which, if need be, he can interrupt him in mid-speech. Mrs Wheatley has a word for it: it is blasphemy: and it is the result of living in a dirty way, and taking photographs of statues like this which show an old woman's breasts, a liberty even worse than showing a young woman's. She wonders whether the old woman actually posed for the artist. She would rather die than have to do that. Miss Brand takes Mr Corker's remark to be an expression of infinite humility in the sight of Our Lord. The fat woman at the back has paid little attention to the words, for it is the pictures she likes and she is wondering whether she will ever be as thin as this old woman.

Mr Corker would like to say: So, it is up to us to find a way. Have you found a way? This is something we should all help each other over. Yet I have not heard it spoken of. Most of the subjects which I find important are not spoken of.

Mr Corker says: But perhaps this is something we should not speak of. Fifteen thousand people died in the Plague, they died like flies.

Like flies, fears Jackie, and two a penny.

Mr Corker says: Four years after the Plague the Turks came – the Turkish infidels to besiege the city for six months. In the end Leopold drove them back, right back, and extended his empire right through the Balkans. Frau Hartinger used to say to me: Herr Corker, you remember how one of our great poets said – Death is a Mussulman and when he is not a Mussulman he is a Slav. That is all Frau Hartinger said about death.

The vicar scrapes his shoes on the floor. So the old woman was a Turk notices Mrs Wheatley.

Mr Corker says: Myself, I've always thought of Death as a man without any face at all.

Is he always so creepy like this? Jackie whispers. Don't be silly, says Alec, he's pissed I keep on telling you; the poor bugger's pissed.

Mr Corker would like to say: Let me tell you my way. I used to think the worst thing that could happen would be to die. Now I think the worst thing that might have happened might have been never to have been born. Imagine – no Father, no Miss Browning, no Mrs McBryde. Not even the glimpse of an idea that we, as we sit in this hall tonight, might exist. Not a glimpse, nothing. The headstone at the grave is better than that. William Corker, Born 1897, Died before 1979. To a few friends known as: Traveller and Thinker. Is that not better? But then supposing when we die, it is as if we had never been born; supposing we know we have wasted our lives? Would that not be the worst of all? To know that one has had something and thrown it away. Wouldn't this be the Turks' most diabolic torture? Wouldn't it? So we must make it impossible. Quickly, quickly. Mustn't we? When I see old men at the Lodge or in an hotel, old men whose trousers have been pressed very sharply and whose shoes have been polished and whose braces have been done up, who have been put into their clothes which no longer fit them and which they haven't even the strength to crease, old men who look like small brothers wearing their big brother's suit, then I know how quickly I must make it impossible, this Turks' torture. Even you, Alec, should hurry. For there is never time to lose. Live where you like! If you hate your wife leave her!

Enjoy your pleasures whatever people call them! Use your talents! Never be ashamed of what you can do! Don't be a door-mat. Don't be a door-mat. It may lead you into trouble this – but no trouble can be as bad as the Turks' torture, believe you me. Let me escort you a little farther, Miss Browning, and give you the chocolates I promised you, and, Miss Browning, you too, don't forget what I say. Take what you want, Miss Browning, take whilst you may.

Mr Corker says: In my photograph you will see that there's sunlight on the old woman's face. I like to think of that as symbolic. The silver lining, so to say.

ST STEPHEN'S CATHEDRAL FLOODLIT

Miss Brand hurries through the West Door to pray to her Lord for her new Master. Her new Master's silver lining is nothing but the love of God. Her new Master knows this but is too shy to say so. She with her Lord's help will succour him and give him strength. She with her Lord's help will release all that is hidden in the good man. The woman with red hair who reminds Mr Corker of Mrs McBryde drapes the cathedral on her lap, for the pattern of tiles on the roof is exactly like the pattern she wants to knit her nephew's rust pullover in. Her son is dead. Dr Sargent lists the German Gothic cathedrals – Vienna, Cologne, Münster – and ponders upon whether it is right to include Strasbourg. Miss Browning would like to find a bar where she could get a whisky. Wolf must be on his way. She sees him climbing the steeple. She tells herself she is unusually on edge because her period is late. One of the old women gets into a coach on a coach tour which goes all the way down the Rhine.

Mr Corker says: I don't know if you know but it takes several generations to build a cathedral. The man who begins building a cathedral never lives to see it finished. This spire here was begun in 1359 and it wasn't finished until

1433. On the other side, the north side, the tower was never finished at all.

The door at the back of the hall is pushed open. A little dim light is let in from the street. Miss Browning turns round immediately and makes out a figure in the door, silhouetted against the feeble light. It doesn't look like a figure to worry about: a woman on sticks. She hobbles to the nearest chair and sits down. It is Irene.

(Miss Irene Corker is 62. Twelve years ago she retired with a pension from the Bank of England where she had worked for thirty years. She retired so early because of the rheumatoid arthritis from which she was already suffering and which since then has grown steadily worse. When she retired she bought the house West Winds. She could afford to do this partly because she had saved all her life but also because she had inherited £10,000 when she was 25. During childhood each of the Corker children was allotted a particular uncle or aunt to be specially 'theirs'. Irene got Uncle Stephen. Uncle Stephen, a paper merchant, was the only brother who became and remained rich. When he died in 1923 he left half his fortune to Irene and half to the D'Oyly Carte Opera Company. He was unmarried and a great lover of light opera.)

> *Mr Corker says:* There's a story about this tower which was never finished. You remember I was telling you about the wines of Wien – and how good they are, only to be equalled by Viennese *music*! And Viennese *women!*

Alec turns to see what has happened, for Corker's voice has suddenly become shrill and he shouted Music! and Women! as though they were orders to a squad on a barrack-square.

> *Mr Corker says:* One year in the middle of the fifteenth century the wine was bad. There wasn't enough sun. We all need

sun and *Peace!* (Peace is shouted like another order.) And
the grapes that year didn't get it. So they went sour. And
the wine tasted *vile!* (Another order.) So *vile* that the grape
growers were going to pour the wine into the streets. Then
the Emperor Frederick, hearing about what was going on,
ordered them not to waste the wine, but to mix it instead
with the mortar that was being used to build the north
tower with. And perhaps that's why the tower was never
finished! The wine was never *vile* enough again, for having
started on wine you can't change to water can you?

Miss Irene assumes that the *viles* are meant for her, as also
the peculiar way of talking. She does not see the Cathedral of St
Stephen's despite the fact that it is dedicated to her uncle's patron
saint. She sees blacks and greys and whites which constitute what
is called a photograph taken by him and projected on to a screen
which he is said to have bought. Nothing about him is genuine
except for the fact that having lived off her for twelve years and
stolen her property, he has just cast her aside. Even if she persuades
him to return, he will have been one of the cruellest men she has
ever met. She considers him, bent now over the projector, the light
making his big nose luminous and all the dark in the Victoria Hall a
pocket for him to hide the truth in. He is in the hands of a woman,
brazenly, and now he hopes to kill her, his own sister, so that he can
settle with his mistress at West Winds. The nose is evil. His hands
are shaking because he is debauched. But she will thwart him.

There was a man in another town, another town, another
    town
There was a man in another town
And his name was Willy Wood.
And he ate up all the good cream cheese, good cream cheese,
    good cream cheese,
And he ate up all the good cream cheese
And his name was Willy Wood

As she remembers the lines, she taps with the rubber-ended stick on the floor. Then she mouths to herself: But this time Willy Won't.

> *Mr Corker would like to say:* Friends, repeat out loud what I have been telling you. Make it clear, if you please, that I am normal. Miss Browning, I shall continue to escort you, and nothing is going to stop me.
>
> *Mr Corker says:* The two nearest towers are much earlier than the rest of the cathedral. They are called *Pagan* Towers and they were put up by the King of Bohemia in the middle of the thirteenth century. The King of Bohemia was staying in Wien then. *Pagan* means ungodly.

THE SPANISH RIDING SCHOOL

> *Mr Corker says:* This is one of the most famous sights of Wien. Why is it called Spanish? For the same reason as I'm called Corker. I'm my father's *son* (barrack-square order) and the ancestors of these horses came from Spain. They are very special horses – as you'll see in a minute. They had to be *bred* specially, for in nature there are always *poor strains* and these have to be got rid of, if you want the best. These horses have Spanish, Neapolitan and *Arab* blood and they combine the best qualities of each. But their original sires came from Spain in about 1560. Twenty or so years later the imperial *stud* was set up at a little place near Trieste called *Lipizza*. There they were bred over the centuries from *stallion* to *stallion* and the finest *stallion* today is the one you can see in front. He is called *Maestoso Mercurio!*

The last two words are chanted like the final spell of a triumphant curse. Miss Irene believes that she understands very well what her brother is saying, and now that her eyes have grown accustomed to the dark she is peering round the hall to see if she can recognize the female. Miss Browning turns round once more to make certain of the newcomer. For a moment the two stare at each other in the dark, then Miss Irene dismisses Miss Browning because the latter looks too well bred and Miss Browning dismisses Irene because she's a cripple and therefore might in the natural course of events come to a talk like this in the Victoria Hall.

> *Mr Corker says:* All these magnificent *stallions* – and there are about eighty of them – have names to conjure with. *Pluto Theodorosta! Favory Kitty! Favory Kitty* – it's almost like a ship isn't it? *Neapolitano Deflorata!*

Miss Brand has a mind to think that her new master might have taken holy orders, for he has a fine voice and the way he reads the foreign names shows how well he could have said Mass. She is sure he can sing too. Sitting as she is in the dark, she dares to believe that she may one day listen to him on the piano. She hopes there is not the insuperable obstacle of his being unable to play. Dr Sargent is bending forward in his seat in a short-sighted attempt to check that they are indeed all stallions. Miss Browning, momentarily satisfied, borrows a cocked hat and a tunic from one of the riders, and rides home with three red rosettes, aged thirteen; at exactly the same moment she knows the difference between a gymkhana and her purpose in being here tonight.

> *Mr Corker says:* In Wien, believe it or not, the squares are like the rooms of houses, and the interiors are like squares. At night you can wander from room to room with a cluster of stars like a chandelier above. And here you have horses being ridden in a ballroom. It was built by the great architect *Fischer* von Erlach. What's called *Baroque* architecture, this is.

He is kicking over the traces, thinks the vicar, but is confused by the fact that the *he* refers simultaneously to Mr Corker and the horse in the new picture on the screen. The leaping horse with its forelegs tucked under, and its hand legs outstretched – flying riderless through the air like a white swan – somehow diminishes the strangeness of what Mr Corker is saying; consequently the vicar, anxious to avoid worry, decides that it is the pictures which matter and probably nobody is listening to the words anyway. He leans across to Mrs Wheatley and says: Most remarkable photograph, don't you find? Mr Wheatley moves his head behind his wife's and replies to the vicar: You need a very fast film. He probably used Kodak Tri-X.

> *Mr Corker says:* Four hundred years of skill have made this possible. Skill in *breeding*, skill in *breaking* the horses in – every rider at the Spanish school has to *break in* his own horse, skill in training. *Mastery*, that's what's needed. *Mastery* and an *iron hand.*

Miss Irene has taken the scarf off her head. She has permanently waved hair, closely set without a touch of grey in it. Seen from behind when her hair is uncovered, she looks like a woman of forty. He could never ride, she thinks, he's always been too soft. She herself is crippled and he is soft. They each belong to the same category: the category of what somebody ought to be sorry for. Not that they themselves need pity: but rather that being the result of sin, foolishness, indiscretion and self-indulgence on somebody's part, they should be recognized as such. One day you'll be sorry, they say. By this token, she and William ought to be making somebody sorry. The difference between them is that she accepts this and tries to behave with dignity, fully recognizing that life is tragic; whereas he hasn't the courage to acknowledge the category into which they have been born and is always twisting and turning in an attempt to evade his destiny. He imagines himself a fine figure of a man: at his age he talks about mastery and an iron hand. Over the years Miss Irene has developed a way of laughing to herself: no sound emerges: but the corner of her mouth twitches and she is aware of an uncontrollable but pleasurable tremor. She feels this tremor now as she reckons the absurdity of her brother's pretensions. This white horse with an eye like an oyster and its four hooves that can pound on the turf so that they may be heard half a mile away, its mane like a white silk fringe on the pelmet of a curtain, its soft and so disdainful muzzle, the nostrils like never-shut mouths, and its skin so tight to its skull and its windpipe like a lanyard worn within – this is a fine animal, this is something in an altogether different category. It is as though horses like this have always leapt over her and her like. She knows what the vaulting of their ribs and the ceiling of their bellies look like from underneath, where she lies like a flagstone. And although in fact her paralysis has crept slowly through her body, Miss Irene finds it easier to understand if she pictures it happening outside time, the result of being struck once and accidentally by the hoof of a white stallion leaping above her in pursuit of a happiness for which she, even before the blow, was strangely unready.

Mr Corker says: Even as he leaps, he is still under control – you can see the reins the rider's holding. The rider is standing on the ground just outside the picture on the left – and the horse, well you might say, the horse is in orbit round him! Eh?

William is feeble and godless and will stoop to anything. He talks of mastery and control and pretends to be an expert about things of which he knows nothing, which are quite beyond him. The most he can do is to sniff at the fine horse's dung like a dog. Miss Irene again looks round the hall searching for a bitch on heat.

Mr Corker would like to say: The lame lady who came in a few
    minutes ago is my sister. Please be the judge between us.
    Please make her believe that I am not a monster. Tell her
    you enjoy the photographs I have taken. Tell her I can
    think for myself. Tell her I have seen something of life.
    Tell her that I shall die before 1979.

Without me William will go to pieces, to pieces.

EIGHT RIDERS SHOULDERING-OUT ON
BOTH SIDES FROM THE CENTRAL LINE

The two massive candelabra are alight above the red sand which
has been hoofed up into little choppy waves. The spectators round
the galleries are silhouetted against very pale green walls which
above and below the galleries extend into darkness. Above the door
through which the horses have entered is a black inscription tablet.
The eight horses are white and their riders wear high black boots.

Mr Corker thinks: I did not take this one myself. It is a colour
    slide which I bought.
Mr Corker knows: My pride benefits more if they think I have
    taken it than if I admit that I haven't.
Mr Corker says: This is a dance they're doing.

Mr Corker's voice has become quieter and more regular,
but to Alec who knows it so well, it still sounds thicker than
usual. The coloured picture looks like a kind of Command
Performance of Bertram Mills Circus in the lounge of a smart
hotel, and he remembers Corker on all fours on the floor under
the bed in the front room. This slide wasn't in the projector then
and no light was shining through it, so nobody could see it then
when Corker was on all fours.

Mr Corker says: They keep perfect time together.

Jackie considers whether, if Corker were mad, it would be possible for Alec not to have noticed it. She believes madness to be more common than is generally realized, and especially amongst old men. A number come regularly into the shop to buy buttonholes for themselves and touch her. It is not their wanting to touch her which she thinks mad – she even feels quite sorry for them on that count; it is all the elaborate tricks and jokes and pretences that they force themselves to go through with monotonous regularity every single time they appear in the doorway, after having stared at her for ten minutes through the shop window.

> *Mr Corker says:* These horses are not born white – although as I'm sure you all know, in English one never refers to a white horse as anything except a grey – anyway these horses are not even born grey, they are born black.

But Corker is madder than any of them, even though he hasn't tried to touch her yet. Corker is a lunatic. He's mad, Ali-Baba, she whispers. Don't be daft, replies Alec, I keep on telling you he's pissed. He's a nut case, insists Jackie. Shh! He'll hear you, says Alec.

> *Mr Corker says:* Their training doesn't begin until they are over four years old. And mostly they live to an age of about thirty.

The fattest woman who makes sandwiches wastes the strain of four centuries and breeds a white farm horse from them in Lincolnshire where she was born. Her school tunic was covered in hairs from his mane. Then her father had to sell the horse and the farm and they moved to Birmingham where he worked in a bakery and wore an old cap covered with flour.

Mr Corker says: The Spanish Riding School has, if I may use the phrase, ridden out revolutions, two world wars, the breaking up of the Empire, the Russian occupation, and today it is again a unique centre of the equestrian art.

Mr Corker blows his nose and glances right towards his sister.

Mr Corker says: And I'll tell you a little mystery story about the Spanish Riding School. It's a true story because it happened to me.
Mr Corker thinks: Irene pretends that everything that has happened to me is untrue because it has happened to me.

Mr Corker walks away from his sister, towards the front of his audience and then stands by the side of the screen on which the eight riders are still projected. He talks in the dark but some of the light reflected off the screen is picked up by his white shirt and his pale hands and forehead. Thus his audience listen to him and can see him but are unable to distinguish his features.

Mr Corker says: One day I decided to go and see the display. To get in you have to queue up in the Josefplatz outside, and then you get a ticket at a kind of little box office – and up you go. Now, in the queue I noticed the man in front of me. I noticed him first because I noticed the smell of the cigar he was smoking. I'd say he was in his forties and he was wearing an almost white silk summer suit. He was a big man too, much bigger than me. When we got up to the gallery – you can see it there in the picture – this man was next to me against the rail. He had a monocle dangling from a ribbon round his neck. He fixed it in his eye and looked over the railing at the red sand. Then he looked at me and smiled – a typical Viennese smile. You are English, no? he said with a very good accent. He must have heard me ask for my ticket at the box office. I said yes I was. You look like an impresario, he said. That's one of the nice things about Wien, people mix much more, they don't all stay together in little separate professional groups. Every man is a man of the world first: then, second, he's a doctor, bank clerk, or whatever. I said I was sorry but I wasn't actually an impresario – although I was concerned with selecting people for employment. I thought I'd lead him on a bit. Something to do with entertainment? he said. I smiled. But you like entertainment? he said. Who doesn't? I said. I've got it, he said, you're connected with the circus, that's why you're interested in horses. By now I thought it had gone far enough, so I told him I wasn't really anything to do with the entertainment business and that I simply wanted to see the Lipizzaners because I'd heard so much about them. Well then, he said, you've found the right person. And he told me he knew some of the riders well and if I liked to meet him next morning, he'd get me into the stalls to see behind the scenes.

Because they can see where he is but not his features, the audience temporarily allow Mr Corker to grow younger. In Wien, they think, he is spry and gay. Even Miss Brand shares in the honour of his being mistaken for an impresario.

Mr Corker says: Well next morning I met my friend in Josefplatz. I thought *he* looked rather like a musical conductor, except of course for his monocle which suggested he came from an army family. They wear monocles much more over there than we do here. People here think it's funny to wear a monocle. But it's always seemed to me that if one of your eyes is all right it's the reasonable thing to do.

Mr Corker would like to say: I am a man of Reason fighting Irene's Ignorance and Prejudice.

Mr Corker says: Anyway we went in by a side door. There was a kind of janitor there and my friend joked with him quite a bit – in Wien everyone always has time for a joke – and offered him a cigar. Then we were shown round, all by ourselves with just a groom who looked like a railway porter. That's another thing they go in for a lot in Wien – peak caps! My friend acted as an interpreter because although I can find my way around by myself, I don't understand other people when they speak. You wouldn't believe it – how those horses live! Like film stars they live.

Mr Corker would like to say: We must demand our rights!

Mr Corker says: I don't mind telling you if there is such a thing as reincarnation you could do a lot worse than be a Lipizzaner next time. It's true they don't live so long, but never mind, it's sweet and short, sweet and short.

As Mr Corker repeats the last two words, he rocks slightly on his heels. He's never been properly looked after, thinks Miss Brand. Miss Browning already suspects that the Viennese friend is a con-man. But this also allows Miss Browning to imagine, like the rest of the audience, that in Wien Mr Corker comes into his own, is a different man, has years taken off him, etc.

MR CORKER A MAN OF THE WORLD IN A FOREIGN CITY

This is no new slide, but behind the doors beneath the black inscription tablet at the far end of the Riding School Mr Corker's experiences are taking place.

Mr Corker says: I was watching one of them having his tail combed in his stall and suddenly there was a great commotion at the other end of the corridor. There was shouting and the banging of doors and all the railway porters sprang to attention and stood there, rigid. From where we were, we couldn't see why. But the groom who was combing the horse's tail did the same. He came to the entrance of the stall and stood to attention, stiff as a post. I asked my friend what was happening. He looked quite surprised and just beckoned to me to follow him. We tiptoed down to the other end of the stables, the opposite to where the commotion was, and tried the door. It was locked. Then my friend muttered something in German which I didn't understand, put his monocle in his eye, smiled and started to march the length of the corridor between the stalls. A man appeared at the other end. I wish I had been able to take a photo of him because it turned out he was none other than the head of the whole Spanish Imperial Riding School, what is called in German The Most Honourable Master Rider. He was very, very tall, and he was in full riding regalia, like you can see here, only his tunic was scarlet and he was wearing two decorations, two huge golden decorations; these decorations were shaped like suns, like the suns you see on old maps, and they must have been carat gold too because they glinted in the sun and seemed to shoot off their own rays. I dare say the Order of the Garter looks something the same, because afterwards I discovered this man was titled as well. He had his kind of three-cornered hat on and white gloves. You thought of all the princes you'd read about, all the victors of unlikely battles against heavy odds, the ones who never spared themselves, the ones who hid their own wounds and were merciless out of pity and could lead men to hell and back for they had a love of honour greater than their love of wife for no greater love has no man.

The confusion of the last sentence passes unnoticed by the entire audience. Suddenly those who are awake are no longer following Mr Corker word by word. They realize they are witnessing something abnormal. Normal questions come to mind to emphasize the contrast. Has he forgotten the story? How long will he go on? What's got into him? But, except for Irene, the abnormality strikes them as in no way grotesque. They watch as a crowd watches a busker in the street, each believing that he or she couldn't get up and do that, not for a hundred pounds. They watch his hands moving in the dark and they watch the horses motionless on the screen, and they wait to judge the performance as a whole, temporarily suspending all other judgements. For a few seconds those who are awake watch Mr Corker as though he were an artist.

Mr Corker says: — in a word a hero, that is to say a man you do not want to hear *bad* about, a man who has faults that are *forgiven* him, one who comes through though not necessarily to victory, and judges himself *harder* than other people and most important of all, pertinent as it is to what I was saying, or anyway what I meant to say – a man who dies bravely, who meets death like a hero. In a word, Friends, that is my idea of a hero and the Most Honourable Master Rider was a hero. He had piercing blue eyes and a scar on his cheek and a chin that would never yield. I noticed all this when I was having conversation with him. It may surprise *some* of you that a man like this should talk to me. A prophet in his country they say don't they —

Mr Corker thinks: Must get back to the story or I'll be late.

Mr Corker says: As it happens we got on very well. My friend went up to him and they had a few words in German together and then I was introduced. The Most Honourable Master Rider didn't speak English so the friend interpreted. The Most Honourable Master Rider bowed and welcomed me to Wien. I thanked him and then the friend told me the Most Honourable Master Rider would consider it a privilege to be my guest if he should ever come to my country. I'd be very pleased, I said to the friend, but what does he mean? The friend explained how he had already offered on my behalf to return the hospitality. Please tell him, I said, it will be a pleasure, but he mustn't expect anything very grand. When this was translated the Most Honourable Master Rider held up a white-gloved hand in deferential protest and lowered his eyes. According to him you are too modest, said my friend. You see what true nobility is! The Most Honourable Master Rider didn't think my little office in Clapham was beneath him! Far from it! He was *interested*, and he asked me all kinds of questions about what I thought our government was thinking. The friend must have translated very well. All the time we were talking we walked up and down the stables. He wore spurs with suns on them, miniature suns like the golden decorations on his chest, only these were silver not gold and whenever we turned round, they touched each other with a jangle. And as we passed the porters, each one jumped to attention and stared straight ahead – this was until the Most Honourable Master Rider told them to relax or some words to that effect. I remember one little incident. I don't see any reason to be prudish about it. We were passing a horse when a natural function had just begun —

My Dear Fellow, starts the vicar, employing one of his rehearsed phrases, I hate to interrupt you in the middle of your fascinating story but we are going to be a tiny bit pressed for time unless we hurry a little.

Mr Corker thinks: He is frightened of me.
Mr Corker says: Well, Father, to cut a long story short then. We talked a while and then we said good-bye and the Most Honourable Master Rider promised to come and see me if ever he should visit London. I was going to give him my card, but the friend stopped me and almost snatched it out of my hand. When we got outside I asked him why he'd done that. He's very eccentric, explained my friend, you want to be careful with that man. You wouldn't think it, he said, but do you know he's one of the wildest gamblers in the world. He's lost hundreds of horses at cards. That's why I tried to lead you out the other way, said my friend. As a

matter of fact he owes me a small fortune, but I don't like to remind him. I can't believe it, I said, a man in his position! Ah! you don't know Wien! said my friend. In Wien we forgive a lot to a great horseman! How long have you known him? I asked. Many years, said my friend, he was married to a cousin of mine once. And now, he said, I want you to meet my younger sister. She's in – how do you call it? – the show business.

Mr Corker again blows his nose.

Mr Corker says: And now comes the mystery. We went to a restaurant just off Josefplatz where he had a rendezvous with his sister. But she wasn't there. We drank an aperitif together and then my friend said he would go and try to phone his sister and we'd order the meal when he came back. And he never came back. He disappeared into thin air. I never set eyes on him again.

Mr Corker walks back towards the projector, disappearing himself from his audience. His audience, with the exception of Miss Irene, is more surprised by the performance than by the story. The fact that Mr Corker is talking as he is in the Victoria Hall tonight is more startling than anything which happened to him in Wien. Behind the Mr Corker they know, there has evidently always been lurking the man they see now: a foreigner in their own country. Miss Irene is the only person to condemn him without hesitation and with triumph because he has proved her right about the dog and the dung.

Mr Corker says: What is the explanation? I've turned it over and over in my mind. Perhaps he really thought I was an impresario and then discovered I wasn't – though even so it's still a strange way to behave. Perhaps he had an accident. Whichever way you look at it, it's a mystery. And

when I tried to ask the waiter at the restaurant he only
shook his head and said Ich weiss nichts.

Ich weiss nichts, Mr Corker repeats the German phrase, after the new
slide has come up on the screen, and adds that it means: I know nothing. Then he pauses and is quite silent. This is one of his favourite
slides. Shining there flat on the silver screen, the façade of the church
is like a huge domed head with a single eye in its forehead.

    Mr Corker thinks: Damn the vicar, and damn the fucking vicar.
    I will say nothing, I'll go slow just to show him.

    I am St Charles's, says St Charles's. And I took you, replies Mr
Corker. The audience stare at the same white dome in the silent
church hall. The foreigner in Mr Corker has mystified them and
made them introspective. They have the impression now in the
silent darkness that as they study the white dome, they are being
studied by it.

    I am the blitz, says St Charles's to one of the old women.
    We were bombed out twice, says she.
    With all the sky lit up livid, and everything going up in
flames, says St Charles's.
    Those Germans! says she.
    And afterwards everything, says St Charles's, burnt to the
ground.
    My husband died in the shelter, the old woman says.

    I am the splendour of your vocation, says St Charles's to the
vicar. But, replies the vicar, how different you are from St
Thomas's and this hall and this lecture of this Corker's. It is
all so ugly.
    In the sight of God, says St Charles's, all are one and verily
there is no distinction even between St Thomas's and me.
    Amen, says the vicar made sadder.

Mr Corker says slowly: This church was built by the same man as the Imperial Riding School. Fischer von Erlach. The two columns either side are meant to represent the Pillars of Hercules.

I am the house of God, says St Charles's to Miss Brand.
Who art in heaven, she whispers.
Hallowed be *thy* name! booms St Charles's.

I am just the shape of a marrow, says St Charles's to Mrs Wheatley.
You are a beautiful church, Mrs Wheatley says.
With two carrots stuck up either side, says St Charles's.
Austrian cooking is meant to be good, says Mrs Wheatley.

I am Corker, says St Charles's to Alec.
You are a church in Vienna.
I am what Corker has seen.
I could see you too.
I am what Corker knows which is more than you, says St Charles's.
Sorry, says Alec.
I am one of the wonders of the world.
There must be others, says Alec.
You're a fool to go. You've never seen anything like me.
Jackie undressed is better.
You can both come in, says St Charles's.
We don't want it, insists Alec, we don't want it.

I am the lights turned on, says St Charles's to Miss Browning.
You are too conspicuous, she says.
Silly Velvet, says St Charles's, people are used to seeing the lights on.
Not after the office is shut, says Miss Browning, for Christ's sake remember that.

I am a royal church, says St Charles's to Miss Irene.

Unfortunately photographed by my unspeakable brother, says she.

I rise above the gutters of the street, says St Charles's, and hold a candle to heaven for the righteous to see.

What have I done to deserve this? demands Miss Irene.

You have been too kind.

I shall stop, she says, I shall stop. I shall drive him like a dark moth, a moth of the dark immoral streets, I shall drive him between the candles you hold to heaven.

Mr Corker says: It is a beautiful sight.

Then he takes out the slide without putting in another and the screen goes white and empty as though in the Victoria Hall a faculty has suddenly failed.

Mr Corker says: And now we shall partake of tea.

A trestle table has been put up in front of the door which leads to the pantry. On it are some cups and saucers, a very large, bright blue metal teapot and plates of little round cakes and sandwiches. Behind the table the fattest woman is serving with the help of her eight-year-old daughter who is also fat. In her blazer pocket is an autograph book and the daughter is waiting for her moment to approach Mr Corker and ask him to write in it for her.

Everybody except Miss Irene is standing in the vicinity of the table drinking a cup of tea. Miss Irene, who has been brought a cup and a plate, remains seated in her chair. It was Mrs Wheatley who brought it to her and who tried to engage her in conversation. Miss Irene had put a stop to the conversation by saying: Now you go back and enjoy yourself – I like to just watch.

And watching she is. As soon as the lights were switched on, her brother made a bee-line for the smart young lady in a hat.

Miss Irene had expected to be ignored herself but the shameless way in which William pushed himself to the side of this young lady made her doubt her previous judgement about the young lady being too well bred. She reminds herself that they say quite a high percentage of *them* come from good homes. If Miss Irene were forced to use a noun, she would say *woman-of-the-streets*. She believes that the word prostitute somehow denotes tolerance.

Mr Wheatley is talking to Alec and Jackie. You must both come to one of our Dances.

Where do you have them? asks Jackie.

Here, says Mr Wheatley, in the Hall here.

Jackie looks down at the rough floorboards and rubs the toe of her shoe over them. Her foot fits into the tiny toe of her shoe as improbably as a tiny hat might sit on the side of her head. Girls wear things as if they are just about to fall off, notices Alec.

We put down some rosin, says Mr Wheatley.

Just ballroom I suppose, says Jackie.

We have country dancing too, says Mr Wheatley.

But no rock?

I beg your pardon.

Nothing, says Jackie, we'll try and come if we can, won't we, Ali-Baba?

Alec, like Miss Irene, is also watching Miss Browning. He cannot understand why she should have come.

When Mr Wheatley has turned round, Alec whispers to Jackie: You see the woman with the hat that Corker's chatting with – she came into the office this morning.

She's quite sexy, says Jackie.

But what's she come for?

Why shouldn't she?

She's not the type, says Alec, does she look like any of the others here?

Like me! says Jackie pertly.

Jack no! says Alec, look at her legs.

Perhaps she's out to catch him.

Who?

Your madman.

Corker?

Jackie nods.

He's not mad, says Alec.

He's not very drunk either, says Jackie.

It's wearing off, says Alec, but he was.

He may be richer than you think, she says.

So what?

So she's after him.

Any city anywhere in the world, Mr Corker is saying to Miss Browning.

But which one most? she asks, encouragingly.

Mr Corker pauses. Then he says: Helsinki, yes, Helsinki.

The vicar takes Mr Corker's arm. Mr Corker turns and with a quick knowing ironical glance into Miss Browning's eyes, says: Was it cut short enough for you, Father?

Could I have a word with you? says the vicar.

Miss Irene sees the vicar take her brother from the woman and walk with him down the length of the hall. The vicar has his hand on William's arm and appears to be doing most of the talking. Hope allows her to imagine that the vicar may be questioning him about bringing such a woman to such a gathering.

Alec goes up to Miss Browning and says: So you did come.

I always meant to, she says.

Do you go to many lectures? asks Alec.

Now and again. I think your Mr Corker is a marvellous speaker.

Alec says: This is Jackie Armstrong, I'm afraid I forget your name.

She too has forgotten her name. The face of the boy opposite her grins and the girl holds out her hand which she must take. It occurs to her that it would be very simple to turn round and walk out and leave this dingy shed and these few people who echo in it for ever and ever. Then, mercifully, it comes back to her: Browning.

You do understand my position? says the vicar.

I have been lecturing for ten years, says Mr Corker.

With a mixed audience, interrupts the vicar.

Mixed! says Mr Corker, mixed in more ways than one! He manufactures and sends off a sneer to knock the vicar's teeth in.

Nobody, continues Mr Corker, has ever complained before.

Please understand, my Dear Fellow, I'm not complaining now – I know a few broad stories myself, so who am I to complain? – I'm merely suggesting —

I'm suggesting, says Mr Corker raising his voice, and I'm suggesting I damn well won't go on with it. You can finish the Talk yourself, Father! And you can explain why too. And I may tell you I know the Bishop of Croydon very well, and I shall be writing to him to give a full account of how I've been treated.

The vicar, like Jackie, is inclined to believe that Mr Corker is no longer drunk.

Miss Irene watches her brother leave the vicar abruptly and rejoin the woman.

The vicar hesitates. Dr Sargent, munching a cress sandwich, approaches.

Well, vicar, says Dr Sargent, one of the most remarkable lectures I've heard. Absolutely fascinating, don't you find?

You have heard the speaker before? asks the vicar.

Goodness gracious, yes. I go to all his lectures if I can. Facts, facts, that's what he's so good on. Has them all marshalled at his fingertips. I remember a splendid talk he gave on the Holy Land – full of facts!

Does he always use – is he always like he is tonight?

Always the same, says Dr Sargent, never changes at all. But new facts of course. I've never heard him repeat a fact, and I've only found him out to be wrong eight times over the last five years. Most remarkable man he is! And they tell me he takes good photos, too. I can't say so much about that because, as you may have heard, my eyes have never been the same since I was in the desert.

There wasn't anything unusual about him tonight?

You weren't fascinated, vicar? Unusual! Yes indeed in a manner of speaking. It's unusual to hear anything so damned good. You're new to these parts, I believe?

Yes, my last parish was in York.

Well, well, you'll find this quite an outpost. No Minster here or anything like it! Ha! We have to stick together and make what we can of it here.

Miss Irene, with the help of her sticks, is making her way to a place in the front row where she will be able to hear as well as see. Mr Corker's back is still firmly turned towards her. Indeed as she moves, his back turns in order to ensure that she won't outflank him. The vicar sits down next to her.

You are a parishioner, Madam? he asks.

No.

But you do live in Clapham?

No.

You came specially for the lecture?

No.

Can I get you another cup of tea?

No.

There is nothing I can do then?

No.

The vicar gets up and tells himself that it is hard to believe he is still in a Christian country.

Miss Irene leans forward to listen to the conversation a few yards away from her.

Alec: Mr Corker, please go on. He's a fool.

Corker: After all, we all know that horses have to excrete! Is that shocking? I ask you, is that shocking?

Miss Browning: Of course it's not shocking! But be an angel and go on. Please. I've come all this way to hear you.

Jackie: What was the story about the horse?

Corker: No, I shall not tell it now. Not within these four walls.

Miss Browning: But you will go on with the Talk?

Corker: I cannot.

Miss Browning: What can I do to persuade you? Anything. But please, please go on.

Alec: You asked me to bring Jackie, remember? Well, here she is.

Corker: I'm very pleased to meet you, Jackie.

Alec: Let's hear it all, Mr Corker. You asked me to bring Jackie specially. And Miss Browning here has chased you right across London. You can't stand two girls up like that.

Corker: On one condition only I'll only go on if the vicar apologizes.

Miss Browning: You're a darling!

Miss Irene's suspicions are confirmed. A terrible loathing overcomes her. There is no longer anything mysterious about her brother deserting her, and the true culprit stands three yards away from her wearing a disgusting, jaunty hat. The loathing is so strong that she forgets the wrong done to her. She no longer feels abandoned, she is visited by a passion which makes William and his smutty jokes utterly insignificant. Her passion demands that Miss Browning should be destroyed. She watches the woman leave the group and introduce herself to the vicar.

Miss Brand is standing by the trestle table near the teapot. She is wearing her best brown velvet dress with a creamy-coloured lace collar. Her big-knuckled hands look almost purple against this dress, as though for the last hour she has been scrabbling with her hands in cold snow for something lost. She is hoping that soon Mr Corker will see her. She would like to tell him how she is enjoying his talk but she fears that this would seem pressing: and so, instead, she is encouraging the little girl with the autograph book to pluck up her courage and go up to him.

The red-haired woman who reminds Mr Corker of Mrs McBryde is handing round another plate of cress and fishpaste sandwiches. When she offers Mr Corker one, she says: Those gardens you had a picture of were ever so pretty.

The Imperial Gardens! says Mr Corker.

Where you saw the French girls, she says.

You are not by any chance related to a Mrs McBryde are you? asks Mr Corker.

McBryde. No. I don't think so. I have a cousin whose married name is Mason, but not McBryde.

You must excuse my asking, says Mr Corker.

Not at all, she says.

But you look so much like a Mrs McBryde I know.

Has she red hair too?

Yes, as a matter of fact, she has.

You'll find we've all got terrible tempers – that's the natural ones, not the ones who are rinsed.

She laughs and moves off with her sandwiches.

Miss Irene is not deceived. The conversation about another woman was for her benefit. William wants to flaunt the fact that he has many women to choose from. He also wants to throw her off the track of the one he has actually brought here. Miss Irene never believed that she herself would have to step so deep into the mire created by the restless stamping feet of women waiting for men. She considers her sticks as weapons.

Miss Browning is telling the vicar about her father's parish near Portsmouth. The vicar begins to become reassured. She is the type of young woman he had hoped to find at a St Thomas's social evening.

Perhaps you remember Barry, says the vicar, Frederick Barry, he was at Ringwood in the New Forest.

No I'm afraid I can't say I do.

Or old Canon Young, he was at Weymouth.

I don't think so, says Miss Browning, I remember the Bishop of Portsmouth of course. He and Daddy used to play chess together.

Did they? says the vicar.

Miss Browning estimates she has given him sufficient encouragement. I always remember, she says confidentially, Daddy being quite funny about outside speakers, and the difficulties they landed him in. Like this old chap tonight.

I've just had a word with him, says the vicar.

He's terribly upset now, says she, he's almost in tears.

Oh dear, says the vicar. I only suggested he might bear in mind the kind of audience he was addressing. I didn't even tell him, I simply hinted at it. Very touchy he must be, very touchy.

Oh I do know, says she, awful. I tried to cheer him up a bit myself. But I'm sure you'd do it better, vicar. He seems to lay great store by what you say.

Is he *compos mentis*? asks the vicar, I mean I wonder if he is normal.

I think just rather old, says she, would you like me to come with you?

It's easy to see, Miss Browning, you've had a lot of experience of church work, says the vicar, I do hope we shall see you here often.

Well thank you sir she says, says she.

One of the old men has a coughing fit.

Chewing tobacco, it makes me sick, Mrs Wheatley says to her husband before she manœuvres the old man pantrywards.

Thank you, sir! exclaims Dr Sargent offering Mr Corker his hand. Mr Corker smiles, as at a bottle of wine placed in front of him.

Miss Irene thinks that it is not worth warning the vicar about the woman. He is too ineffectual.

The vicar and Miss Browning approach Mr Corker.

My dear fellow, says the vicar, what are we going to have the privilege of seeing in the second half?

Is there a second half? asks Mr Corker with maximum sarcasm.

Of course there is, says Miss Browning with emphatic cheerfulness, and like all good lectures it will get better and better, I know it.

Mr Corker grunts happily.

My dear fellow, says the vicar, I'm sorry if there's been any misunderstanding. For my part I can only say that I look forward most keenly to what you are still about to tell us.

We shall go to Schoenbrunn. Mr Corker pats his stomach. There he says, you have a setting if ever there was one.

Thank you, says the vicar.

Good, says Alec.

Yes, says Jackie.

William! says Miss Irene. She is up on her feet and sticks.

Mr Corker has no choice but to turn round. Hello, my dear, he says, I didn't know you were here.

William, won't you introduce me to your friends?

Mr Corker introduces his sister to Alec, Jackie, the vicar and Miss Browning.

You must forgive me, Miss Irene says, for not shaking hands, but I need both hands for these silly old sticks.

I'll fetch you a chair, Miss Corker, says the vicar.

No need, she says, I'm on my feet to go. I just wanted to say hello to all you young people before I went.

You're killing me, William, wasn't true, decided Alec, nobody is murdering her.

I expect some of you see more of my brother than I do, Miss Irene is saying, and as she speaks she jerks her head repeatedly towards Miss Browning. But none of you can have known William so long as I have. I have known him as man and boy, haven't I, William?

Mr Corker is trying to hide his large elderly face in a small teacup.

Alec remembers her voice saying: You're going to be sorry, William, very sorry.

And you'd be surprised how much he still depends upon me. I was lucky when I was a young girl. William has always been unlucky. You wouldn't believe how much we've always shared things. What's mine is his. What's his is mine! (This last phrase is hissed out almost under Miss Browning's nose, for the old lady now leans right forward on her sticks as though she had a mind to butt Miss Browning's breasts with her head.) I think I may see one or two of you later – I think I may – and you too, William. You know how glad I am to meet any friend of yours.

Are you really going already? says Mr Corker.

I shall wait up for you, she says.

But I shan't be coming back to West Winds tonight, says Mr Corker, I told you. I'm staying at the office.

Alec watches the expression on Miss Irene's face. She smiles very slightly, and it seems to him that it is the smile of somebody who is quite merciless.

I know, William. I shall wait up. Good night, vicar. Good night, all you young people. Good night – did William say your name was Browning? I have a bad memory for names, but I never forget a face, a kindness or an insult. (Again, she hisses the last word.) Good night, Miss Browning.

She makes for the door. The vicar follows her, anxious to do the right thing, but also to avoid being snubbed. He follows her therefore like a bodyguard. Mr Corker whispers gently: It's the pain, it's the suffering that makes her like that. Miss Browning is thinking very fast. Jackie squeezes Alec's hand and pulls him aside. They walk towards the other end of the hall.

Did you ever see her before? she asks.

No. But I heard her over the telephone. I told you. You're killing me, William, she said. And then she said he wouldn't get a penny out of her.

She looked mad to me, says Jackie.

You think everyone's mad.

No I don't.

You said Corker was mad.

So he is.

He's not, says Alec.

Well, *she* is.

She must be hell to live with, concedes Alec, a real old maid.

She can't help that, says Jackie.

Alec gives a quick look round to see if they are being observed. Then he kisses her inside her mouth quickly. For an instant they both close their eyes, and their two tongues are like two whales. Quickly they separate and lean against the wall, side by side.

They hate each other, says Jackie.

Who do?

Corker and his sister!

Oh Them!

Jackie inserts her hand between the wall and his bottom.

She's got the lolly I think, says Alec, but he just couldn't stand it any longer. I don't blame him either.

Look at him, says Jackie.

Mr Corker, greatly relieved by the departure of his sister, is telling the Wheatleys about the café violinists in Wien. He is miming the way they play.

Any road we persuaded him to go on with the Talk, says Alec.

Do you think you'll leave him? asks Jackie.

I don't know.

I hope you do.

You've taken against him, haven't you? But he's better than that old cow in your shop.

She's just an old cow.

What's the matter with Corker then?

He's double-faced.

Double-faced *and* mad!

Alec's penis is becoming erect.

He's soft and silly, Alec, but that gun you said you'd found, he'd use it too, I think. I bet he treats the people who come and see him like dirt. I bet he does.

Let's again soon, says Alec.

187

Yes, yes, says Jackie, but where?

Miss Brand observes everything that happens in the hall in case it should lead to Mr Corker coming over towards her. When she saw them kiss, she estimated the shame due to be felt by Mrs Gooch. An illegitimate baby would result and, born unwanted, it would be put in a home and brought up as she was brought up. She says now to the girl who is nervously balancing on one leg by the table, and still clutching the autograph book in her sticky hand: You go up to him, dear, and ask him, he's not so busy now. Go on.

We must find somewhere, says Alec, we must.

It's not easy, says Jackie.

I'll find us somewhere, see if I don't.

Ali-Baba, says Jackie.

Like the girl with the autograph book, Miss Browning is also waiting for her opportunity to claim Mr Corker's attention. She wants to follow the crippled sister. She fears that the sister may be on her way to her brother's office. She hopes she is wrong, and it is all the result of being overwrought for what with Corker threatening to stop the Talk, and the old sister's strange behaviour, and waiting for the curse, and the unusual fears which have haunted her since the morning, it wouldn't surprise her at all if she was beginning to imagine things. Yet for this very reason she dare not let the crippled sister go unfollowed. She dare not lose the chance of being reassured by being proved wrong. Whilst if she is right and if the first stupid idea of coming to the Talk was indeed the result of a genuine premonition because it has turned out that by being here she is uncannily in a position to prevent an unforeseeable danger threatening her Wolf, if with a woman's instinct (despite waiting for the curse) she has been right all along, without realizing why, to treat this job with special care and her only mistake has been to doubt her own intuition, then all she has to do is to intercept the old woman – but quickly.

Mr Corker, she begins, a dreadful thing —

Mr Corker, echoes the schoolgirl, having first repeated the sentence six times under her breath, will you be so kind, please, and sign your name in my autograph book?

Of course I will, says Mr Corker and, smiling at Miss Browning, he adds: Do you think you'll be able to sell it for a lot of money one day?

I'm terribly afraid, says Miss Browning —

What of? asks Mr Corker facetiously as he opens the book.

Seriously, says Miss Browning grinning. I've just realized what the time is and I've got to go or I'll miss my train.

But you can't! says Mr Corker, you haven't seen half yet.

It's dreadful. There just isn't another train, you see.

Where have you got to get to?

Near Camberley. I promise to come again to the next lecture and I'll arrange it better.

We could have dinner first, says Mr Corker.

Why not? says Miss Browning whose teeth are so white.

But I am disappointed, says Mr Corker.

So am I. You must write something suitable in the book, Miss Browning says to change the subject.

Mr Corker pauses. What's your name? he asks the girl.

Yvonne.

Well isn't that a coincidence! he exclaims. Here's another Yvonne, you see. He pats Miss Browning on the arm and beams at them both as though he has just christened them.

Mr Corker writes in the book: To Yvonne from Uncle Corker.

We are ready when you are, says the vicar, my Dear Fellow.

In the ensuing commotion of handling during which the little girl takes back her book and says Thank You Very Much, and the vicar puts his hand on Mr Corker's shoulder and Mrs Wheatley takes the plate Mr Corker is holding, Miss Browning says 'Bye 'Bye and Mr Corker distinctly feels her gloved hand in his. It feels to him like a present which as a child he would delay opening in order to prolong the pleasure of wondering. The lights go out.

VIEW OF WIEN FROM THE BELVEDERE

Mr Corker says: That's looking back at the city we've been in. There is the spire of St Stephen's.

Mr Corker's audience are inattentive. They have already been there. They want to see something new. Jackie's nipples are standing up like tiny domes.

Mr Corker thinks: Thank God Irene's gone.

THE GATES OF SCHOENBRUNN

Mr Corker says: I wonder how many of you have been to Versailles.

Dr Sargent begins counting the French palaces.

Mr Corker says: Schoenbrunn is more beautiful than Versailles. There is something intimidating about Versailles – but at Schoenbrunn you feel like an invited guest.

Mr Corker's audience peer through the bars and the wrought iron. They haven't received the invitation, but a small curiosity stirs within them.

Mr Corker says: This was the country seat of the Hapsburgs. It was first begun by the Emperor Leopold and the architect was the same Fischer von Erlach.

Mr Corker pronounces the now familiar name in a rhythmic voice as though it were the refrain of a poem. Although they recognize it, none of his audience is quite certain what the name actually is. In several cases they recognize it by the picture it suggests: the picture of a fisherman in oilskins standing alone in the middle of an icy stream, fishing for salmon in Scotland.

> *Mr Corker says:* Leopold was building it for his son Joseph. But when Joseph died, work on the building stopped and it remained unfinished until 1744 when the great Maria Theresa asked another architect called Pacassi – not Picasso (laugh from Vicar) – to complete it.
> *Mr Corker knows:* This is not the truth I want to tell.
> *Mr Corker thinks:* Thank God Irene's gone.
> *Mr Corker says:* It's beautiful eighteenth-century iron-work, isn't it?

Mrs Wheatley would like a grate in the lounge like that. She is proud of the fires that burn in her house. She would rather go into a room and feel a good fire burning than anything else in the world. Miss Brand kneels before the gate of the altar and wishes to dwindle until she is small enough to slip through the bars and upwards. Alec's hand and eyes are aware of the contrast between two substances. This awareness scarcely becomes thought. There is the wrought iron, wrought with a pattern like lace, but hard, inflexible, sharp-edged, dark-coloured, obstructive. There is her breast that fills his hand as though his hand were a bowl and her breast is malleable, changing, warm, fair-skinned, as though that part of her body was a few stages nearer to being a fruit.

> *Mr Corker says:* I think I can take it that we all have our dreams, that is to say we can all imagine the life we would like to lead but can't. We would all like something better – not merely in the next world, which after all is the vicar's province – but here and now in this one. I don't know about you, but I do the pools every week. I'm not ashamed to admit it. How would you spend it, if you won? I'm sure you've asked yourselves that question.

She'd buy a bottle of port, the old woman whose husband was blown to pieces by the Germans decides, and get a chicken for once and save the rest.

Mr Corker knows: I must say what I would like to say.

Mr Corker would like to say: It's not football pools though that I want to tell you about. It's something else. Leopold and Maria Theresa knew what they were doing when they built Schoenbrunn, they must have done. They were building an ideal setting. And if you go there today, you can still understand what that means. The last time I was there, I planned some changes in my own life, changes very much for the better!

Mr Corker finds himself saying what he would like to say.

THE SOUTH SIDE OF THE PALACE OF SCHOENBRUNN

Mr Corker says: The Palace! Do you know how many rooms there are in it? One thousand four hundred. If we shared it out between us we'd have a hundred rooms each.

Just one, thinks Alec, so that we could lie down.

Mr Corker says: Nobody could keep it up nowadays. But as we walk through we can imagine what it was like to live here, it gives us ideas of how we could change things of our own. Like I told you I did. Some of the changes you can't get carried out these days – you couldn't get anyone to paint a picture on the ceiling above your bed, for instance? Yet why not? Why don't they manufacture ceiling papers with pictures on them – there's an idea for you with money in it, I dare say. After all it's logical. We spend more time looking at the ceiling above the bed than we spend looking at any walls. Well don't we?

Jackie giggles and Alec presses her face against his chest to stop her. As she lifts her head up, he slips his hand between her skirt and tummy and, keeping close to her, feels his way over her suspender belt, up again and inside her pants until he reaches her curly hair.

Mr Corker says: What is happiness?

THE GREAT GALLERY

Jackie keeps her legs tight together.

Mr Corker says: Not to be hurried, that is very important for happiness. A leisurely pace as we wander towards the door at the far end. What is the hurry? I always say. To get one thing done just to do the next? Behind that door is another door and in the end you come to the exit, so why hurry? I like to sort things out for myself in my own time. A room like this is leisurely, isn't it? Look at the mirrors, one after the other after the other and the same with the windows. It's a stroll from one end to the other and you can look into the mirrors as you walk and see reflected there the gardens passing by, because the windows look out on to the garden. We don't have time for each other these days with everybody rushing in and out of rooms banging doors. But you just can't do that in a room like this. If only every-body had time to explain themselves! What a difference that would make to happiness too. Take the word *patience.* We say I'm losing my patience and then we begin to quar-rel. But patience is feeling you have enough time. And if you're in a room like this you can't feel rushed, you have to feel you've got all the time in the world. All the time in the world. It's my opinion we'd cut down our quarrels by fifty per cent if we lived in rooms like this. I've never known an architect well, but I'd say architects ought to look up how their buildings affect the divorce rate. Pacassi the old architect here could have made many happy homes, I think. It's all a question of thinking things out. One day we'll have the world fit for heroes to live in. Not in my time, not in yours either. But one day when they've worked everything out. People will live in rooms like this, not only Emperors but dustmen too and they'll be proud to know each other. Far-fetched? But why not? When people are happy they get on with each other. Imagine a happy world! A world confident enough to enjoy itself! A world where if anybody complained they would be treated as if they were ill.

Mr Corker thinks: I'm free now.

THE FISH POND AT SCHOENBRUNN

Mr Corker says: A world where we could all be ourselves. Free. A world in which we could all feel at home. I can imagine that when it is very hot people might lie in a pond like this amongst the water-lilies, just as now they lie in deck-chairs on a veranda. The Romans, as you know, were great believers in public baths, and I've often thought it was an idea worth reviving. What better setting to talk and philosophize in – so much better than a cocktail party where everybody stands up. The water-lily leaves could be used as little tables for putting drinks and delicacies on. The fish – there are shoals of them, silver and red and golden – would drift between us – instead of cigarette smoke at a cocktail party – tickling a foot here, a shoulder there. And we would lie in the water – the water of course would have to be specially purified and warmed – around our hostess in the middle – you can see the statue of her here naked as a goddess.

Mr Corker thinks: Miss Brand would be a waste.

Mr Corker says: Far-fetched? I ask you were the Romans far-fetched? It's all a question of changing conventions. We in

Clapham don't think of taking our clothes off in public, but that's because of our climate and because there are so many sex maniacs about. When our summers get hotter and we've got rid of all our sex maniacs – we're too soft about them at the moment, if a man knows he's going to get flogged, where were we?

There is absolute silence in the Hall: the silence accorded the tight-rope walker.

Mr Corker says: Yes, of course. When our summers get hotter, the conventions will change and your grandchildren may think nothing of going to a bath party on a July evening. What about the mosquitoes? you may think. But by then we'll have got rid of mosquitoes. We live, my friends, in a time of change. I am no longer as young as I was, you can see that for yourselves, but nevertheless I say: Let us embrace the new, let us discard the useless.

Mr Corker thinks: If the new will embrace me!

Mr Corker says: Taking the opposite – I told you that's what Wien did, didn't I? Turning the inside out. Here the garden is like an interior – perhaps the Garden of Eden was like that too, vicar? A kind of indoor garden that still has the sky above. Here is our hostess as I've shown you and our Roman bath, and here behind are the corridors and galleries between the lines of trees that are cut exactly like walls. Topiary. That's the word for the art of clipping trees. See how straight they are clipped! And when the sun is out they give cool shade, smelling of leaves like a good soap should. Smaller groups stroll there, leaving the water when they've had enough. The secret is never to overdo anything. Strolling there as many of the great have strolled, making up their minds, planning the future, taking fate into their hands – Napoleon walked here without a doubt.

Mr Corker thinks: All is possible.

Mr Corker says: I know some people say the only sensible things to grow are vegetables – because you can eat them. But I don't hold with that at all. There are pleasures for the eye too. These hedges are a joy to see and to wander down. It is an ideal setting. It is the same with certain beautiful members of the fair sex, they are not always the best conversationalists but what does it matter? There are more ways than one of appreciating. Many more.

Mr Corker decides: Mrs McBryde or one like her.

Mr Corker says: We have become too materialistic today: we think all the time about efficiency. But as you look, Friends, does it seem that efficiency is the most important thing in life? Or Duty either? Why must we always put off what we want? Why do we all postpone our happiness?

THE MILLION ROOM

Mr Corker says: It is too easy to do it once too often. Some of you may want to know why this is called the Million Room. You see how every panel right up to the ceiling is filled with a picture? Hundreds and hundreds of them are there, like tiles? And each one is a miniature Persian painting. In this one room are some of the most beautiful Persian paintings in the world – so I'm told. It was Maria Theresa who had it done and it was one of her favourite rooms in the whole palace. But it was dear, it cost a million florins. That's why it's called the Million Room. Now in my opinion there should be millions of million rooms. This is one of my ideas. Every man ought to have his own Million Room. Not the same as this with Persian miniatures, I don't mean that at all. But we should all have a room of our own which is not a bedroom or a dining-room or an office, but a room where we can think in, a room of a million and one ideas. As I see it, one of the great needs today is for people to know what they are doing. If people knew what they were doing, they wouldn't be so discontented and we wouldn't have all these strikes. Take dustmen, for instance, if they knew that the health of everybody depended on their doing their job properly, they'd be proud to be dustmen. But the trouble is that nobody has the time or the place to think in. That's why we need Million Rooms. Take the coal miner. Just think what he could think about – all the uses to which the coal he has dug out has been put! To cook with, to warm people, to make electricity, to run trains, to make bread – there's no end to it and if he could only realize what he's doing he would be a happy man. It was personal experience which first made me realize this. I was looking at all the books in my office and suddenly I thought of all the millions of jobs in London now being done as a result of people coming to us over the years. I'm not advertising now. It's just an example of how thinking can make a difference. Maria Theresa sat in this room and could think about all the events of Persian history: we need somewhere to sit where we can think about what we do. Otherwise we do things automatically and are ignorant about what we are really doing.

Mr Corker knows: I am saying what I would like to say to *them*, but not what I would like to say, for the sake of the relief granted me when the words, instead of choking me like feathers, float away in the air and the darkness.

Mr Corker, still leaving the slide of the Million Room in the projector, comes again to the front of his audience as he did when he told the story of his adventure in the Spanish Riding School. Once again, too, his audience can see his hands but not his face. Miss Brand, near to him in the front row, grants Mr Corker every right to speak out because he is clever, and also because in her experience the ideas gentlemen entertain have no connexion with anything else.

Mr Corker says: There is so much wrong. Our feet stick in it – and all that is wrong holds us back. There are dangers on every side – we know them even if it offends our sense of occasion to mention them. They wait like debtors, the dangers. To be destitute is one, to fall victim to a disease is another, to lose one's sanity and be buried alive, to be robbed by those who will stop at nothing, to give way to one of the weaknesses which will make outlaws of us, to fall victims to the utterly indifferent world. Dangers on every side, and if we survive, we survive to die. Why? Tell me why (Mr Corker begins to shout) I show you pictures of Schoenbrunn?

Only the vicar scrapes his feet on the floor.

Mr Corker says: You don't know. Of course you don't know! Because you never look up from the ground – you never hold your heads high enough. Pride! The vicar will tell you pride is a sin. And I will tell you that pride is what you have left when you have been stripped naked. Pride is your right to say: I matter! I matter! (Mr Corker thumps his chest with his fist.) Despite the wrongs and despite the dangers! Pride is the moment that comes even to the worm when it turns. Pride is what allows me to say, if you'll excuse me, vicar: my dear, your red hair is lovely, lovely.

Dr Sargent gets to his feet and walks to the door. As the door opens a yellow bow of light traverses the Million Room projected on to the screen. The vicar clears his throat to speak but hesitates a fraction too long.

Mr Corker says: Let him go. He's late for an appointment. But if you're not late for your appointments, I still have something to say. I do not believe that life can go on like this. It has to be different. I don't understand it. I don't understand why people are so callous to people. I don't understand why we always have to be frightened of the abyss into which we may fall. Why can't we fill in the abyss? Why can't we live in peace together, and give each other pleasure? Everybody wants just that. Or nearly everybody. I don't understand why it doesn't happen? It doesn't have to cost us a million florins. It's just a question of arranging it.

Mr Corker knows: I am withholding some of the truth.

Mr Corker says: Have any of you ever been desperate enough?

Alec's hand hot, and his finger wet, lies still all of a sudden by her silken cunt.

Mr Corker says: You need to be desperate, you need to have nearly suffered the Turk's torture – did I tell you about the Turk's torture? I forget now what I have said and what I haven't – you need to be near the end of your tether anyway, before you decide that the alternative is happiness. Perhaps therefore the world will get worse before it gets better.

Jackie glances up at Alec to see whether he is worried. He is staring hard at Corker. He feels her looking at him. He is mad, he whispers. No, not all the time, he isn't, she says solemnly. Then she puts her hand on Alec's trousers to feel how comfortably big he has grown in the bleak hall. Mr Corker remains motionless. The vicar, superstitious at the best of times and convinced that in every dear fellow there is a raging demon, fears that if he interferes now, he may make it worse and prevent it getting better. Mr Corker peers at his audience in the dark. His audience mostly tell themselves that they have never heard anything like it, at least not since they have known it to be true. Slowly Mr Corker walks back to the projector and changes the slide.

Mr Corker says: But in case it is of any help to you, let me tell you that I have chosen. I have made the choice. There it is. Happiness is there. There for the taking. Like a fruit, like the apple in the story of Adam and Eve, for there were other apples on that tree and it was their misfortune to choose the one they did. To the best of our ability we must choose happiness. That is my choice. I may be interrupted, prevented or defeated by circumstances but at least now I know what I want and what I am doing. I am making myself happy.

The old woman who lost her husband in the blitz begins quietly to cry into her handkerchief. Each sniff sounds in the dark like pieces of paper being rubbed together.

Mr Corker says: We have been built for it. Our bodies such as they are, our minds such as they are, even our hearts whatever they may feel, have been made in such a way as to be capable of it, indeed to need it.

Mr Corker's audience can see on the screen a photograph of a gentle sloping field and on the brow of the hill a colonnade of triumphal arches with a bronze eagle twenty feet high and wings outspread, above the centre arch. Mr Corker appears to have forgotten that he has changed the slide for he gives no explanation of what this one represents, and only those of his audience with good eyesight can read the mysterious title at the bottom.

Mr Corker says: My advice to you all is to do likewise.

Mr Corker delivers the last phrase like a slogan, and then changes the picture on the screen.

A STATUE IN THE PHEASANT WALK

Mr Corker says: Young love!

To all of Mr Corker's audience the stone couple look like a couple saying good-bye. In a second he will lower her to the ground, and she will kiss him once more and then walk away. And he will wait until the train or the bus or the walking figure turns the corner, out of sight. It is hard to say to what degree this is the effect of the sculpture itself, the lighting of the photograph, Mr Corker's previous words, the unprecedented events of the evening, or the old woman's sobs. As if following the example of the statue, Alec withdraws his hand from between her sweet, sticky legs, and Jackie presses his other hand against her blouse as girls do as they near the bus stop. It occurs to everybody that they may soon be saying good-bye to Mr Corker himself. He sounds like a man who is leaving. Miss Brand is suddenly frightened, not for him, but for herself.

Mr Corker says: We're as young as we feel.

THE WIENER WOODS NEAR HORN

Mr Corker says: No trip to Wien is complete without a visit to the Wiener woods. They are woods full of sunshine and wild flowers and babbling brooks. I went here one Sunday with Frau Hartinger and her son who had come for the week-end from Munich. We hardly met a soul and I remember how it occurred to me that if you went to sleep on one of these slopes, and if you didn't wake up like Rip Van Winkle for twenty years, you wouldn't know that more than a minute had passed. It is all so gentle and folded in, the most peaceful scenery I have ever seen, and although Frau Hartinger kept on saying that it was all different now and the little village inns had become expensive, I couldn't believe it, and I could easily picture my nurse, because when I was young, I had a Viennese nurse, walking here in these woods and picking the flowers and pointing out the different kinds of birds – she knew a lot about natural history, and was very clever too at arranging leaves. Do you believe in ghosts?

Mr Corker's audience are willing to be guided by Mr Corker, walking behind them to ensure there are no stragglers. The red-headed woman, who was embarrassed but also bucked by his peculiar but gallant reference to her hair, shakes her head: she does not believe in ghosts. The vicar also shakes his head, not because he is so sure but because he feels it his duty to offer some guidance to his flock whilst not out of the wood yet under the care of the usurper Corker.

Mr Corker says: I don't. But if there were such things and if there were such things as happy ghosts they'd live, I'd say, in these parts, playing like children, climbing the trees, collecting feathers, making ambushes, pretending to die heroes' deaths – Look! Look! I'm going to fall off this tree trunk without putting my hands out – Look!

Mr Corker's voice changes as he said this. It sounds as if he were imitating a woman's voice. The fattest woman shivers. It sounded like a ghost voice but he said he didn't believe in ghosts. Mr Wheatley glances up at the cross-beams in the roof, as though to assure himself that they are still in position and that what is happening is happening despite the improbability of it in their own Church hall.

Mr Corker says: Going to bed under the leaves, hiding – You'll never find me, never, never (Mr Corker uses the same shrill voice). Ready! Scrapping, fighting —

My mother and your mother
Went over the way
Said my mother to your mother
It's chop-a-nose day.

Fishing in the streams and the largest fish to be caught to be given to Liesel because she is favourite and never dead in the morning, and eating berries and running downhill – and pretending to fall over to be tickled. Yes, yes if I was going to be a ghost and happy again I'd live here. But as I told you I don't believe in ghosts, nor in the life after death, Father.

Miss Brand becomes certain that Mr Corker is not going to offer her the post, for he is a man who says things he does not mean.

A STREAM NEAR HORN

Mr Corker hurries on: Just look at the water, always moving, but quite cold because it comes from the Alps, and so fresh, pure as pure. And all the time bubbling. It's continuous, you see. That's why you can always look at water, spend hours just looking at it and thinking because it's continuous. It never stops, it never repeats itself, and it is never exhausted. You can learn a lot from the stream. Some people prefer the sea. But the sea's too big and it always faces you full on. What is so nice about streams is that you can stand by the side of them. You can let them go past you. This was a very fast one even in July, and I'm quite proud of this photo. It's caught the way it all gets tangled all the time because it's so fast. Even the shrubs and bushes on the bank look as if they're being blown by the wind in the same direction. But there wasn't any wind that Sunday. Not a breath. They must grow like that clutching at the stream as it passes. There was a story about this stream. We found a dog there who kept on jumping into the water and facing upstream. And barking at the river he could see advancing towards him, and snapping at the white foam and the bubbles. Then he would clamber out and race downstream along the path there and jump in again to have another go at stopping the current. It was a white dog. I don't know what breed, a mongrel I'd say. Frau Hartinger's son tried to catch it. He said dogs were not allowed to roam about the woods unaccompanied and it must be lost, and it was a law that every dog had to wear a collar with its name and address on it, so if he caught it he would know where to report it. In Munich Frau Hartinger's son works for a firm that makes special ball-point pens, called German Scribes. I've got one. The dog was too quick for him. It came quite close to Frau Hartinger's son and as he tried to grab it, it bounded away, so Frau Hartinger's son had the idea it might be easier to catch him as he climbed out of the water. He got down to the water's edge and stood on a stone. When the dog came near he bent over to catch him and lost his balance and one of his legs went in right up to the knee. It didn't matter much because he was wearing leather shorts. Lederhosen they're called. But he was made very angry and whilst he was emptying the water out of his boot he swore and cursed and started throwing stones after the dog. None of them hit him but he went on throwing stones at it and stones into the stream as well. I tried to stop him but he took no notice and his mother did nothing but smile and she whispered to me: Just like when he was a boy. That kind of thing makes me quite cross, so I walked ahead on my own. I knew I couldn't get lost because in that part all the main walking paths are marked – you can see a little signpost there nailed to the tree. The path followed the stream all the way. I tried to work out where it could have come from and where it was likely to be going, this stream. Most likely it comes from a spring in the hills. Schoenbrunn! You'll remember how that means

Beautiful Spring! Gushing out of the rocks, clear as clear, and sparkling. Then babbling down the hills and through the woods to join the Danube. With the Danube it might go through Dürnstein where Richard Cœur-de-Lion was imprisoned and Blondel his faithful page found him, and later through Budapest and Yugoslavia and Rumania until at last it reaches the Black Sea. You can't talk of the mouth of the Danube, it has many mouths. Its delta covers an area of a thousand square miles. It's a thought, isn't it? The water you can see here, so fresh from the spring, eventually reaching the Black Sea. In a few weeks' time the Turks from Constantinople may be fishing in it! Later it will evaporate in the heat of the Black Sea and form clouds. So, if there is an east wind it is just possible that it might come back to Horn and permeate through the rocks and the pores of the stones again. But if there is a west wind, it will go over the Caspian to Asia.

Oh to be dead and to be the element I ought to be, thinks Miss Brand. The vicar looks at his watch. This Corker babbles worse than his stream. Alec holds his left hand up to his face for it smells with a sweet familiarity, which no single life may explain, of Jackie's sex.

> *Mr Corker says:* What a power! eh? Driving the water round the world, ceaseless and remorseless. What a power! eh? They say nature abhors a vacuum, don't they? And why? I'll tell you. It's because nothing happens in a vacuum, nothing changes.
>
> *Mr Corker thinks:* Nature abhorred West Winds for the same reason.
>
> *Mr Corker says:* But I must finish the story about the dog, poor dog.
>
> *Mr Corker knows:* I should like them to see me as the man I am. I should like them to know what I know.

Mr Corker says: It kept up with me as I walked ahead. All the while it kept up with me. Sometimes it ran along the path. Sometimes it jumped into the water and barked at the current. After a bit I didn't take any more notice. I could see the wood was coming to an end and there were fields ahead and some buildings. By this time the dog seemed to have dropped behind and disappeared. The buildings turned out to be a saw-mill, by the side of the stream. It wasn't working because it was a week-end but obviously it was all in use. Most of the stream was diverted into another channel which went over a weir: then the water, deep and black-looking, flowed under a brick building. The water-wheel must have been inside the brick building. I sat down above the weir and waited. As I told you I can watch it for ever, continuously. I started to dream, and then the next time I looked up I saw something white in the water about ten yards away. It was the dog. And it was in difficulties, you could see that easily. It was trying to swim against the stream but the current here was too strong for it, and it was being forced slowly backwards. Foot by foot. It had its nose pointing right up to the sky, almost vertical. It had a funny fixed stare too. I must say I have a horror of drown-ing, always have had.

The fattest woman closes her eyes because she doesn't want to listen.

Mr Corker says: I jumped up to try to find a stick to help it. I thought if it could bite the end of a stick, I might be able to pull it to the shore. I couldn't find a stick, but I found an old bit of iron like a poker. It was leaning against the side of the brick building. It was quite heavy because it was iron. However, I tried with it. The dog was only a yard or two from the weir now. It was only a little weir, but still. There were palings along the top to prevent things being

swept over, and I thought these would save it if I couldn't.
I held out the poker thing right in front of his nose, but he
wouldn't take it. Isn't that funny? He just wouldn't take it.
He didn't even try to bite on it. He just went on staring up
with that fixed stare at the sky, his eyes wide open and his
front paws going like a white mouse's.

Mrs Wheatley takes Mr Wheatley's hand and holds it. The
story that Mr Corker is telling is not in itself disturbing to a
woman like Mrs Wheatley who learns every week how to maintain order, life and contact after two H-bombs have fallen in
the Greater London area. It is the speaker's tone that disturbs
her. The Civil Defence instructors are efficient and comradely.
Whereas, since he began talking about the dog, Mr Corker has
been speaking as though he has forgotten his audience and
doesn't himself know where the story is going to end. It sounds
unstable and unplanned. Madness, she fears, could lie that way.

Mr Corker says: He just wouldn't take it. I shouted at him but
it didn't make any difference at all. He just wouldn't take
it. There he was slowly being driven back only about three
feet away from me. I shouted at him again: Dog! Dog! I
shouted. (Mr Corker shouts) *Hund! Hund! Hund* is German
for dog. Please! Please! He was so close to me, yet I was
quite helpless. All I could do was to wait till the palings, the
bars, stopped him. But they didn't. I suppose there were two
or three missing. He was half stuck there for one moment,
with his front paws out of the water, still scrabbling. The
next moment he was gone. You know what the water over
a weir is like? It looks like a kind of curtain. Well, he slid
over the edge and he must have fallen behind the curtain. I
didn't see a thing after his feet in the air when he was stuck
between the palings. I didn't hear his splash at the bottom.
Not a trace of him. You'd have thought you would have
seen him through the curtain, but no. Not at the bottom

either in the black water, after all he was a white dog. But I couldn't see a sign of him. So I rushed round to the other side of the brick building where the stream came out and waited there. I waited for five minutes but nothing came out, only water and a few leaves. I thought perhaps he was inside. I tried the door. It was locked. I tried to listen but all I could hear was the rush of the water. Then I tried the other side where it was brick and a bit farther away from the channel. I put my ear to the bricks, but it was hopeless. All I could hear was the rush and something turning in the water.

Miss Brand believes that in the Old People's Home it will be like it was for the dog in the brick building.

Mr Corker says: I couldn't hear anything that sounded like a dog. Nothing. He just seemed to have disappeared off the face of the earth. I listened and listened. That's what I was doing when the Hartingers came up. They burst out laughing and said I ought to be a water diviner. As a matter of fact, I have done it once or twice. But I didn't tell them that. And I didn't tell them about the dog.

Mr Corker thinks: Your hair is lovely, and I'll say it again.

Mr Corker says: It just goes to show though, doesn't it? You can't be too careful. Even in an ideal setting, you want to be careful – whether it's a river, or traffic or electric blankets or oil-stoves or the tide coming in, it's always, always better to be safe than sorry —

Mr Corker knows: I am prepared to risk all to be happy.

Mr Corker says: If you're a dog!

The woman who cried laughs at the little joke because she wants to be cheerful.

Of all the slides that Mr Corker has shown his audience this strikes them as the dullest. It is a photograph of a few stones under water and the grass of the meadow coming down to the stream. There is nothing in it. At first Mr Corker himself can find nothing to say about it. He merely explains that it's the same stream, photographed farther on in the meadows. Everyone looks at it silently and blankly. Projected on to the screen it doesn't really appear to be a photograph at all. It doesn't appear to be a *picture* – this is the word that occurs to the audience. It is as though the objects themselves were there, dreary and inert: stones like a wall in the rain, grass like sacking, leaves like weeds or garbage. It is what can be found on any waste lot. Mr Corker's audience have seen gardens and fountains, carved statues and domes floodlit, fabulously expensive shops and white stallions – and now they are offered the mud by an unimportant river-bank. They are not, however, disappointed. On a level at which none of them bothers to observe, they expected this: not this particular photograph but the assertion that it makes. For to each member of Mr Corker's audience except Alec, this slide is a reminder of how problematical and distant the rest has been. Despite the fisherman-architect and the Empress and the wide boulevards and the Pheasant Walk and the wrought iron, they do not believe in the promise of the constructions they have seen. It would be naïve in the extreme to count on the fact that Schoenbrunn exists. To do so would be to build castles in the air. Each knows, according to his financial means, what has to be considered as real: the cinder path they are making from the back door, one scuttleful of coal to last three days, the remaining twenty-five jars of last summer's jam, the back gate that blows in the wind because one hinge is half off, the damp patch in the front room, the mortgage still left to pay, the weekly instalment on the telly. Yet they do not consider themselves deprived. Unlike Mr Corker, they are not certain that those who live in Schoenbrunn are happier, or that they would be happier if they lived there. They use the rules of another branch of common sense. Life, they say, is like this. They have learnt how near the mud always is, how quickly the grass grows over, how easy it is to drown. They do not put the lesson they have learnt into these words, and each one uses different words. But the principle is the same for them all. It is a hard job to maintain any position. The forces against you are so strong that you have only to glance away for a second for everything to revert to its inhospitable, inert, winter state. The principal force to be contended with is given a different name by each person. For Mrs Wheatley it is the essential stupidity of people, for the vicar it is this century, for the old woman who lost her husband it is the rising cost of food, for another old age pensioner it is the greed of her landlord, for Miss Brand it is her own body, for Jackie it is old age itself, for one of the old men it is the unconsciousness that prevents his knowing he is urinating. Alec is the only exception. This morning he would have named it ignorance, not knowing the proper rules. Now he has his own rules. If he wants something, he will find it. If he doesn't know something, he will learn it. If he has Jackie, he has what he wants. And so it happens that when Mr Corker, after a silence during which he can think of nothing more to say, remembers the birds in the meadow and tells his audience about them, Alec is the only member of the audience who responds as Mr Corker intends. Mr Corker explains how the birds are circling high in the sky above the stream. He is not now sure what kind of bird they are. Might they be pipits? he asks. He then proceeds to give an imitation of their cry. Coee-ee-curi. Coo-ee-curi – coo-ee-curi-coo. Coo-ee-curi-curi. Coo-ee-curi. Coo-ee-curi-coo. Curi-coo. Coo-ee-curi. There is something about making this noise which seems to please Mr Corker. He continues like a year-old child, delighted to have discovered another shape in which to put the mouth and make a noise. Nobody present knows anything about birds, so nobody recognizes what kind it is. But all of them admit, considering the age of the speaker and the unusualness of the Talk, that it is quite a fair imitation of a bird. None of them would for one moment be deceived by it: it is clearly a man, and an old man at that (who may have difficulty with his teeth) pretending to whistle like a bird. But Mr Corker's audience recognize at this point that he has a talent, which he ought to have done more about. Why, with a gift like that he could have been on the radio, the woman with red hair will explain in the pub next Friday night. But when he did the bird song it was *clever*, wasn't it dear? Mrs Wheatley will say to her husband when they are agreeing that on no account should he ever be invited to any St Thomas's function again. Mr Corker's audience recognize his talent and, to some degree, are carried away by it. They cannot forget it is a man, Mr Corker, whistling behind them in the corrugated-iron shed, the Victoria Hall. On other occasions some of them have seen real birds, who have flown in through the door and not been able to find their way out, and have perched on the gravy-coloured beams and beaten their wings against the hardboard, until shooed out by the late Father Bean with a long stick that is still kept in the church for opening the window high on the South Wall. There is no question of those who have seen them being reminded of these birds by Mr Corker's cries. But they and the rest of the audience do *picture* a kind of bird as they listen. Some imagine a large one, others a small one, some think of it as white, Jackie imagines it golden, others black. Yet they all, except Alec, imagine the bird, whatever it looks like, crying in the air over flat ground. The ground is a kind of marsh, an extension in every direction of what they can see on the screen: wet stones, mud, weeds. This marsh is dangerous unless you know how to cross it. Treacherous. *Treacherous* is the word most of them would apply. Treacherous as the wind, as cancer, as madness, as winter, as the sun when it is hot, as hoping too much. The bird's cry is plaintive. *The cry of a lost soul* are the words for it. Yet it does not seem sad to Mr Corker's audience. They imagine it with pleasure, for it is a confirmation of what they have learnt: life is like this. And when they *picture* it so bleakly – a single bird's cry flung up over the inert marsh – they know, for a moment, that just living, they have triumphed. How different this is from what Mr Corker intends! Mr Corker remembers the summer meadow full of flowers, the sunshine and the supper he had with the Hartingers that night. He has already forgotten the dog. He is aware that he has only one more slide to show: his Talk is coming to its close. It is time for him to sum up and underline his message, and although the notion of imitating the pipits first came to him because he hoped that somebody might on the evidence of his imitation decide whether they were pipits or not, as soon as he begins, discovering first that he can't exactly remember the pipit song, and second that for some reason tonight, some reason far stronger than Kummel, he can do exactly as he chooses, he has the idea that this song can serve as his Summing Up. The objection that bird-song contains no words is instantly swept aside. It is impossible to understand the words in the greatest arias. It is feeling that counts, feeling and spontaneity. The song of a pipit is like the song of a lark. And what more apt than a lark to express the aspiration and freedom of his theme? The ascent to happiness! Mr Corker might have succeeded better with another audience. He succeeds only with Alec. Cooee-ee-curi. Cooee-ee-curi. Cooee-ee-curi. To Alec, Corker's whistling sounds like a man whistling. But a man whistling sounds carefree, and Alec feels an onrush of certainty and confidence. He will leave Corker. He will get a job where he can use his hands. He will take Jackie away with him. He will find a room for them to live together. As Corker pauses to gain breath, Alec whistles three notes of the same song. Corker looks across at Alec and waves.

A LAST LOOK BACK TOWARDS WIEN

Mr Corker says: The song of the birds who know no frontiers! But us? We, unfortunately, we are near the frontier and the end of our trip. This was taken not far from the German border in the Tyrol. We are looking eastwards, in the morning, back towards Wien. It looks as though it's going to be a hot day, doesn't it?

For Mr Corker's audience the Talk is over. In their minds the light has already been switched on. There is no longer any other time and place but here and now. It is as irrelevant to say: it looks as if it's going to be a hot day, as it would be to announce the date of the next total eclipse of the sun. They have to get home, it must be late, it has gone on longer than they expected. There is another reason too for their impatience. They have come to their conclusion. They suffer the responsibility of being right. Life is as they know it in Clapham. For a short while they had no objection to being beguiled with unlikely accounts of a distant city, but when it is over it is over and a fiction. They cannot now get involved in another story. Necessity and duty call if positions are to be maintained. The old man with the weak bladder already fears the end may be too far off for him.

> *Mr Corker says:* The sort of day when you have breakfast on the veranda in the sun, with semmels and apricot jam. The end, of course, is always a little sad.
> *Mr Corker thinks:* When the light goes on they'll start staring at me.
> *Mr Corker says:* But I always say to myself: I shall be back. And right from that moment, the last Austrian breakfast on the hotel veranda, I start anticipating my next trip. Anticipation!
> *Mr Corker thinks:* I'll go on for just a little longer.
> *Mr Corker says:* There is a gift for you! The art of enjoying something before it has happened, the art of gaining pleasure from the future.

Bloody stupid! says Alec but without looking at Jackie. What's the matter? she whispers. Nothing, he says.

> *Mr Corker says:* I can see myself now setting out again and leaving my flat in time to catch the boat train from Victoria. My housekeeper is at the door waving.

It is not me, concedes Miss Brand, he won't see me waving. She hopes again that she will die soon.

> *Mr Corker says:* And so it was when I took this photo. I could have said to myself – This is the last picture of Austria, *Auf Wiedersehn Wien!* (Mr Corker makes the German sound almost like a bird cry.) That means Good-bye Wien. But I did no such thing. Instead I said to myself – This will be my first sight of Austria when I come back next time, *Grüss Gott Wien* (another bird cry), which means: God bless you, Wien! And I'll tell you something else too. When I have given this Talk before, not this same talk because I always vary what I say according to the occasion, but another talk on Wien, City of the Blue Danube, I have actually used this as the first slide!

For Alec this admission is enough. It demonstrates how it is all a trick, how Corker's talk is just talk. With disappointment Alec tells himself: Corker is not killing his sister. Corker will never fire the revolver. Corker's business will never never expand. Corker's housekeeper will be Bandy-Brandy who will nag him to death. *He is playing with himself* – are the words Alec repeats – *playing*.

> *Mr Corker says:* The first shall be last and the last shall be first! That's right isn't it, Father?

Alec tells himself that there is no seriousness in the man. Corker wouldn't even cry out for *Help!* What does he need help for?

> *Mr Corker says:* Friends, I have enjoyed talking to you tonight.

Alec grips Jackie's leg above the knee. Jackie can feel the difference of purpose in his touch. This is not for its own sake, but is the result of what he is thinking. Her leg is no longer her leg. He is borrowing it. She lends it gladly.

> *Mr Corker knows:* Tonight I have been free as never before in my life.
> *Mr Corker says:* And I hope you have enjoyed it. Do not forget Wien – it is a city well worth a visit. But as I have tried to show you, it is more than that, it is an example. We must have the courage of our convictions —

How can he be helped? Her leg proves Alec right. It is soft either side and hard on top and he can feel the warmth of it through her skirt. Corker has never had his hand on such a leg and his hand wouldn't appreciate it if he had. Corker has missed everything and everything is wasted on him. Her leg proves him right. There is muscle and energy in it and sex down all one side such as Corker couldn't support. Corker is frail and fragile and there is no strengthening him. There is nothing in him to strengthen. Her leg proves him right. Maja's leg may feel the same. But Corker only has a picture of her.

> *Mr Corker says:* We must pursue what we want and live as we like, most people don't think for themselves and so they just quietly take what they're given.

Corker was brought up with money or he wouldn't have the little he has. Let him keep his wardrobes and soup plates and his round bloody table. Her leg proves him right. There is nothing that he should give Corker.

> *Mr Corker says:* This is not necessary. Friends, this is what I hope I've shown you. Wien is there as an example. It *can* be done, civilization *is* practical.

What does Corker need help for? *Fiddling with his slides.* Alec ticks it. Then, releasing his grip, he slides his hand along Jackie's thigh. Her leg proves him right.

Mr Corker says: We can make a happy life for ourselves.

The vicar at last takes the initiative by beginning the clapping. Mr Corker's audience claps because it is over and now that it is over Mr Corker, a character, can be said to have given generously of his time. Alec does not join the others in their clapping. He feels ashamed for the old bugger. To Mr Corker the clapping in the dark sounds like a fire he has lit.

Part Four

Corker as Desired

1

The street is just such a one as made Albert Immonds, the van driver from Coleford, think of the stumps of a felled forest. The brown houses are narrow and low and identical on either side of the street. The street is on an incline running down to a crossroads and a coal merchant's yard at the bottom. The houses are separated from the street by about eight feet of garden. Between the front gate-posts are low purple brick walls. The chimneys and roofs of the houses towards the top of the hill are silhouetted like heaps against the sky. There are a few chinks of light showing through curtains in upstairs bedrooms. A tall man in one of these front gardens could almost touch the bottom of the front bedroom window. Miss Corker is half-way down the hill. She is making good progress and is already within three hundred yards of her brother's office. In her handbag which hangs from her wrist is the spare office key which she has found at West Winds. She uses each stick in turn to lean her weight on. From the top of the hill it looks as though she is trying, first with one stick and then with the other, to pin a black invisible leaf on to the road: each time the leaf is blown a little farther on so that she is forced to take another step and jab again.

The sight of Miss Corker is a great relief to Miss Browning who has run most of the way from the Victoria Hall. Now, at the top of the hill, she slows down to compose herself before shouting out.

Miss Corker! The old woman appears not to hear, and Miss Browning dislikes the feeling that her voice can probably be heard in the houses which are standing shoulder to shoulder the length of the road. She quickens her pace down the hill.

Miss Corker, I'm catching a train too, can I offer you a lift in my taxi?

The crippled woman does not stop and barely looks up. Mr Corker sent you after me, she says.

I told him I'd look out for you since I was going the same way.

That was most thoughtful of you, wasn't it? And most thoughtful of Mr Corker too.

No, no he didn't send me, I offered since I had to leave anyway, you see, I was very sorry to leave actually because I thought it was a splendid talk, didn't you, Miss Corker?

There is no reply.

If we turn left at the bottom, says Miss Browning, we'll get into the main road and there we'll get a taxi I think – if we are lucky! She gives a little laugh, and puts a hand under Miss Corker's elbow.

Miss Corker gives a jab with her elbow to push the hand away and says: I'm not going to the station and if I was I'd have no wish whatsoever, none, to share a taxi with you.

Are you going to the office, because Mr Corker said if you were —

It is none of your business where I'm going.

There is a sound of a television voice from the house they are passing. This voice sounds very fluent compared to the awkward and excited dialogue of the two women in the road.

He said it would be better to wait for him, we could go and have a cup of tea together if you like, if we turn left —

Most thoughtful again! Miss Corker, to emphasize her sarcasm, says this in a sweet, polite voice. The voice, like her hair seen from the back, suggests a woman twenty years younger. Most thoughtful to be so kind to the sister of your friend.

Shall we do that then, Miss Corker —

I am going to the office. You can tell Mr Corker I'm quite capable of looking after myself. You can also tell him I shall be waiting up when you arrive.

I told you I'm catching a train, Miss Corker.

Then I suggest you catch it.

Miss Corker veers to the right, away from the turning to the main road and towards the coal merchant's yard. There she leans with her back against the wire-mesh fencing to rest and take the weight off her hands. Miss Browning stands awkwardly beside her. Miss Corker points with one of her sticks towards the main road. Catch it! she says. Catch it!

Look, if we get into the main road we could have a cup of coffee together and you could explain to me what's the matter and afterwards I'll see you back to the office. Shall we do it like that?

The matter! I'll tell you what the matter is, my woman. The matter is that Mr Corker won't have a penny left. He hasn't much anyway, but soon he's going to have even less. I'm going to make him repay every penny he owes me, every penny he's had from me. He is not going to be able to afford *anything*, anything he's promised.

Miss Corker leans right back against the fencing which sags a little beneath her weight. On the other side of the fencing is a bunker of small, household coal.

We can't talk here, says Miss Browning, but I do think we may have things to talk about. I'll catch the next train. I've almost missed it already —

Catch it! This time Miss Corker swings one of the sticks round in a semi-circle at knee level. Miss Browning steps away.

Listen —

Catch it! Miss Corker lets her head fall back against the wire which vibrates with the blow. Momentarily she closes her eyes.

Miss Browning folds her arms. She calculates that at the worst she can keep the old woman talking here.

Miss Corker regrips her sticks, preparatory to moving off. Since opening her eyes, she hasn't glanced at Miss Browning.

She is pretending that Miss Browning is no more than a lamp post. A man comes out of one of the houses, looks cursorily around, notices two women talking by the coal merchant's yard and hurries up the hill. He can let himself out of his own front door, imagined Albert Immonds, travel several miles in a bus, walk along streets almost indistinguishable save to the experienced eye from those he left an hour before, arriving at where he is unknown and cannot except with the greatest difficulty be traced, and there find the means and those willing to allow him or entice him to become somebody totally unconnected with what he is and with what he is believed to be behind his own front door. Miss Corker moves forward. The office is no more than a hundred and fifty yards away, at the end of Summerbourne Road.

Miss Browning is at her side. All right, she says, so I'm your brother's mistress. Now let's talk.

Miss Corker hobbles faster than before, without looking up.

Don't you see, says Miss Browning if I'm his mistress I can help you, you tell me what you want and that'll help me to help you, don't you see?

Miss Corker still says nothing, but seems intent on watching the ends of her sticks.

Don't you see? Miss Browning's question hangs in the air like the whine of a child.

They reach the end of the wire fencing. In that corner of the coal merchant's yard there is a dump of used tyres.

Leave him! says Miss Corker. Her voice has become like the shrill cry of a bird, and as she speaks the words, she jerks her head like a bird pecking.

Miss Browning goes ahead and, bending her knees slightly, walks backwards so that the crippled sister can see her face level with her own.

But I love him, protests Miss Browning, I love him. Please stop so we can talk.

I've told you, says Miss Corker pecking hard at the proffered face, but not for one moment slackening her speed, he has no money.

Miss Browning desperately abandons the frontal position and comes round to the side again. Now she leans over the old woman and whispers into her ear. I want to see him happy, she says, help me!

He was always happy, cries Miss Corker, always.

They can see the traffic in Croydon Road which runs across the end of Summerbourne Road.

Miss Corker, I appreciate how difficult it is for you because you think I'm no better than a prostitute and a family like yours has certain standards, values to keep up, believe me I appreciate your position. Her hand approaches the cripple's elbow. But for your brother's sake let's try to work out something, the two of us. The hand grasps the elbow. I tell you I love your brother. The hand pulls backwards. I'm prepared to sacrifice myself for his sake. The two of them slow down almost to a standstill. Couldn't we, if you care for him too —

Hold your tongue! cries Miss Corker.

We both want the best for William, shouts Miss Browning, can't you see? We both want the same thing for him.

Miss Corker stops and, tapping with one stick to emphasize her words, says: I shall drive him like a moth between the candles.

Miss Browning does not know how to put a stop to the silence which follows and seems endless. A bus passes the end of Summerbourne Road. She is now almost convinced that nothing will stop the old woman, who is as obstinate as she is frail.

Finally Miss Browning finds these words: Do you know William is ill? Miss Corker, I'd like to tell you about the disease he has.

Miss Corker raises a stick and Miss Browning in order to avoid being struck on the hip, grabs Miss Corker's raised arm. Miss Corker is crying out: You Filthy Person! But as she cries and Miss Browning takes her arm, she begins to fall.

She falls towards Miss Browning. Both Miss Browning's hands grasp at the clothes. The sticks clatter to the ground. It is at this moment that Miss Browning loses her temper. She deliberately relaxes her grip upon Miss Corker's clothes and drops her. Miss Corker slithers to the pavement and stays there.

Miss Browning steps over her so that she need not see Miss Corker's face. She looks down at the twisted body. It is lying with all its weight on what might have happened, but has not. The old woman's handbag is on the pavement at the foot of the wooden fence. Miss Browning picks it up with the intention of giving it back to her. She does not like the idea of them being separated. She bends down and says: Miss Corker! Miss Corker! The old woman's face shows no reaction. The eyes are open but staring fixedly. Miss Browning touches the flesh near the mouth. It is damp and cold. Miss Browning suffers the illusion that the drop has killed Miss Corker.

Irene Corker cannot move. The paving-stones seem to be on top of her lower limbs, not beneath them. One of her hands is in the gutter and she is aware of it resting on something soft: otherwise all that she can feel, except for the air that breathes on her face, is stone. There is silence all around her and when she makes a noise in her throat to break the silence, she hears nothing. The continuity of her thoughts up to the moment of her fall has been completely broken: like her two legs they seem to have been severed from her: she cannot now conceive of any other condition save the one she is in: the condition of waiting, entombed. The only variation open to her comes through the use of her eyes, for, despite Miss Browning's impression to the contrary, she can in fact see with them, and therefore can also change the direction of her gaze. Yet even when she does do this, the significance of what she sees remains exactly the same, so the variation afforded her is more apparent than real. She can see the creosoted fence that juts out on to the pavement and prevents her seeing any passer-by who, walking along Croydon Road, crosses the end of Summerbourne Road in which she lies. Above the fence she can see a window with lace curtains across it and some kind of liquid-container, shaped like an upended pebble, standing on the window sill. Above that she can see the backs of the roofs of the tall dark brown buildings that face her brother's office across the main road. Two drain-pipes from these roofs run parallel, part, come together again and then join to become one larger pipe. This pipe is swollen at its top to accommodate the commotion caused by the meeting of the downrush of the two smaller pipes. But whether Miss Corker looks at the bricks, the slates, the lead-pipes, the window, the liquid container, she is struck to an equal degree by a quality which they all have: the quality of their permanence. When she has been moved they will still be there, just as they were there too before she fell. They have functioned. They function. They will function. Whereas she has ceased to function. And all that remains in her mind of the evening's events is the knowledge that only if and when she rejoins the functioning world, can she become interested again in her own ambitions.

Miss Browning is no longer conscious of what she is doing. She finds herself in the Croydon Road and only then realizes where she is, because of her acute awareness of the danger threatened by the people whom she is passing as she walks as quickly as she dares to a telephone box. This unconsciousness of all the intermediate steps she is taking is not the result of numbness or shock. It is a violent and terrible form of absent-mindedness. Her mind is full to the exclusion of everything else with the inevitability of what has happened. The crippled sister is on the pavement where she dropped her. One minute ago it hadn't happened. However much her reason tells her that that minute cannot be relived, she clings to a wild prayer: if with God's help she can put enough distance between herself and the street where it happened she will find herself somewhere else where it didn't happen, where the critical second passed unnoticed, and where she will be as she was before when she thought too little about God. Now she finds herself coming out of the telephone box, some keys in her hand; the separated handbag has been left behind. Her mind is full of the enormity of the risk of going back. She must cross the end of Summerbourne Road again. The risk is that she will be forcibly attached to the crippled woman lying on the pavement for the rest of her life. She finds herself outside the front door of the office. It is locked. She finds herself in the dark, the door shut behind her. There is no sound from upstairs. Her mind is full of the darkness in which there is not a crack of light. She strains to listen but can hear nothing but herself. She finds herself staring by the light of a match at a notice on the wall which reads: You Will Want The Jobs We Have. Come Up. The match goes out and her mind fills with hatred of the old man who allowed himself to be deceived and the complexities of whose life have trapped her, even in the dark in which she is hiding, as she has never, never been trapped before. Then she finds herself outside on the common, crying and running with blood at last flowing down her legs.

2

Mr Corker leaves the Victoria Hall, practising what he has preached. He is happy. He is wearing his blue, belted gaberdine macintosh and his blue-grey felt hat. He has a habit of turning down the rim of this hat at the front and back which gives him a somewhat foreign if slightly soft appearance. Other Londoners in better circumstances achieve the same effect with astrakhan collars. He is also wearing a pair of fur-lined leather gloves (a Christmas present from Irene), and carrying an attaché-case. Inside the case are his slides and notes: all the evidence he has used of Wien.

When he reaches the first corner and is out of sight of the Hall, he looks up at the few stars visible through the light cloud and remembers the sentiment of his own words at the beginning of the Talk: Everything that people have done is there all the time, inextinguishable as the stars. This inspires Mr Corker to call himself a free man. He has truly acted according to his own free will. The direction in which he is walking proves it. He is walking away from the station, towards his own premises.

The doubts that assailed him during the afternoon have dispersed. He has felt his own power. He has been able to share his ideas and experiences: he has been able to tell things he has never heard told before. The originality of what he has felt and told lends authority to the originality of his decision and his plans for the future. Nobody was able to stop him, not even the fool vicar: nobody sniggered. It is true that Dr Sargent left, but during the tea-break Dr Sargent had congratulated him, and so probably the Doctor did indeed leave because of a previous appointment. It seems to Mr Corker that his whole Talk was consistent. The distinction between those parts in which he said what he meant to say, and those in which he only wished it, has been altogether lost in the general triumph of having spoken out and been listened to.

But Mr Corker is a practical man and so, as he walks, he budgets and bargains with himself. He is making applications to himself for shares in his newly found freedom. Each application has to be carefully considered on its own merit and in relation to all the other applications, for Mr Corker is fully aware that his freedom can never be larger than his income. During this budgeting and bargaining process Mr Corker continuously changes his role as a representative. One moment he is Mr Corker, householder: the next he is Mr Corker of Clapham, businessman. And always between whiles he is the arbiter: Mr Corker, managing director.

The representatives use promises to strengthen their claims: but they are not above using threats as well. Each appears flanked by success and disaster. The managing director must manœuvre and judge between all the possibilities which he himself provokes in the world, the world being as it is.

The Corker of Clapham comes first to present his claims, for without his interests nothing would be possible. He has a bankrupt beside him without collar or tie and he pushes him forward and Corker, the bankrupt, says: It can happen. But immediately the Corker of Clapham takes his place and stepping out of a plane in Madrid says: Think of all the Spanish girls who are coming over to England for jobs, there's a fortune to be made out of them! The managing director suggests that business should first get better in Clapham, but agrees that the move should help to make it better because less time will be wasted travelling and more time can be spent on business in the evenings.

The Corker of Clapham says: We must give Alec a rise or we shall lose him. Is he worth a rise? asks a Corker who has done well by being single-minded. We could try staying open an hour later in the evenings, says the managing director. Corker the photographer comes out of a dark room, newly constructed. I need time, he says, look at him! and pushes forward a Corker who has no front to his face and appears to be facing away from whatever direction you look at him: You can't afford to waste your talents, he explains. The Corkers are beginning to descend the hill where the purple brick walls run along the fronts of the gardens no larger than a bed. And look at this! He produces a secret photograph of something never photographed before. The managing director does not know what it is: he only recognizes that it took courage to take it. Corker, the photographer, is proud: I need time, he says. Materials are expensive, reminds the managing director. You will be saving on fares, says the photographer.

A naked Corker in his bath with the grey hairs on his chest like smoke in the water, interrupts: I need the saving on fares towards the housekeeper. Look! He produces Corker the already familiar bankrupt: A man can go to pieces if he's not cared for. The Corker of Clapham takes over from the bankrupt. An idea! he says. Why not use the Reception-Room for a little exhibition of photographs and I could persuade some of our employers to buy them. The television set is still on and the voice still suave. Excellent, approves the managing director. The Corker out of his bath and in his dressing-gown suggests: With a good house-keeper I could teach her to develop and print. How much are you going to pay her? asks the Corker who has done well by being single-minded. Six pounds, answers the managing direc-tor. That's not much for somebody who is able-bodied, says the Corker mysteriously back in his bath.

What'll happen to her when we're away? asks Corker the trav-eller on the site of the Parthenon. Still have to pay her, says the naked Corker, she'll need a holiday too. I'll be able to give more talks, being freer in the evenings, says the Corker before the Coliseum. And if you give more Talks, you'll be able to charge more, says the Corker who has done well by being single-minded.

If we are careful, says the managing director, we should be better off all round. We'll need to entertain, insists a Corker who is discussing the Holy Land with the Bishop of Croydon. Look! and he points at a friendless Corker's funeral procession with not a mourner in sight. They are passing the coal merchant's yard. Entertainment need not cost much, claims the Corker who has done well, it evens out, what you offer and what you take.

Kummel! says a Corker who is a genie inside a bottle. Look! And he pushes forward a Corker who denied himself everything: This Corker is hobbling on sticks like Irene.

In moderation, decides the managing director, we need to be careful for there is no help in the world if we fail or overstep the mark. When we are free, we are also alone.

All the Corkers appear as faces reflected in mirrors arranged like the facets of a crystal. They all have the same face.

It is only necessary for me to make a slip, says the managing director, savouring the courage necessary to recognize the truth, and it could be the end.

Mr Corker in his blue gaberdine crosses the road so that he is now walking on the opposite side from where, a hundred and fifty yards farther on, Irene lies.

We have ten thousand on our books and have been established for seventeen years, says the Corker of Clapham. We are not a little business done in the front parlour.

I am in good health, says the naked Corker.

I could always get a job, says the photographer Corker.

Or I might get married, says the naked Corker again.

Or we could settle abroad, says the traveller Corker, Frau Hartinger would help for one.

We are all right as we are, says the Corker in the Kummel.

Count your blessings! orders the managing director.

The business is our own.

We have a flat to ourselves which costs nothing.

We are young for our age.

We are solvent.

We are free.

The managing director presents the bankrupt Corker to himself. The bankrupt Corker says: I've done most fucking things. The managing director dismisses this other Corker: I cannot tolerate you happening to me.

My week-ends will be my own, says the naked Corker, and I shall lie in bed in the mornings and eventually reach the stage of saying:

My dear, your red hair is lovely, lovely. The householder Corker, taking off his velvet smoking jacket, puts on the brown overall and climbs up a pair of steps and says: There's a lot to be done first. Look! He opens the sitting-room door and there inside are armchairs pulled up to the fire, and polished fire-irons, and pictures of foreign cities on the walls, and a bookcase and a table with glasses and a decanter on it. That's how I want it, so there's a lot to be done.

This is the point in Summerbourne Road where Miss Browning protested her love.

We must make do with Mother's furniture for the moment, says the managing director.

Is that some knitting I see in the armchair? enquires the naked Corker. Six pounds a week is not enough to attract the best, I must offer seven. I can't get a McBryde for six. Is she more important than anything else? asks the host Corker, surrounded by masonic friends and local members of the Royal Photographic Society. The Corkers pass Irene sprawled on the opposite pavement without noticing her.

Your friends will come all the more to see you, says the naked Corker, if she has red hair which is lovely. Six pounds ten maximum, says the managing director.

We might advertise in the Spanish press straightaway, says the Corker who has done well by being single-minded. I had better go and make inquiries at the Spanish embassy, says the managing director. Why not ask for an introduction from Gibsons the sherry importers? asks a Corker who mixes well and never forgets a name because he uses Pelmanism. Last Christmas they gave us two bottles, says the Corker in the Kummel, and I took them both home and never set eyes on them again.

It's going to be different now, says the managing director.

Mr Corker in his blue gaberdine hums as he leaves Summerbourne Road and crosses Croydon Road.

And so say all of us! And so say all of us!

When he reaches the front door, he looks up at the sign above: *Corker's of Clapham, Employment Agency.*

All the Corkers now recognize this as their place, chiselled out for them. Even the address – 84 Croydon Road – means far more to them than the number of a door in a street. They will inhabit these premises and the livelihood which they promise, as the young Corker once inhabited the name *William.* When the Corkers are instructing a stranger how to find the premises they often tell him to look out for the Co-op, for they are above it. This is meant literally – the Co-op is on the ground floor, and they begin on the second floor. But the address and the signboard place them in a metaphorical sense too. Here they are *above* certain consequences and habits and *below* others. When they are inside and the door is shut, certain people and certain possibilities are shut out. Of these the majority are unwanted, and a minority are desired but known to be beyond their means. Farther down the road, near the traffic lights, a drunk is singing quietly but hoarsely to himself. The Corkers are *above* that, just as they are *above* the untidiness of the pavement, littered with old paper and scraps. On the opposite side is a large furniture stores, with a reproduction Jacobean dining-room suite in the window costing £290. They are *below* that. Along the length of the road and then throughout the whole greater London area, extending below ground and up into the sky, there are millions upon millions of events, offers, commodities, actions, words which can be categorized in the same way: either they belong to 84 Croydon Road, or 84 Croydon Road is above them or below them. This is not to say that the Corkers are snobs. They would call themselves realists – and the depth and nature of the emotion they feel as they now look up at the signboard would be impossible to explain in terms of snobbery. They feel confirmed. They feel that reality admits them as they are. They are aware of the pressure of all that is below them – it includes most of what they can see along this bleak South London road; and equally they are aware of the pressure of all that is above them, which includes part of what they can imagine. The confirmation lies in the blessed comforting fact that the two pressures are in equilibrium and in that equilibrium, by the sign with the name of their business on it, they can live and have their being. It is as though a man alone in endless space suddenly discovered that, whenever he wanted, he could hear a voice addressing him personally. The signboard assures the Corkers that they are neither alone nor accidental. The scheme of things has left a place, and a pleasant place, for them.

Mr Corker, in his blue gaberdine, fits the key into the lock and opens the door. As soon as he is inside he takes his hat off. Then he feels along the wall for the light switch. Illuminated, he climbs up the steep, stone stairs.

Now that he is at home, he recognizes that he wants to go to the lavatory. But the lavatory door is locked. It is always kept locked to prevent waiting clients (or worse still undesirables who have climbed up the stairs for that purpose alone) using it. The proper place for the key is the left-hand top drawer of Mr Corker's desk in the Inner Office. Only he and Alec know this. If Alec wants to go to the lavatory, he asks Mr Corker for the key. If a client happens to be in the room, they use a code. Alec says: I think, Mr Corker, the typewriter needs a new ribbon. Whereupon Mr Corker hands over the key of what will be presumed to be the store cupboard. Mr Corker has always enjoyed this little plot, but now clearly some new arrangement will have to be made: he can't go and fetch the key from his desk every time he needs to go to the lavatory.

It's not practical, says the host Corker, we must have another door let in which doesn't open on to the landing. Hurry, hurry, insists the naked Corker, I'm uncomfortable.

Mr Corker opens the door between the Waiting-room and the Inner Office. The top of his desk is piled high with the contents of its own drawers. The revolver lies on the table. The safe has gone altogether. Mr Corker can see the wall, a different colour because less faded, the length of the shelf where his Books have stood for seventeen years. He steps gingerly forward. Eight or ten books have been thrown on the floor; the rest are missing. There is no clock on the mantelpiece.

Help! whispers Mr Corker. And all the Corkers echo it till it seems that the whole of 84 Croydon Road is full of that whisper.

Part Five

Corker's Continuation

(Over two years have passed and it is 1962. The events already described have run their course. The consequences have become known. Miss Irene Corker has died. This was nine months after her fall in Summerbourne Road. She left all her property and money to the Radley Rheumatism Clinic. She did not die before Miss Browning, thanks to Miss Corker's detailed description, was arrested on a charge of assault and battery. Miss Corker maintained to both the police and an Insurance investigator that Miss Browning, who was her brother's mistress, had struck her on the head to prevent her reaching 84 Croydon Road because there her brother in collaboration with Miss Browning had 'arranged' the burglary in order to be able to claim the Insurance money. Various facts made this revengeful allegation more credible than it might otherwise have been. There was no trace of the front door of 84 having been forced. Mr Corker, after his half bottle of Kummel, had in fact failed to shut it properly when on his way to the Victoria Hall. The safe, in which Mr Corker claimed there was nearly £250 because it included the money he intended to pay that week to a travel bureau for his summer trip to Calabria, had not been broken into, but had disappeared without trace. The Books of his business, which Mr Corker declared were worth more to him than the cash, the clock or the silver from upstairs all put together, had not been included in the property evaluation on which he paid his premium.

When Miss Browning was arrested in July, three months after the burglary, the police found a photograph of Wolf in her handbag. Checking in their records, they discovered that this was a photograph of a man with a record of housebreaking and robbery with violence. They started a search on the grounds that he might be able to help them in their investigations, but failed to find him. Miss Browning therefore was tried alone. To protect Wolf she agreed that she was Mr Corker's mistress but pleaded innocent of striking Miss Corker over the head. Mr Corker denied in court that there was any liaison between himself and Miss Browning and suggested that his sister was out of her mind. Miss Browning was given a two-year prison sentence for assault and battery.

Since this appeared to confirm Miss Corker's allegations, Mr Corker's Insurance Company refused all liability for the burglary on the nominal grounds that the front door must have been left open when the office was unattended.

Wolf, whilst Velvet was in prison, found himself another, less excitable woman. Miss Brand entered an Old People's Home in Islington. Alec left Corker within a week of the talk, and took Jackie to Reading, where he obtained a post as a laboratory assistant in a chemical manufacturers': he is still there. They are married, they have a six-months'-old baby, and they live in one large room because they can find nothing else which they can afford. A few weeks ago, and by accident, Alec saw Corker on a Sunday in Oxford Street. He spoke to him and asked him, as he asks everybody, if he knew of an unfurnished flat with a reasonable rent. Corker said it was a pity he had not known a year ago, for then Alec could have had part of 84 Croydon Road, but now he had given it up. They each thought the other had aged.

Mr Corker was forced to shut his business in December 1960. The loss of the Books and the money was a serious enough blow, but the scandal which accumulated was worse. All the local talk maintained that there was certainly something between him and Miss Browning and that he had unchivalrously lied his way out. Some went as far as his sister and alleged that the burglary was 'faked'. Over seventy per cent of his 'employers' ceased to notify him of their vacancies. The police were reluctant to bring a case against him for fraud, but a solicitor advised him that it was useless to appeal against the decision of the Insurance Company.

Strange as it may seem for a man with his previous experience, he found it difficult to get a job. He was 64, and unqualified. He tried several jobs in the Clapham area. For a few weeks he worked for Mr Soloveichik in Streatham where Miss Marlow, promoted to personal secretary, wasted no time in establishing her authority. Mr Corker took the letters she typed to be posted. He decided to leave the area.

He obtained a job as a warehouse clerk in Cricklewood. Here he earns £9 a week and lives alone in a bed-sitter for which he pays £3. At first his landlady agreed to give him supper for an extra thirty shillings a week, but the conversation between her, her husband and her daughter was so trivial and acrimonious, in Mr Corker's opinion, that he asked to be released from the arrangement. Usually he now eats his evening meal in the café of the local Odeon cinema. He has been unable either to travel abroad or to continue with his photography. But he still gives public Talks, although the circumstances in which he gives them have changed. Indeed his weekly Talk is now the climax and justification of Mr Corker's week. Every Sunday afternoon for the last nine months he has been one of the speakers in the corner of the Park at Marble Arch. The first time he climbed on to his box, he climbed down again immediately. But with experience and the indulgence of the second Sunday luxury he allows himself – three or four glasses of Kummel with a sandwich lunch – he has become more confident and assured.)

The placard board is hinged to the box so that both can be carried as one unit and when shut, the placard board acts as a lid. In the box Mr Corker keeps his pamphlets. On the placard board, which is white, is the emblem of a sun. The sun is painted golden but is chipped in places. On the sun is a red cross. Over it is written the word *Paneuropa*, and beneath, in italics:

Unity in essentials.
Liberty in inessentials.
Charity in all.

Mr Corker is standing on the box behind the placard board. About ten sightseers stand around him listening. None has been there for more than five minutes. He glances down at them occasionally, but most of the time he addresses his words to the third-storey windows of the buildings on the far side of Oxford Street. Not a word he says is audible more than fifteen yards away. Twenty or thirty other speakers are enjoying the same freedom of speech in this windy corner of the Park and the air is full of the noise of words, haphazard as blown leaves. Two policemen wander casually among groups of sightseers. Most groups are larger than Mr Corker's, but a few are smaller.

A child says: Can we go to the zoo now, Daddy?
Mr Corker says: The second Europe was Rome —
The child says: Can't we, Daddy?
Mr Corker says: The third Europe was Charlemagne's.
A man shouts: Charlie who?
Mr Corker says: The third Europe was created by the Migrations of the Peoples. The fourth Europe was the Europe of the Roman Church. This was at the time of Innocent the Third.
A man wheezes: Innocent!
Mr Corker says: At the time of the great Crusades against the Turks! The fifth Europe was the work and dream of one man alone – Napoleon Bonaparte!
A woman, drunk, giggles: Who does he think he is – Napoleon?
Mr Corker says: Napoleon's plans were defeated and his dream turned to dust over a century ago. Now it is our turn! We must take our destiny into our hands! We must create the sixth Europe – the United States of Europe! Paneuropa! The Sixth Europe! The Permanent Europe!

Two young men clap ironically. Mr Corker looks down at them, and from behind the placard-board hands them one pamphlet each which they stuff straightaway into their pockets.

Mr Corker has had the pamphlets specially printed according to his own design. They contain several long quotations from Count Coudenhove-Kalergi and at the bottom a questionnaire to be filled in and sent back to Mr Corker.

> *Mr Corker says:* These days you hear a lot about the Common Market but make no mistake about it this is only nibbling at the job – and the ones who are nibbling are the big financiers! Especially the German financiers. Let me remind you that Europe covers an area of 600 million square kilometres – that's the same size as China – and includes far more countries than the Six. Remember Portugal, remember Spain, Greece, Yugoslavia, Finland! And further let me make it quite clear that Paneuropa is not just a question of tariff agreements – Paneuropa means Federal Government, nothing less, Paneuropa is concerned with the spiritual as well as the material, Paneurope means the whole of Europe – all 600 million square kilometres of it – coming together and recognizing its common inheritance and blood and ancestry. Europe, we say, is a family – one of the families of man!
>
> *A young student asks:* What about Munich?

Mr Corker is now addressing all the multitudes too far away to hear him.

> *Mr Corker shouts:* I am asked What about Munich? And I take this to mean – What about Chamberlain and his famous words 'I bring you back Peace in Our Time!' We all know how wrong he was. But what I would ask is – Why was he wrong? What was Neville Chamberlain's mistake?

Mr Corker's voice attains the rhythm and almost the tone of a bell-buoy.

> *Mr Corker shouts louder:* His mistake was to begin too late. He allowed himself to be blinded – and then he allowed himself to be tricked, tricked by a guarantee which was not worth the paper it was written on! I would not say that Mr Neville Chamberlain was a villain, I would rather say he was an old fool.
>
> *A woman shouts:* Like you!
>
> *Mr Corker shouts:* If ten years before Europe had united – and already the great Count Coundenhove-Kalergi from Vienna was advocating this – if, I say, Europe had united in 1930 what chance would the Nazis have had, what country I ask you could Germany have overrun if Europe had been united?
>
> *An old man says:* The Soviet Union.

Mr Corker adjusts his glasses and gazes at the faces beneath him. His voice still has the rhythm of a bell-buoy, but now he looks at the faces whilst declaiming and tries, as it were, to push them away with his words so that, lost in the distance and the mist, they can become grateful and numberless.

> *Mr Corker shouts:* We must live with the Russians, but Russians, remember, are not Europeans – any more than the Americans are Europeans. We are Europeans! You are Europeans! And if we could only recognize the power we have within us, if we could only understand how easily removed can be the differences between us, if we all saw what we have in common, if one fine morning we all rose up and said: Enough! Today we are going to claim our heritage – Unity in Essentials – if we did this together one day, we would be free, and by we, let me make it quite clear, I mean all of us all over Europe, we would no longer

be imprisoned by the petty interests of nationalism and competition, we would be citizens of the greatest power on earth – greater even than the Americans or the Russians – the United States of Europe – and as citizens of this power we would have access to all the variety and riches of our wonderful civilization, we would become the future whom our ancestors dreamt of – there, ladies and gentlemen, is a thought – we would be the citizens of what was once called Utopia – Utopia! Imagine it! The beautiful Renaissance towns of Italy, the industry of Germany, the music of Vienna, the wines of France —

A young man whistles and says: The women!

Mr Corker shouts: It is no laughing matter – what stops us? Only our own apathy, only our own lack of confidence, let us rise up —

The young man says: – and poke her.

Mr Corker shouts: Let us sweep away all that belongs to the past. I would like to see the British army and navy swept away, the customs swept away, the pound note, the House of Lords, Greenwich Mean Time, the Union Jack —

A man says: Fucking traitor – listen to him – doing the Russians' work for them – that's what he is – a fucking traitor.

Another man says: He's always here.

Mr Corker shouts: I am used to interruptions! It is the penalty of being ahead of your time. Six hundred years ago it seemed Utopian to think of a united Switzerland.

A young girls says: Cuckoo!

Mr Corker shouts: Five hundred years ago it seemed Utopian to think of a united France. Four hundred years ago it seemed Utopian to think of a united Britain.

The drunk woman says: And what about the Irish Free State – and *your* murdering soldiers you sent us!

Mr Corker shouts: Three hundred years ago it seemed Utopian to think of a united Hungary with the Turks driven out of Europe! Two hundred years ago it seemed Utopian to think of a United Greece – the Greece that the great Byron died for! One hundred years ago it seemed Utopian to think of a united Italy – the Italy of Garibaldi. And look at Italy today! I ask you. Was it Utopian?

A man imitates Mr Corker: And twenty-two years ago I ask you it was damn funny to think of Manchester United! I ask you.

Most of the group laugh and several begin to stroll away. Mr Corker re-addresses the third-storey windows in Oxford Street.

Mr Corker shouts: Can you still with your hand on your heart go on saying that it is Utopian today to think of a free, united Europe – a truly European life? We must learn from history! We must learn or go under. That is the thought I will leave you with this Sunday afternoon: WE MUST LEARN OR GO UNDER.

As soon as he has stopped talking Mr Corker steps off his box and disappears from sight behind the placard board. In the box along with the pamphlets is his old blue gaberdine which he puts on. He finds it hot work addressing the public and afterwards he must always take care not to catch cold. Whilst he is doing up his belt (which is twisted several times at the back) a well-dressed man comes up to him and says: Excuse me, sir, will you be so kind if I ask you a question? The voice and accent are foreign. Mr Corker beams. I am delighted, he says. What about Egypt? asks the foreigner, I want to know how you would consider that country's contribution to European culture, and also Poland's. Yes, says Mr Corker, a very complicated question, and puts his hat on. That is so, says the foreigner. They both hesitate, looking into one another's faces. The foreigner is probably twenty years younger than

Mr Corker and holds himself militarily upright. He is from Hanover. Mr Corker's hair is longer than it needs to be. He has also become shabbier in other ways. He no longer notices, for example, the sleep in the corners of his magnified eyes. A little owlish, a little prophetic, a little dowdy but with the clean nails and soft fingers of a gentleman, he could be mistaken for an English eccentric. And now is. Would you care to have a cup of tea? says Mr Corker. That is very kind, says the foreigner, Gunter Ruhling. He stands upright. My name is Corker, says Mr Corker, W. T. Corker. First I must just attend to this. He indicates the box and placard board.

Herr Ruhling stands tactfully aside. Mr Corker folds the placard board in half. It is hinged across the golden sun. He bends over the box. The pamphlets inside are done up in bundles of fifty with an elastic band neatly round each bundle. Mr Corker slips out one pamphlet to give to the German gentleman who has expressed interest. Then he touches with his two middle fingers a picture which is stuck on the inside of the bottom of the box. It is a colour picture from an illustrated magazine showing a Dutch film star in a décolleté black dress. She has long red hair, the colour of a red vixen. Mr Corker's two fingers move down the hair, going from side to side and once going back on their tracks to make a complete circle. Quickly afterwards he bangs the placard board down on to the box like a lid and picks up the whole thing, holding it against his stomach with two arms, the letters of the word Paneuropa under his chin.

I leave it across the road, he explains. Herr Ruhling's dilemma shows on his face. Politeness demands that he should help the old man, yet at the same time he would hate to be seen carrying a placard. Mr Corker comes to his rescue by saying: Perhaps this would interest you. He nods at the pamphlet in the hand he can't move because the unit is heavy. Herr Ruhling gently plucks it from between the thumb and forefinger and says: Indeed, very much indeed.

They cross to the Edgware Road. Mr Corker has often thought as he carries his equipment this hundred yards how much he misses Alec. He believes that Alec would have made a good speaker too.

The equipment is left in a tobacconist's. Herr Ruhling waits outside. Windy today, says the tobacconist, many people? Fairish, says Mr Corker, but we mustn't grumble I suppose. Shall I leave it here? Just dump it in the corner – will you be up next week? Definitely, says Mr Corker, next week is Palm Sunday. All right, says the tobacconist, I'll get it out ready. Mr Corker puts two and six on the counter (his weekly rent for storing the unit) and says: I'll see you're given the Freedom of Europe! The tobacconist laughs for the old man says the same thing regularly every darned Sunday.

Now, says Mr Corker to Herr Ruhling outside on the pavement, now for some tea and some real Viennese pastries, do you know this part of London? Not well like some. Well, I'll show you the way, we cut through this little street.

Mr Corker hurries along, fiddling with his gaberdine belt and with a kind of shuffle as though wearing carpet slippers. Herr Ruhling walks with his hands clasped behind his back, and is very careful where he steps.

Do you hold meetings often? asked Herr Ruhling. Every week, weather permitting. It is so typical of your country, says Herr Ruhling, this freedom you have so that every people can get up and say what they like, you do not find the same thing anywhere else, not in Paris, not in Bonn, not in Brussels, indeed this is why it is so famous this free speech of yours. All countries, says Mr Corker, have their contribution to make, in Germany – you are German? Herr Ruhling smiles in assent. In Germany you have the best workers in the world, believe me, they are real workers. Herr Ruhling says nothing. And Beethoven too! adds Mr Corker, the musical genius of Germany is unquestionable, unquestionable.

They pass a small restaurant with iced cakes and slices of ham in the window. Herr Ruhling slows down as though to enter. No, no, says Mr Corker, we're going somewhere special, I'd challenge anybody to go where we're going blindfold, taste one of their pastries and say whether they were in London or Wien.

What we do not see eye to eye, says Herr Ruhling, is where Europe ends and begins. For us Europe is our own country, France and your country, that is the pure Europe. But, says Mr Corker, the glory that was Rome, Greece, Athens! I speak of Modern Europe, says Herr Ruhling. Surely we are what we are because of what has been, says Mr Corker, hurrying. I would say, says Herr Ruhling, we must become what we want. True too, too true, says Mr Corker, and here we are.

They enter a restaurant with candelabra hanging from the ceiling and tables on golden legs and a deep red carpet. Along one side is a glass counter on which there are silver dishes a yard long. On the silver dishes are the pastries. Most of the customers are women with silver and golden hair swept up and held in place under hats as apparently light as the pastries.

You can smell the coffee! whispers Mr Corker, real continental coffee!

They find a table in a corner and Mr Corker insists upon taking their coats to the cloak-room. When he returns he says: Europe needs every square kilometre that belongs to it. We Germans, says Herr Ruhling, have had many kilometres taken away from us by the Russians and the Poles. I know, says Mr Corker, but you see you must stop thinking of We Germans, it is We Europeans!

The waitress comes up and Herr Ruhling is still smiling at the innocence of the old Englishman who has invited him to this strange tea in a place where nearly all the customers are women. Mr Corker orders lemon tea and a selection of pastries including especially several rum babas and two *indianerkrapfen*. I expect you know far more about all these delicacies than I do, says Mr Corker, blinking and touching his tie which still has the pearl pin in it. Not at all, says Herr Ruhling.

Mr Corker leans back in his chair. Now tell me, he says, your point of view. I agree, says Herr Ruhling, with the large part of what you are saying – Europe has the need to come closer together, we have the same blood and the same interests and it is my view this will happen in our common front against communismus. Mr Corker's eyes are watching the waitress selecting the pastries from the glass table, but he nods at Herr Ruhling's speech. But one thing please I must say. This internationalness you have spoke about, this is dangerous fire you play with. It is true what you say, but to speak it in the street – that is dangerous because to people who do not use their head – Herr Ruhling points at the precise centre of his forehead – it seems like what the communists say. The only communist country I've been to, says Mr Corker, is Yugoslavia. Yugoslavia, says Herr Ruhling, is not real communist – you believe me. You want to go to Czechoslovakia or East Germany to see what communism is.

The tea and pastries arrive. Mr Corker rubs his hands softly together. Shall I be mother? he says. Herr Ruhling looks puzzled. Sugar and lemon? asks Mr Corker. Please, please. I will tell you I have a cousin in Dresden. From time to time he writes to me. They never see a lemon there – and there are long, long lines for meat. Try a baba, says Mr Corker, they're made with the best Jamaican rum. And all the time they are watched. You Englishmen you do not understand how lucky you are!

Delicious! says Mr Corker, do try one. Thank you, says Herr Ruhling and puts up his hand. I have travelled a lot, says Mr Corker, to eleven different countries in Europe, and although they say there's no place like home I've often thought I'd like to live in another country. I know, says Herr Ruhling, the English they live everywhere, but still you are lucky – you have not suffered like the rest of us, not even in the war. Believe me, Herr Corker, there are things I have seen which I would not wish to tell you, I was in Berlin when the Russians came.

The *indianerkrapfen* is beautiful, I'm sure it's made with real cream, do let me persuade you. Herr Ruhling reluctantly accepts the little bowl piled with white foam. Scenes out of hell, Herr Corker. I am sorry, says Mr Corker.

It is part of your charm in England – the way you have escaped, the way you always believe in fair play – even your free speech – you do not know how lucky you are. Mr Corker purses his lips together, and smiles slightly, and then says: Sometimes we are lucky and sometimes we are unlucky. It all depends how you measure it and that changes too. I'm lucky today.

He puts his tongue out to lick the last piece of chocolate from the spoon with the imitation amber handle. Herr Ruhling looks puzzled. Please, I must tell you this, he says, a pride in your fatherland, to be a patriot as you say, this is the best defence against communismus. When Herr Ruhling smiles, his teeth are as white as his collar. May I ask if you know Count Coundenhove-Kalergi himself?

Mr Corker pours out more tea and signs the waitress to bring some more hot water. Yes, lies Mr Corker. Is that so? says Herr Ruhling. A man of the highest principles, says Mr Corker, a man with a vision whom it is a privilege to know. One of nature's gentlemen, we say in English. How did you first know him? asks Herr Ruhling. Another? inquires Mr Corker. *Nein danke. Bitte schoen*, says Mr Corker smiling at the use of one of his lovingly polished German phrases and helping himself to another pastry.

I met him last year at Berne, quite by chance. We were staying in the same hotel and started talking one evening and then discovered we had many ideas in common, so we went up to the mountains and spent a week together above the world. It's something I'll never forget. The old count opened his heart to me up there.

Of course he's an old man now, we're both old men. Mr Corker peers at Herr Ruhling and adds: I'd put you at forty-five. Forty, says Herr Ruhling, lying. A young man still, says Mr Corker, with your life before you. Please excuse me just a moment.

Mr Corker walks slowly towards the toilet and disappears. As the door closes behind him he congratulates himself. This is the third time he has succeeded. He takes his hat and coat from the cloakroom, goes out into the street through a side-door and, as he walks away, tots up the bill that Herr Ruhling will have to pay. He makes it eleven and threepence.